Advanced Praise for
The Ambulance Chaser

"In *The Ambulance Chaser*, readers meet Jason Feldman, a morally com-
promised attorney who finds himself embroiled in a dangerous plot that
is way above his pay grade. Divorced from his DA wife, estranged from his
son, hobbled by addictions, and stuck in a lonely life with his cat and a chiropractor girlfriend who is his only source of clients, Feldman still draws us
in with his humanity and desire—no matter how thin—to finally get things
right. With the sudden appearance of a long-lost friend and a long-disap-
peared dead body, Feldman's long-held secrets threaten his very life as he
is drawn into a terrifying cat-and-mouse game with sinister players. A not-
to-be-missed, twisty, fast-paced legal thriller that keeps the reader guessing on subjects as fascinating as the Odessa Mafia and illicit trysts on a
Pittsburgh incline. I, for one, hope to see more from debut novelist, Brian
Cuban, in the future."

— Deborah Goodrich Royce, author
of *Finding Mrs. Ford* and *Ruby Falls*

THE
AMBULANCE CHASER

A THRILLER
BRIAN CUBAN

Post Hill PRESS

A POST HILL PRESS BOOK
ISBN: 978-1-63758-241-1
ISBN (eBook): 978-1-63758-242-8

Post Hill Press
New York • Nashville
posthillpress.com

Published in the United States of America
1 2 3 4 5 6 7 8 9 10

To my father and the most important lesson you taught me, even if I didn't always listen. "Today is as young as you will ever be. Live like it." I think about you and miss you every day.

Norton Cuban, 1926–2018

CHAPTER 1

This must be what hell feels like, standing at a busy downtown Pittsburgh crosswalk, waiting for the light, while sweating my ass off in my court-room-blue pinstriped suit. I reach behind and tug at the lower back of my sweat-drenched shirt. The day is expected to exceed the century mark, as it has the two days before in a city that previously had never experienced a one-hundred-degree day, spurring on cable and online punditry about global warming, and the possibility of rolling blackouts.

The ten-minute trudge to the courthouse might as well be an hour in this oven. I mop my forehead with a handkerchief and peel off my suit jacket to inspect the off-color perspiration splotches. There isn't one smile in the crowd of people bumping shoulders. I'm silently cursing my failing deodorant and the agonizingly long red light when my cell phone vibrates in my pocket, and I glance down to see a text message. It's a URL, but there is no name attached to the phone number. One of my steadfast rules of life is never to answer calls or return texts from numbers I don't recognize. Spam from political action committees, robocalls for extended car warranties, and links from the occasional porn purveyor are common. This one is about to be exiled to the trash folder when another comes through.

Heather Brody is back. Open the link.

I text back: *Who is this?*

A blast from the past. David Chaney. Read the story.

Holy shit. I haven't heard from him in decades and frankly would have been content dying of old age without contact. My hands shake as my thumb presses down on the screen, leaving a sweaty print.

I fixate on each word in the tiny headline, reading it repeatedly in the hope that my vision is playing tricks on me.

"Human Remains Linked to Heather Brody."

"Oh my God," I mutter to myself, stepping off the curb. A horn blasts, and a woman screams as I glance to my left to discover a bus bearing down on me. For a split-second, I consider whether to make a dash for the concrete trolley medium, but I'm frozen in place like a raccoon staring into a pair of headlights on a desert highway. A strong hand yanks me back by the collar as ten thousand pounds of steel with an advertisement for my law firm on the back accelerates past, pushing a wave of wind that clogs my nose with noxious exhaust fumes. I catch a glimpse of astonished faces and hands pressed against the windows.

I run my fingers over my chest and down my pants legs to ensure I'm still in one piece, then turn around to thank my savior. A middle-aged guy with a baseball cap and beard is shaking his head like a disappointed father. "That was close," I sputter. "Thank you. I cross at this intersection every morning and should know better."

He admonishes me, "You almost crossed over all right. I can't imagine anything so important it couldn't wait until you got to the other side of the street."

His lecture fades into the background as I scan the horrified stares of people probably wondering what special kind of idiot doesn't look both ways before crossing a city street during morning rush hour. The little green man changes from flashing to solid, signaling a safe journey through the parallel white lines. My savior waves and traverses the crosswalk, but I hang back to gather my composure and come to grips with the life-changing revelation. I didn't find time to access the Web or read the paper this morning, but David obviously did.

"Construction workers excavating a vacant lot in the Hill District unearthed bones wrapped in a tarp. While the police have not issued an official statement, a department employee speaking on condition of anonymity because he was not authorized to speak publicly, stated that personal items found in the shallow grave are linked to the Squirrel Hill teen who went missing over thirty years ago."

You shouldn't text and walk. That's how accidents happen. Call me.

What the hell? I eyeball every person milling around the intersection, up and down the sidewalk, and across the street. He's watching me, but from where? And how would I recognize him after all these years? My mental snapshot of David is fossilized at seventeen years old. I size up each pedestrian gathering for the next opportunity to cross the roadway. A fifty-ish guy in jeans and a Steelers T-shirt returns my gaze and presses the silver button on the stoplight box. He's about the right age, but what else? How can I be sure?

"Are you David?" I ask.

He shakes his head. "Nope, I'm Frank, sorry."

David and I were once inseparable. We took our naps on the same blanket in kindergarten and shared our milk cartons. We were best friends in elementary, junior high, and high school. But he disappeared our senior year, and I haven't spoken to him since then.

I've dredged the Internet, but it's like he's erased from the Web with no Facebook, Twitter, Instagram, or LinkedIn accounts. No news stories, obits, marriage announcements, birth notices, or mugshots. How does someone walk the planet for over forty years without even a mention?

My hand is clammy and trembling as I dial, causing me to botch the number twice before hitting the correct sequence of digits. I cover my left ear with my hand to muffle the ambient street noise.

"Hello, Jason. Did you read the story?"

His voice is calm and unhurried, like we hung out and drank beer last night.

"Yes, I did. Where are you? Are you following me?"

"I'm in town and need to see you."

"Why?" I ask, glancing at my watch. My pretrial conference is in twenty minutes.

"Why do you think? Meet me at the Cathedral of Learning."

"I can't. I'm headed to court."

"I know. You're a lawyer, your ex is the district attorney, and you have a grown son named Sam."

The realization that he's been monitoring my life and daily movements is unsettling. My head swivels from side to side, but everyone blends into the same person. Suits, dresses, and high heels all moving in a synchronized swarm.

"The building has thousands of rooms. Anywhere in particular, and what time? I asked you if you're tailing me."

"I'll text you the specifics."

"You've obviously kept tabs on me. I've tried to find you over the years. It's like you moved to the dark side of the moon."

"I've been kind of off the grid," he says.

I caught a *Dateline* segment about people who decide to "go dark" by not using computers, getting rid of their phones, buying everything with cash, and using solar power. They sever all connections to the world we take for granted and count on to live a normal life.

"Yes, we need to talk about Heather, but why were you following—"

"Don't abandon me again," he says, cutting me off. "Be there."

"David?" I say, but the line is silent.

Vanished again. Just like he did thirty years ago without even saying goodbye. We were best friends. Who does that? I'm the one with the grievance. The light changes again. I carefully look both ways, and sprint across the street.

CHAPTER 2

A blast of chilled air sends goosebumps cascading up my arms as I step from the oppressive heat into the courthouse. My suit jacket, belt, phones, keys, and briefcase slide through the x-ray machine while I contemplate my world being turned upside down. Before stepping through the magnetometer, I glance back toward the entrance, paranoid and distracted at the worst possible time. A lack of courtroom focus results in lower settlements and the words all plaintiffs' personal injury lawyers dread: *We, the jury, find for the defendant.*

As I put my belt back on, my stomach inflates with gas in objection to the three cups of dark roast coffee I drank this morning. I beeline to the public restroom in the lobby, not only to relieve myself but also to finish the cocaine hidden in my wallet.

Entering a lavatory with the intent of engaging in illegal activity that, if discovered, could result in my disbarment, imprisonment, or both, requires meticulous multitasking. I make a visual risk assessment of the space before the door shuts behind me. My eyes rove the sink, the urinals, and finally the bottom of each cubicle, searching for feet. Satisfied I'm alone, I enter the stall farthest from the entrance, hang my jacket on the steel suit hook, and drop my pants.

After extracting a miniature translucent baggie from behind the Platinum American Express card in my wallet, I use my index fingernail to break the seal and sprinkle a tiny pile of blow on top of the briefcase. In less than ten seconds, I'll be awash in renewed confidence and clarity. Of course, I'm cognizant of the fact I'm breaking the law, but I also ceased to care about that a long time ago. Life is a matter of choices. This is mine.

Yank. Yank.

The steel latch prevents the door from opening. The surprise intrusion, however, causes my knees to lurch upward, propelling my briefcase with them. A mound of white powder and the remaining contents of the open Ziplock burst into the air like a freak July snowstorm, settling on the floor, my lap, my shoes, and my shirt.

"Sorry, I didn't realize this stall was in use."

The nasally and irritating voice of His Honor Josiah Steelman.

My pulse races and my hands sweat like a bad high. Why is Steelman using the public restroom when judges have private facilities for their use and their staff?

"No problem, your honaghh..." The words stumble out of my mouth in unintelligible gibberish. I attempt to camouflage my panic by hacking out a faux sneeze while extracting a sliver of toilet paper from its stainless-steel receptacle and blowing my nose...twice.

"God bless you."

Steelman shuffles into the cubicle farthest from me. The soft metallic thud of the bolt is my signal to extricate myself from the embarrassing and potentially dangerous situation. I survey the battlefield. Cocaine shrapnel is everywhere. I hurriedly brush the white flakes from my clothes and flee the bathroom. After waiting five tense minutes for the malfunctioning elevator to the third floor, I hustle to the courtroom and check messages. The text from David is timestamped ten minutes ago.

> *Cathedral, —Italian room, 3 p.m.*
> *Confirmed,* I respond.

Phone use while court is in session is verboten and getting caught can result in a contempt ruling and a five-hundred-dollar fine. I power down and push through the double wooden doors. The courtroom is packed. Multiple conversations crisscross the room as lawyers speak with clients while waiting for Benny, the tipstaff, to call their case. Benny cups his hands around his mouth and bellows, "Mr. Feldman, the judge, and the defendant's counsel are waiting in chambers."

I rush up front and follow Benny out through the back corridor to Steelman's private office. During Steelman's twenty-plus years on the bench, he has occasionally expressed disdain for the low-end, meat-and-potatoes auto accidents that provide a living to me and many other attorneys in Allegheny County. He considers us "rapacious, ambulance chasers, nuisances as litigators, and the scourge of the civil justice system." An anonymous op-ed in the *Tribune* last year accused him of treating personal injury lawyers and their clients with a "level of scorn customarily reserved for rapists and child molesters."

Benny eases the office door open and announces, "The lawyer for the plaintiff is here, Your Honor."

Steelman acknowledges my presence with a curt nod and a tug on his bow tie. "We'll start the motions docket in fifteen minutes," he says. "This won't take long."

"I'm sorry I'm late, Your Honor. The elevator malfunctioned."

He taps the crystal of his wristwatch. "I'm not interested in your excuses. Everyone in this room but you arrived when he should. I'll cut you slack this time and won't hold you in contempt, but in the future, be on time."

The insurance company representative, Merrit Crombar, is a slovenly claims lifer I've come up against multiple times. We've never been in a room together where he hasn't exuded an *I slept under a bridge last night* vibe, and today is no exception.

Steelman points at Crombar and says, "Where do we stand on resolving this nuisance matter?"

"I've extended a substantial settlement offer to Mr. Feldman. His client sustained minor sprains and a scratched rear bumper on his vehicle." He places his hand on the shoulder of the lawyer representing the insurance company and boasts, "My able counsel believes I'm being too generous and he's chomping at the bit to bring in a defense verdict."

I'm tempted to blurt out, *"The correct term is champing, doofus,"* but also want the case to resolve so I clamp my mouth shut. I remove the medical reports from my briefcase and pretend to study them.

"Mr. Ellis suffered permanent damage to his neck and back, missed two weeks of work, and is still in considerable pain," I say.

Crombar rolls his eyes and cracks, "I've had hangnails worse than your client's injuries."

Steelman sighs and glances at his wristwatch again. "Cut the crap, both of you, and come up with an agreeable number. I have a crowded courtroom waiting on me."

I want to settle as badly as he wants to get rid of us but can't roll over or Crombar will lowball me on every case we have together. Regardless, neither side is interested in going to trial. The negotiation lasts thirteen minutes. The case settles, and I pocket a much-needed ten grand and change.

CHAPTER 3

The revolving courthouse exit is still spinning as I tap "Heather Brody" into the Google search bar, which brings up multiple stories about last night's discovery. Construction has halted while investigators sift through dirt and dig their own holes, searching for clues to how she died and ended up in a shallow grave miles from home. I contemplate a crime scene drive-by, but there is other urgent business to take care of before I meet David. The toilet snowstorm wiped out my personal drug stash, so I'll have to pay Kevin a visit.

I take the bat phone out of my briefcase and type "reup" into the secure messaging app.

Kevin Goldman doesn't fit the gangster stereotype of a narcotics trafficker. He earned his PhD in philosophy and an MBA from the University of Pennsylvania. Two years ago, *Pittsburghprenuer Magazine* named his rideshare venture, WARP, the hottest startup in the city and a stout local competitor to mega-stalwarts Uber and Lyft, operating under the tagline, *We pick you up and drop you off at WARP speed.*

The mission statement describes WARP as socially conscious and philanthropic. In lieu of tipping the salaried drivers, passengers choose from a list of nonprofits to receive the gratuity. What the story doesn't mention is beneath the hood of social respectability are the *select* couriers like me.

Instead of picking up passengers, we deliver cocaine, marijuana, and heroin to a discreet, upscale clientele.

When I went to work part-time for Kevin as a side hustle to my law practice, his insistence that I use a company "bat phone" was at first a pain in the ass. I hate carrying two phones. It makes people suspicious, especially girlfriends. The logic, however, is sound from a security standpoint. Messages are not stored on a server, and they self-delete in sixty seconds. All of Kevin's select drivers use bat phones, and business-related communications using any other device is grounds for immediate termination.

I'm in the parking garage when Kevin calls.

"I'm on my way over," I say.

"No good. I'm swamped. What do you want?"

What does he think I want? Read the text. "I need a refill."

He sighs audibly. "Get over here pronto. I also need you to work tomorrow night."

I slump back against the seat and bang the steering wheel with my palm. I was hoping for a night out with my girlfriend, Mary. "How many deliveries do I need to do?"

"We will discuss when you arrive. This is more of a favor but an important one."

"Yeah, fine," I mumble, starting my car. "I'll be there as quick as I can."

Kevin answers the door donning a WARP branded T-shirt. All of his regular drivers are required to wear them, though his drug couriers are expected to dress more in line with the upscale clientele we serve. The thin fabric hugs his broad shoulders and impressive biceps like an extra layer of skin. He's a workout fanatic and constantly gets on me for my devotion to Primanti Brothers sandwiches. I've known him since we were kids. We attended different high schools, but the same synagogue and Hebrew school. His grandparents, like mine, immigrated from Eastern Europe. His father is the head rabbi at Temple Sherith Israel.

Kevin steps back and motions for me to enter. "You got here fast."

I follow him into the kitchen where a cocaine-filled baggie is lying in full view next to a cup of steaming coffee on his circular, glass-topped breakfast table. The hazelnut aroma mixes with the unmistakable, ether scent common to high-quality blow.

"What's the favor?" I ask, fixating on the happy powder.

Kevin takes a sip of coffee. "One of my angel investors in WARP asked me to supply a driver for his daughter's sixteenth birthday bash tomorrow. I need someone to make sure they arrive safely and are driven home without incident."

"Can't one of your other drivers or Yak handle this?" I ask, crossing my arms in front of me, already angry at my impending weakness.

Kevin's eyes narrow. The godfather doesn't like rejection. He leans into me and says, "Yes, I could, but I am asking you. I trust you the most, and Yak has his own duties. He's not a chauffeur."

This sucks. I have job descriptions as well. I'm a lawyer and a high-end drug courier, not a babysitter.

Kevin slides the baggie of cocaine to me across the glass. "This is on the house and should ease your pain but let me remind you: I bailed your ass out when your dad was about to be evicted from that senior care facility for non-payment of funds. Should I fill out the scorecard of what I've done for you?"

I fold my hands in my lap and sit mute in my chair, unable to deny that he rescued me from a financial abyss. Caring for my dementia-ravaged dad to the tune of twelve grand a month at Rolling Oaks Luxury Assisted Living means my law practice must net one hundred twenty thousand dollars annually before I buy my first quart of milk. That's not including sixty-five thousand to my paralegal Stacy in addition to miscellaneous office expenses.

I wasn't about to throw my dad into a substandard, understaffed nursing home drenched in his own piss and covered in bedsores. A buddy of mine sued one of those facilities. I'm haunted to this day by the horrific photos of neglect and abuse he showed me. They were high-definition vivid in my head when I accepted Kevin's illegal offer and stepped over the line. He fronted me a forty grand loan to bring my dad's rent up to date. There was no tiny angel tapping on my shoulder and whispering I was doing wrong. I knew damn well.

"Different topic, but did you read the story about Heather Brody in the Tribune?" I ask.

"Yeah, she didn't show up at home after a Pirates game thirty years ago. They found her remains yesterday. Crazy shit. I hope she and her family finally receive some justice. I bumped into her around the neighborhood, but we didn't run in the same circles. Didn't you know her?"

"Not well. We had some classes together, but she hung out with kids who drove Beemers and snorted blow. Way out of my league."

Kevin places his coffee cup in the dishwasher and says, "I'll text you the address. They live in the Virginia Manor area of Mt. Lebanon. Her dad is a real-estate developer. His name is Roger Hambrick."

I'd rather pull out my toenails with my teeth than chauffeur a bunch of privileged brats, but he's right. This is part of the job. "How many partygoers am I taking?"

"Four or five at least. You'll need to come by here and pick up the WarpMobile. The party is on the Gateway Clipper. The boat leaves at seven and returns about ten p.m. After it docks, collect the kids and drive them back to Roger's place."

I snatch the baggie and wiggle it at eye level to distribute the powder evenly. "I haven't been on the Clipper since high school."

"You won't be a passenger. My personal security will handle things on the water."

This might work out. I'll ask Mary to join me for dinner, and the evening won't be a total bust.

"One more thing."

I drop my head, let out an exasperated puff of air, and mutter, "What else?"

"While the kids are birthday bashing, I'd like you to rendezvous with Yak."

Shit. I knew there had to be more to this favor. So much for dinner with Mary. I like the shaved-headed, muscle-bound Ukrainian, but conversations with him are exhausting. The heavy accent. The broken English. His cartoonish Eastern European bravado.

Kevin picks a brown paper sack off the floor and upends it. Five half-quart Ziplocs of cocaine tumble onto the table along with a massive roll of currency, secured with two rubber bands. He peels off three crisp Benjamin Franklins and methodically lines them up next to each other one at a time like he's dealing a poker hand.

"Consider this an additional weekend bonus. Yak will meet you at Three Rivers Bowl."

"Do you mind if I do a bump?" I ask.

"Knock yourself out. How's your old man doing?"

I tilt the clear plastic baggie toward the table, dispersing the fine particles and coating the glass with a thin film the size of a quarter. "He's as well as can be expected, I guess, given the circumstances. I wouldn't wish dementia on my worst enemy. I understand now why it's called the 'long goodbye.'"

Kevin nods in agreement. "The former cantor at our synagogue has advanced Alzheimer's. My dad visits him weekly and talks with the caregivers. They've taught him a lot about the disease. You should speak with him. Have you checked out any support groups?"

I bristle at the implication that I don't know what's going on with my own father, but the reality is I've made little effort researching this awful scourge that stabbed him in the mind and me in the heart. What's the point? His cognitive function has deteriorated rapidly over the last three years. It won't be long before he doesn't recognize me, his only son. The best I can do is make sure he lives out his life in dignity and luxury.

"I appreciate your concern, but I'm on top of it and doing fine."

I grab a butter knife from Kevin's kitchen drawer and slide the tip of the blade through the white powder.

"Are you going to join me?" I ask in jest, knowing he's going to decline.

"Yeah right, you'll colonize Mars before I put that shit in my body."

When I first mentioned the paradox of a sober drug dealer, he said in his best imitation of his rabbi dad, "The Torah states, 'A person must distance himself from things that destroy the body and accustom himself to things which heal it.'"

He wasn't kidding either. Kevin will drink a beer and coffee now and then, but other than that he doesn't ingest soda, sugar, or anything processed.

"I know you're Mister Jewish Clean, but your contradictory lifestyle still vexes me."

Within seconds of inhaling, a tsunami of self-love washes over me as dopamine receptors activate and cocaine-drenched neurons fire like a cerebral lightning storm. My eyes roll up and quiver shut. A wave of goosebumps cascades over me. I stand too quickly and topple forward. Only my outstretched arms prevent me from face-planting on the tabletop. These kick-ass highs come with less frequency these days.

Kevin puts the cocaine back in the bag and hands it to me. "Primo shit, isn't it? There's no conflict. It's a business, and I'm filling a need that should be legal and has been part of the human condition since Adam and Eve."

"The Official First Couple did blow?"

Kevin laughs and says, "Doubtful. They were into apples. I'm talking about the need for pleasure. Text me after you drop the kids back at Roger's and show yourself out. I need to change for the gym."

CHAPTER 4

Dating a chiropractor has its advantages. Mary and I first met four months ago when I referred an auto accident client to her. The more we got acquainted with each other, the more it became clear how much we had in common, particularly our love of animals and gangster flicks.

"Walsh Chiropractic Clinic, how may I direct your call?"

"Is Dr. Mary available? This is Jason."

"She's finishing with a patient. I'll let her know you're on the phone."

I spend the dead airtime furiously working the Google search engine for new developments on Heather.

"Hey, sweetie, how did the hearing go this morning?"

"We settled. As always, I appreciate you sending Mr. Ellis my way."

"Of course. My patients love you. I just examined an elderly woman who is perfect for you. A rear-end collision. The trunk of her car is smashed like an accordion."

"Outstanding. When can I visit with her?"

"She's coming in for a manipulation tomorrow. I'll email you the details."

"Sounds fantastic. I'm in Oakland, heading to meet an old friend at the Cathedral of Learning." I roll down my window at a red light. A kid with a backpack exits the Dirty Dog, an iconic University of Pittsburgh hot dog joint. He's chomping on an extra-long frank with chili con carne oozing over the sides of the bun. A soft breeze guides the frankfurter equivalent of a cocaine high into my nostrils. The car behind me honks as Mary's voice jostles me back to the present. "I hope your reunion goes well. Are you still coming by tonight? I thought we'd grab dinner and take a romantic stroll on Mt. Washington."

"Let's do that. There's a new hamburger joint I want to try," I say, scouting for a hard-to-find campus parking space.

"Hmm, I'm thinking sushi. We need to break you of your junk food addiction. Before you know it, you'll be spinning with me before work. Won't that be fun?"

Mary is a spin fiend, but I see no enjoyment in perspiring my ass off with fifty other people in a cramped room, spraying sweat onto each other, then going home and posting their scores on social media like they won the Tour de France.

Her voice goes hushed and smokey. "Have you ever done it on the incline? Faire l'amour?"

I don't need Google Translate to catch her drift. Public sex on one of two city inclines chugging up the side of Mt. Washington is the Pittsburgh version of the mile-high club. I miss an open spot, slam on my brakes, and put the car in reverse. Unfortunately, the driver behind me—one who's probably not preoccupied with an unexpected offer of voyeuristic *concubito*—slides in before I can back up.

I clear my throat twice. "Can't say I have, but it sounds intriguing."

"Get ready for an exhilarating ride," she whispers. "My next patient is here. Enjoy your time with your friend."

The last time I wandered the halls of the Cathedral of Learning was as a student at the University of Pittsburgh School of Law. At the time, I lacked appreciation for the architectural grandeur of the building, one of the tallest in the city, rising forty-two floors and 535 feet above the ground.

I push through the double doors with no clue why David chose this place. This is also not the most inconspicuous location. Days and early evenings, the lush green space surrounding the structure is alive with activity.

The first-floor hallway is bustling with people entering and exiting classrooms and different nationality rooms. The extravagantly decorated homages to countries around the world are a huge tourist attraction, especially during the summer and fall months. Each room is designed and furnished for an authentic experience of stepping on foreign soil.

David texts: *Don't worry about the sign. The door is unlocked.*

The Italy Room comes up on my left. A square piece of cardboard covering the window reads, "Temporarily Closed for Renovation."

I'm not sure how long I stare at the entrance before turning the doorknob.

The lights are off, but the mid-afternoon sun is high and penetrating the arched windows. Rays of sunlight diffused by iron mesh protecting the glass crisscross the window frame, giving the room an angelic aura. The rich oil smell of antique furniture fills the room like I've walked into an ancient Florence monastery. David sits in a wooden pew staring up at a mural of a petite woman in a white, flowing dress.

Our eyes meet as he stands, walks past me, and locks the door. His are sullen and ice-cold, like a February dusk. Straggly brown hair with streaks of gray sprouts from his ball cap, dropping below his shoulders in sharp contrast to his neatly coiffed beard. His skin appears weather-tanned and age-lined in a dignified way. He has the appearance of a time-worn outdoorsman emerging from deep in the wilderness after thirty years of solitude. That beard and hat. I run my thumb over the edge of my collar where a Good Samaritan latched on and saved me from being roadkill.

"That was you this morning wasn't it. Why didn't you identify yourself instead of ambling off like a complete stranger?"

He shrugs and says, "I didn't expect you to do a Stevie Wonder into the path of a bus and reacted on instinct. The timing wasn't right, and we are in fact, strangers."

He's right. I don't know this bearded enigma. With time to think, would he have left me in the street to become a hood ornament? It could have been poetic payback for doing the same to him in the storeroom when we were kids, but what was I supposed to do?

"You've obviously been tailing me. Why?"

"I wasn't following you."

David glances at the door as if he expects someone to enter.

"Well, that's quite the first contact after thirty years. The video would make a nice feel-good story. Long-lost friends reunited in life-saving act. Whatever you were doing there, thank you again."

I offer my hand, but he doesn't reciprocate. His right hand remains at his side and appears deformed with three fingers crooked and bent at odd angles. Possibly a car accident? Maybe the best course of action is to slow down. He wasn't on the sidewalk by happenstance, but I don't want to agitate and drive him away.

"Where have you been all these years? I've tried to track you down, but it was like you left the planet."

A thick silence saturates the room as David adjusts his cap awkwardly, grabbing the brim with his right thumb and pinkie. He slides it downward making it more difficult to see his eyes. "I didn't want to be found."

"How's your dad?" I ask.

"He's dead." There is no hint of sorrow or reflection, as if he's reading a random obituary. I resist the urge to ask how he died.

"I'm so sorry, David. May his memory be a blessing."

David crosses his arms and stares at the polished hardwood floor. I stand in silence, waiting. Loud voices in the hallway contract my chest muscles in paranoid twitches. I walk to the door and position my ear flush against the glass window.

"I locked the door from the inside," he says.

Famous last words, I think.

"Is anyone in your life?" I ask.

David cocks an eyebrow as if I've asked the stupidest question ever. "What?"

"Do you have anyone? Wife, girlfriend, kids?"

David takes a deep breath and picks at his fingernails. "Not at the moment. Never married. I didn't see the point."

"Why did you choose this place?"

The screech of an approaching siren draws my attention to the window. David and I move toward the glass in unison as the wail intensifies, then stops. A car is pulled over, and the officer is at the driver's window writing a ticket. We look at each other, shake our heads, and both release a stuttered laugh of nervous energy.

"Remember when our parents took us here?" he asks. "We made believe we lived in different countries and pretended to speak the native language."

I grin and nod. "I had forgotten about that. We had a blast creating our own version of pig Latin."

Reminiscing is fine, but I need to somehow budge the thirty-year-old elephant in this room.

"What are we going to do about Heather?" I ask. "Have you spoken to Trent?"

He removes a folded piece of paper from his pocket. "Do you remember the Odessa Club?"

How could I ever forget?

New Year's Eve, 1988. I was sixteen years old. David and I were watching *Unsolved Mysteries* at my house when Trent Stodge called.

"Yo man, the 'rents are throwing a charity poker game at the Odessa Club," he said. "I'm home alone and popped the new Super Mario into the Nintendo. Come on over. We'll knock down brews while we play."

A week before, Trent bragged he was flying to Vail with Heather Brody. They had been dating since they met at a party last Halloween. The relationship took me by surprise—other than their families both having money, they were so different. Trent, a year older than me, had been kicked out of a Jewish private school for selling weed and worked at his dad's toy store nights and weekends. He continually boasted he would one day take over the family business. She was a National Merit Scholar with visions of Harvard and medical school.

"Very cool but I thought you'd be in Vail with Heather," I said, excited at the prospect of Super Mario. My dad couldn't afford Nintendo, but Trent always had the latest video games.

"I planned on going, but her parental units had a cow when they found out I was showing up—Heather's bitch of a sister snitched to them that I got expelled from school, so now it's like I'm not good enough for her or something. Our house is bigger, and my dad drives a way nicer car than her old man. The trip would have been lame anyways with her parents spying on us. Come on over."

I looked at David. He wasn't a fan of Trent's bragging and considered him a poser, but he loved the Steinway baby grand piano in Trent's living room. I knew he would tag along.

"Sure, we're on our way," I said and hung up.

We threw on our coats and gloves and trudged the quarter mile to Trent's place from the have-nots side of the track, to a world of house-keepers, in-ground swimming pools, and summer trips to the Pocono Mountains, or as my dad often called the area, the Jewish Riviera.

Trent greeted us wearing jeans and a T-shirt emblazoned with, "Stodgehill Toys—Get Your Yahtzee On!" We followed him into the living room.

"How about those brews?" David said as he sat down at the Steinway.

"Tickle those ivories, Mr. Piano Man," I quipped.

For the next few minutes, David mesmerized me with a spot-on rendition of "New York State of Mind." When it was over, he stood, faced me, and bowed. I clapped and slapped him on the back.

"You're going to be famous, dude."

David wasn't talented in the way a guy hitting most of the high notes in a karaoke bar was. He was truly gifted.

We had stopped playing Super Mario and had moved on to black-jack when I noticed the clock on the wall was ticking close to midnight. Gesturing toward the television, I said, "The Times Square ball is about to drop. Turn on the tube."

"Fuck the ball," Trent replied with a dismissive wave of his hand. "I have something way more fun."

He walked to the front door and stepped onto the porch. A few seconds later, he came back inside, closed it, and turned the dead bolt. He strode back into the living room, shoved his hand into his pocket and, with two fingers, eased out a tiny, clear plastic baggie filled with white powder.

"Anyone up for a toot?" he asked, grinning. The kind of unsettling grin an evil clown makes before he drags you into the sewer system.

I stared at my feet. My dad didn't talk to me about drugs, mostly I think because he was always exhausted from work. He'd come home from a double shift at the post office, eat something, catch the morning news, and go to bed. The closest I came to drug lectures were the anti-marijuana, war-on-drugs PSAs on television. I imagined my brain as bubbling eggs in a frying pan, even if all I ever did was puff on a joint.

As Trent tipped the baggie and sprinkled a small pile of cocaine onto the coffee table glass, I stole furtive peeks at the foyer as if there were an unseen SWAT team waiting to kick in the door or worse, Trent's parents returning from the Odessa Club. Trent lifted a playing card off the top of the deck and drew it backward through the almond-size mound of powder, creating two equal lines of blow. He then pulled a ten-dollar bill out of his wallet and rolled it into the shape of a straw. He offered it to David whose eyes narrowed into an are-you-fucking-kidding-me expression.

"I don't do that shit. I'm on my way to Julliard next fall." *

Trent howled in laughter and said, "Dude, you smoke more weed than a Jamaican. I know your dealer."

David shrugged and said, "That's different. It chills me out."

Trent tilted the money tube in my direction. "Jason's going to do it. He's not a pussy, right?"

The force of Trent's glare melted through my fake bravado, leaving behind a nervous and unsure little boy.

"I don't think so," I stammered.

"Lay off him," David said, glaring at Trent, who ignored him and shoved the rolled bill so close to my face I thought he was going to jam it into my nostril. "It's your turn, wuss."

David's voice seemed a mile away. "Don't snort that shit, Jason. Your pops will skin you alive if he finds out." I wish Trent's parents hadn't been at the Odessa Club that night. I wouldn't have been at his place and taken the straw from him.

The wail of a child crying in the hallway jerks me back into the real world. "Yeah, I remember the place," I say. "It was above the toy store. Trent's dad hosted parties, and there was lots of gambling as well until his dad got busted for tax evasion and went to prison. He died a couple years after he got out."

David reaches into his pocket, takes out a folded piece of paper, and hands it to me. It's a 1929 article from the *Pittsburgh Press*. "The club's lineage goes a lot farther back."

I squint, reading the tiny print, which is illuminated only by the natural lighting in the room.

"'Society for Odessa Aid Firebombed.'"

David doesn't wait for a question. "The Society for Odessa Aid was the precursor to the Odessa Club. In those days, it was in the Hill District and run by Ivan Stodchenko, Trent's grandfather. I guess he shortened the name to Stodge at some point."

"What does this have to do with Heather?" I ask.

David hands me another ancient news story.

"'Odessa Society Bombing in Hill District Linked to Jewish Rackets.'"

As I read, pieces fall into place. I knew that Stodgehill Toys got its name because it started in the Hill District, but I had no clue that Trent's grandfather, Ivan, also had a piece of the Prohibition-era numbers rackets. He also ran a speakeasy, serving bootleg booze out of the Odessa Society. Like father, like son? The apple falling right underneath the tree?

"Holy shit," I say.

"Yeah, holy shit."

David uses the back of his hand to blot sweat from his forehead. "The past isn't your fight, and I think I can take care of this, but I needed to warn you. I owe you that. Watch your back. You don't want to mess with these people."

I pace back and forth in front of David, struggling to find words that articulate my confusion. I can't believe this is happening.

"You still haven't answered whether you were shadowing me the other morning, I say."

"I wasn't following you; I was following them."

A disarming tear seeps out from the corner of his right eye and slides down his cheek. Growing up, I don't remember ever seeing him cry. He quickly blots the damp skin with the back of his mangled hand and turns his head away from me. Did he ever make it to Julliard? I'm not sure how he will respond, but I wrap my arms around him, pulling his body to mine. His arms are at first limp at his sides but eventually make their way to my back, pulling me tighter. He buries his head in my shoulder, and his body convulses. He's wrong. I can't run from our past any more than he can. David releases his hold, steps back, and wipes his eyes. The corners of his mouth twist up into an awkward smile. He places his hand on my shoulder as he walks past me to the door. He turns the lock and peeks into the hallway.

"David? Who is them? Where are you going? What are you going to do?"

He looks back at me tight-lipped and stands in place for what seems like an eternity. He then pulls the door wider and slides into the hallway, gently shutting it behind him. That's it? I rush to the door and inch it open. The crowd has thinned, and David's nowhere in sight.

I text, *Where are you going? Text or call me! I can help!*

No response. I open the door wider, push through a tour group, and double-time to the exit.

CHAPTER 5

I flop down on a concrete bench in the green area outside the Cathedral. Lovers are kissing. Dogs are barking. Students lie on blankets with their textbooks spread out. Who was David following? Everyone is suspect, and my head is spinning. I'm a moron for allowing him to walk out and have no clue how I'll find him. Kevin may be able to help, but he'll want something in return.

I open the Google app on my iPhone and once again, for what seems like the one-hundredth time, search Heather's name.

"Allegheny County District Attorney Sonya Kim-Feldman will hold a news conference tomorrow at three p.m. to announce what her office says is a major break in the Heather Brody disappearance. Brody didn't return home after attending a Pittsburgh Pirates baseball game thirty years ago and has not been seen since."

A red Frisbee bounces on the pavement and skids to my feet. I pick it up and search for the thrower. A smiling kid with a shaved head and a goatee waves at me.

"Over here, dude!"

I draw the disc back across my chest and fling my arm forward. The Frisbee spins evenly and straight toward his outstretched hand. The rotation of the red saucer is on a trajectory for a perfect landing when his arm drops to his side, and it flies by him, skidding in the grass. He runs toward the Cathedral and yells, "Holy shit."

A crisscross of screams, hysterical outbursts, and calls for help saturate the air.

"He jumped!"

"Call 911!"

"We need a doctor here!"

"Is he dead?"

I instinctively run toward the motionless body sprawled face down in the grass. A man and woman kneel on either side of him. She announces she's a doctor and checks his vital signs. The man has his ear close to the ground as if the injured person is speaking. He nods his head, turns to the doctor, and says, "His name is David."

Two police officers push by, yelling into their walkie-talkies.

"Make room. Stand back. We have a jumper at the Cathedral of Learning and need to secure the scene."

I step backward, out of the gawking mass of onlookers. Phones are raised high, no doubt taking video and snapping photos. The voyeurism sickens me. I should have gone after him. I'm responsible. The ear-piercing screech of the ambulance siren ends, and moments later paramedics rush by, pushing a gurney. The open lane collapses behind them like the Red Sea, obstructing my view. I spot a gap in the crowd and head for the opening. They stabilize David's neck with a brace and gingerly lift him on his side, sliding the stretcher under him, while the cops compare notes.

One says, "He jumped. They're transporting him to Shadyside Hospital. Let's head over."

I turn and sprint to my car. I'm about to back out of my parking space when my text alert pings.

I'm looking forward to the incline tonight. :o)

Shit, dinner with Mary.

I reply, *My old friend tried to kill himself. I'll call soon.*

She replies immediately: *OMG call when you can.*

Many of my clients end up in the Shadyside Hospital emergency room after auto collisions, so I'm on a first name basis with most of the nurses and doctors. It also happens to be where my friend and next-door neighbor, Dr. Frederick Allen, is on staff. I arrive and jog through the automatic door, straight to the nurses' station where I'm greeted by the not-so-friendly face of Registered Nurse Sarah Adelman. Sarah and I had a month-long romance two years ago after meeting on one of those swipe-right dating apps. The morning after spending the night at my place, she discovered cocaine residue on my bathroom vanity and broke off the relationship, telling me she had dated enough cokeheads for two lifetimes. As I approach the desk, Sarah is busy scribbling on a chart while also talking on the phone. She glances up at me, and hangs up.

"Mr. Feldman, why are we graced with your presence this evening? New client? I'm not aware of any accident victims today."

Ouch, I guess bygones are not bygones.

"Nice to see you as well, Sarah. I'm here about a person who was wheeled in five or ten minutes ago. His name is David Chaney."

She jots on a yellow notepad. "That's his name? He was unconscious and had no identification when they brought him in."

I steal a look past Sarah toward the ICU. "Who's back there with him?"

"Dr. Allen."

"Mind if I wait around a bit?"

Sarah is back on the phone and scribbling. She covers the mouthpiece and juts her head toward the waiting room. "You know where everything is."

"Would you please tell Dr. Allen I'm here?"

She nods and returns to her phone conversation. The Shadyside Hospital ER waiting room isn't designed to comfort traumatized family members who are waiting for good or awful news from a doctor or nurse. Two coffee tables and four equal lines of red and blue hard-plastic chairs make up the furniture in the room. A game show contestant is smiling and clapping on a thirty-two-inch television bolted to the wall. I pick up the remote lying on a three-year-old edition of *People* magazine and announce in a soft but demanding voice, "Unless anyone objects, I'm changing the channel."

No one says a word, so I switch to the local news and turn up the sound. There wouldn't be any reporting on David this soon, but Heather should be dominating the airwaves. Mary is also waiting on my call. I press her name in my phone favorites while keeping one eye on the tube. The weather anchor has a grim look with a red Heat Advisory banner flashing next to the predicted high of 102°F.

"Mary, I am so sorry. I'm at the hospital."

"How is your friend doing?"

"I'm not sure. I'm waiting to speak with the doctor."

"Do you want me to come down?"

I glance toward the nurses' station. No sign of Doc Allen yet. "Don't trouble yourself schlepping all the way here. As soon as I speak to the doctor about his condition, I'll text you."

"How are you holding up?" she asks.

A loaded question with more layers than a wedding cake. How should I answer? We haven't reached the confess my sins stage of our relationship, and there are certain transgressions that never ripen enough to peel back the layer of shame protecting them.

"I'm stressed out and exhausted."

"I'll pray for your friend. Try to sleep well tonight."

"I'll try. Thanks for understanding and being so supportive."

Her tone morphs to genuine surprise. "What else would I be?"

She's right. What else would she be? Why did I expect something different?

I'm about to check online news when the smiling face of a young girl in a graduation cap flashes on the television. I've opened my high school yearbook on multiple occasions to study her every feature. It's Heather's senior photo. I can't hear what's being said but don't dare turn up the sound any louder. The picture changes to video at what appears to be the construction site where her remains turned up. Yellow crime scene tape ropes off the area. I decide to chance pissing off a few people and am about to press volume up on the remote when Doc Allen enters the waiting room.

"Good to see you, Jason. I'm sorry it's under these circumstances. Nurse Adelman tells me you're acquainted with the patient. Are you family?"

I shake my head. "He's an old friend. His name is David. David Chaney."

"Does David have family we can contact? He's in tough shape, and from what I'm told, incredibly lucky the injuries are not more severe. A four-story fall is nothing to sneeze at."

The fourth floor? I assumed he exited the building after leaving the Italian room. If he wanted to kill himself, why not jump from higher? It's the second-tallest university structure in the world.

"There's no one I'm aware of."

"No parents or siblings?"

I shake my head. "His mom left when we were kids. His dad is deceased, and David's an only child. How bad is he hurt?"

Doc Allen crosses his legs and leans back in the chair.

"He sustained multiple fractures and a concussion, but there's no internal damage. He has a lot of healing to do, but as things stand now, I expect him to make a full recovery."

"Did the police tell you where he fell from?" I ask, wondering what else the cops know that I don't.

"Yes, they did, and they acted like jagoffs. One complained he had better things to do than wait on me for a suicide attempt."

"Can I visit him?"

Doc Allen stands and shakes his head. "He's heavily sedated and can't receive visitors."

I employ my best puppy-eyed *I'm all he has left* face. "Right now, I'm his family. Let me in for five minutes."

"He's unconscious, Jason. He won't know you're there."

"Then what's the harm," I press. "Five minutes. I won't stay a minute longer."

Doc sighs and scans the area as if to gauge the privacy of our discussion. There are people scattered around the waiting room, but they appear consumed with their own problems. In the rear corner, an elderly gentleman, at least in his eighties, sits quietly with his head bowed. A woman in courtroom-style business attire is seated next to him, her head on his shoulder, her right hand on his. There are waves of visible ripples in her throat with each swallow, one after the other. She raises her head and dabs at her suit with a tissue. A child of about four or five is on her lap, oblivious to their grief and engrossed in a book my mom read to me, *Curious George*. My favorite line was, "You never know what's around the bend. A big adventure or a brand-new friend." At the front of the room, a woman is rummaging through her purse. Tats cover both her arms. Her face is gaunt, tired, and raw. Her eyes project a resigned hopelessness. She pulls out an empty cardboard Narcan box, shuffles over to a trash container, takes a deep breath, and releases. Did she use the overdose-reversing nasal spray to revive her boyfriend or husband? As she sits and buries her face in her hands, Kevin's moral prostrations about free choice and drug legalization seem less compelling.

No one in this room gives a damn about our conversation.

Doc apparently agrees and motions for Sarah to come over. "Will you please escort Jason to Mr. Chaney's room and stay with him while he briefly visits?"

She walks past me toward the ICU hallway. "I'm happy to, Doctor. Please follow me, Mr. Feldman."

CHAPTER 6

I follow Sarah down the sterile, white hallway, and into David's room. I've been in countless hospitals visiting clients but never adjusted to the nauseating odors of disinfectant and latex that often propel me back in time to my mother's hospice deathbed, where she laid bald, skeletal, and dying of stomach cancer. Sarah removes David's chart from a plastic holder hanging on the back of the door. Seemingly satisfied nothing has changed for the worse, she makes a hieroglyphic notation on a whiteboard, then checks his IV and the monitors. David doesn't open his eyes or acknowledge our presence.

"Dr. Allen says I should stay with you."

"Sarah, this is my best childhood friend. Can you give me three of the five minutes in privacy? I'm going to pray for him."

"Well, I'm not supposed to leave the room."

I sit in the chair next to David's bed and take out my phone.

"I'm going to say a Jewish prayer for the sick and dying. You are welcome to join in with me."

Sarah fidgets with her nurse's badge, and her gaze shifts to the floor.

"I guess it's okay. I'll wait outside."

She backs quietly out of the room and pulls the door shut. I haven't formally prayed on any level since my son's bar mitzvah. Now, in case anyone is listening, I must recite a prayer I last heard at my mom's funeral. I was ten years old and couldn't stop crying. My father took my hand and led me into the bathroom where I sobbed until my throat muscles ached. He dropped to one knee, wiped my tears, and recited the mi shebeirach. I repeated each line and mourned for my mother as only a child can. Was she not coming back? If I prayed and cried hard enough, she would surely be waiting at home, but when we walked in the door, she wasn't there. What was the point of prayer if it couldn't bring my mom back?

After Googling the prayer, I place the phone on David's bed, kneel, and begin reciting.

"May the one who blessed our ancestors, patriarchs Abraham, Isaac, and—" Shit, David's left arm quivers and raises off the bed, rigid and out-stretched, as if he's reaching for something. I check the door and apply pressure to his wrist until it lowers flush on the mattress, then press my lips to his left ear and whisper, "You're going to be okay. I'm sorry I haven't been there for you, but I'm here now." David's eyes flutter open, and with a gasp, he raises his head off the pillow and moans in a muted, raspy voice, "I didn't."

As his head collapses onto the bed, the door opens. In addition to Doc Allen, two frowning faces in sports jackets with gold badges hanging from their suit breast pockets are visible in the hallway. Doc steps into the room, and points to the visitors.

"These are Pittsburgh police detectives. Can you please step outside?"

The female appears in her mid-to-late forties. "Mr. Feldman, I'm Jeanette Keane, and this is Jeffrey Romo. We're detectives with the Violent Crimes Unit. Dr. Allen tells me you're a close friend of David Chaney?"

Violent crimes? Why are they interested in this?

"We were childhood friends, but today is the first day I've seen him in at least thirty years."

Romo flicks his head toward the waiting room and says, "Let's sit down and have a chat. We'd like to ask you some questions."

"Do you mind if I grab a bottle of water from the vending machine down the hall? The air in here is awfully arid."

Romo shrugs. "Suit yourself. Don't take too long."

Doc Allen places the drum of his stethoscope to David's chest while pressing two fingers over the inside of his wrist. "I don't think I'm needed. I'll stay and tend to my patient."

I keep one eye on the detectives as I slide my money into the slot and wait for my water to slide forward and drop. Why are they here? Attempting suicide isn't a crime. Maybe they happened to be in the vicinity? The watchword is listening. I won't volunteer anything more than the painfully obvious.

I return to the waiting area and take the seat I was in fifteen minutes earlier. The Narcan girl is gone, and the same elderly man and his family are standing at the nurses' station. A stone-faced doctor is speaking with them. The old man's chest heaves erratically, and the woman is sobbing while a little girl tugs her arm. "Don't be sad, Mommy." The child will eventually lose all memory of her grandmother. I wonder how long they were married, probably forever.

Keane positions the chairs so she and Romo face me like I'm in the principal's office. She has a Detective Olivia Benson from *Law & Order: SVU* vibe to her with wavy, dark-brown hair dropping below her shoulders, high cheekbones, and an *I always get my man* expression in her determined eyes, which size me up through conservative, black-rimmed eyeglasses. She begins the inquisition.

"Let's start with easy stuff. What's your friend's name?"

I steal a glance down the hallway toward David's room. Has he spoken again? What's going on in there?

"His name is David Chaney."

Romo nods and scribbles. "That's what the nurse and doctor told us."

"I'm the one who told them. He and I were childhood friends, but as I told you, I hadn't seen him for a long time before today."

Romo takes his turn. "If the first time you saw him in thirty years is here at the hospital, how did you find out about his suicide attempt?" His tone is one of *I caught you in a lie, and now you're mine.* My gut feeling is he's the bad cop in every sense of that phrase.

"I didn't say this was the first time. I spoke to David this morning. He texted me the other day, and we agreed to meet at the Cathedral of Learning."

There is no reason to obfuscate the basics. CCTV security cameras are in abundance on campus. One of the gawkers might also expose my presence by posting video on social media. I've learned something from long and painful personal experience and countless witness cross-examinations. While spontaneous bullshit often makes sense at the moment, the liar rarely considers the almost infinite external variables which eventually cut right through to the ugly truth. The moral of the story is if you're going to fabricate, pick your spots. This isn't one of them.

"Why did he want to get together?" Keane asks.

"I guess he wanted to catch up. We chit-chatted about old times, and we both left. He seemed fine."

Keane leans forward in her chair, resting her chin in her right palm. Her stare is soul-piercing, as if she knows every lie I'm going to spout before it leaves my lips.

"Why the Cathedral of Learning?" Keane asks. "Does the location have significance to either of you?"

"Our folks took us there as kids. Nostalgia, I guess."

"Are his parents alive?"

"David mentioned his father had passed. I don't know about his mom. Like I told the doctor, she took off when we were young. I don't remember him ever talking about her."

Doc Allen finally walks out of David's room and heads in our direction. He sits down next to me, facing Keane and Romo.

"David is conscious but heavily sedated. He's banged up good with multiple fractures, but his injuries are relatively minor compared to how much worse they could be, given the fall."

Romo scribbles in his notebook. "Give me the fifth-grade version, Doc."

Doc Allen reads from his clipboard. "David sustained a concussion, three fractured ribs, a broken right wrist and left ankle."

The hospital intercom blares, "Dr. Allen to ER, stat."

We turn our heads in unison toward a commotion at the emergency room entrance. Paramedics are wheeling in a child covered to her neck with a blood-soaked sheet. Doc bolts to his feet and rushes to meet them. Two police officers are next through the door, struggling with a male fighting to get out of his wheelchair. Keane jumps up and says, "Wait here. We're not done yet."

Romo yawns and says, "You got this, I'll keep Mr. Feldman company."

"You're not going to assist your partner?" I ask."

While two cops pummel the guy back into his seat, Keane handcuffs his wrist to the metal armrest.

Romo grins and says, "Did it look like she needed my help?"

"I guess not," I say, tapping the empty chair next to me. "Detective, I've been sitting in these uncomfortable hunks of plastic for well over an hour, waiting to learn about the condition of my friend. I'm exhausted and going home. Here's my business card. My cell number is on the back."

Romo studies it and says, "A lawyer, huh. What kind of law do you practice?"

"Personal injury."

"Give us a few more minutes of your time and you can go home. Why didn't you alert the officers at the scene that you knew David?"

"After visiting with my old friend, he takes a nosedive out of one of the tallest buildings in the city. I was in shock, and by the time I pulled myself together, David was in the ambulance. I got over here as fast as I could. Why are you interested in this? Attempting suicide hasn't been a crime in this state for many years."

Romo stops writing, cocks an eyebrow, and says, "I'm aware of that, counselor, and I didn't even go to law school."

I point to the circular clock on the wall. "The evening is late, and I'm tired. You have my contact information. Goodnight."

"Your name is familiar," Romo says. "Weren't you married to the district attorney?"

"Yeah, I was. Why are you asking?"

"No reason," he says.

Bullshit. Cops don't ask a question without a reason.

I exit the waiting room. Keane is down the hall, still speaking with the paramedics and uniformed officers. She snakes her head around in my direction for a moment and returns to her discussion. Sarah is wiping tears from her cheek while talking on the phone.

"I'm devastated, Mom. She couldn't have been more than thirteen years old."

Sarah raises her head. Her eyes are bloodshot and puffy. Streaks of makeup stain her cheeks. The phone's receiver shines damp with tears.

I lean over the counter as far as I can. "What's wrong?"

She says, "I'll call you later, Mom. I love you too."

Sarah juts her chin at the now beaten and bruised guy moaning in his wheelchair.

"A wrong-way drunk driver on Forbes Ave." She dabs another tear.

"How bad is the girl hurt?"

Sarah slides another tissue out of the box in front of her. "She didn't make it. The drunk barely has a scratch." She bawls quietly.

I want to say, "If it's any comfort, he now has more than a few scratches after that beating." Instead, I put my hand on hers. "I'm so sorry. May her memory be a blessing."

She swallows hard and says, "Death goes with the job, but losing children always rips me apart, especially when alcohol is involved. It haunts you."

I feel her pain. Memories like that can haunt us for a lifetime.

I text Mary: *My friend is banged up but will be ok. Headed home.*

She texts back: *I'm so sorry sweetie. Do you want me to come over?*

I text: *I'm crashing the moment I walk in the door. Call you tomorrow.*

Ok, get some rest.

CHAPTER 7

A summer storm last night broke the heat wave and ushered in a cooler, cloudy morning, allowing me to decompress on my back porch with a cup of coffee and my laptop before driving to the hospital to check on David. The expansive, timber, oil-stained deck extending into a privacy fenced backyard was a key selling point in the decision to buy the 1800-sq.-foot, 1950s original wood-frame home in Schenley Park. Sonya and I envisioned countless evenings sipping tea on the porch while watching Sam play. The fantasy oasis of inner peace insulated her from the evil she dealt with daily, but even the seven-foot-high fence couldn't shield me from my past.

I first met Sonya Kim-Feldman when we were students at the University of Pittsburgh School of Law. Her black hair falling to the small of her back and ocean blue eyes stopped my heart the moment I ogled her seated in the law school lounge. At six feet, she was the tallest girl in the school, standing out like the Mona Lisa hanging next to paint by numbers. She was also brilliant, with the ability to engage on any topic, from sports to intricate constitutional law concepts. It's a cliché, but I knew right off she was the girl I would marry.

I devised a plot to get her attention by delivering a bouquet of red Valentine's Day roses to her apartment. The holiday came and went, and Sonya was her usual cheerful self but said nothing about the flowers. I was heartbroken but knew something wasn't right. Sonya wouldn't ignore a romantic gesture. She'd say something, even if letting me down gently as she had done with other law students who vied for her affection.

I returned to her building, and the roses were still in front of her door, wilted and long dead.

As I picked up the vase, a door across the hall squeaked open. An elderly woman in her bathrobe leaned into the hallway.

"Did you leave those flowers?" she asked in a cranky voice.

"Yes, ma'am, I did. I guess I had the wrong apartment."

"You sure as hell did, young man. Lilly and I were best friends, and she died last week. You have some nerve leaving red roses at her door."

"Ma'am, I'm sorry. I made a mistake."

"You don't live in this building and shouldn't be here. I'm calling the police."

I sprinted down the hallway to the elevator and collided with Sonya who was getting off.

"Jason, what's with the bouquet? Do you deliver them part-time?" She winked. "You know they're dead, right?"

I sucked in all the oxygen my lungs could hold and exhaled, thinking, *Now is the time heroes, cowards, and boyfriends are made.* "Sonya, you're not going to believe this, but..." She laughed and told me her mailbox didn't match her unit number. The mission, however, was a success. The brilliant, first-generation Korean American law review student was dating the middle-fifty-percent-ranked Jewish schlub. After graduation, we married, and nine months after our wedding night, Sam was born.

I shower, brew my java, then bang around the Internet for thirty minutes in a fruitless search for new information on David and Heather, I power down, dress, feed Willie, and head out to visit David.

As I'm opening my car door, my phone vibrates.

I'm out of here. Don't try to find me and B careful.

I stop the car and respond, *Where are you? I'm on my way to the hospital.*

Within seconds, I get an auto-text: *Error: Invalid Number. Please re-send using a valid mobile number or valid short code.*

I try again. Same response.

I slam my foot on the gas pedal. Tires spin on the wet pavement and catch, propelling me backward into the street. I juke the steering wheel to avoid crashing into a parked car. The acrid odor of burnt rubber filters through the air conditioner as I race to the hospital. Walking in, I don't recognize the nurse at the ER desk. He's conversing with a doctor who is also a new face. Her name tag reads, "Dr. Cheryl Fleming." I catch bits and pieces of chatter about the two dead kids yesterday and Dr. Fleming's irritation at the beating the drunk driver took from the cops.

"I had to console grieving family members and suture up the injuries that asshole took from the police on top of it. Don't they know we end up cleaning up their mess?"

The nurse, whose tag reads, "Chris Jenks," nods sympathetically and says, "I heard he was combative so they had no choice."

"Yeah, but still..."

"Excuse me," I say, reaching for the pump bottle of hand disinfectant on the counter. I push down on the plunger, and a dime-size blob drips into the palm of my right hand.

The doctor sighs, glances toward the entrance, and says, "I hope the drama this morning isn't a predictor of how this day goes. That guy was out of his mind to discharge in his condition, but I couldn't talk any sense into him." She picks up a clipboard and trudges down the hallway.

"Chris, I'm here to see David Chaney. He's in room 134."

"Mr. Chaney is no longer a patient here."

I had hoped David was kidding with his text. Why would he leave in his condition?

"He's not here? Are you sure you have the right person? His name is David Chaney, admitted yesterday after an attempted suicide."

"Yes, he left this morning."

I glance down the hallway toward David's room, fighting the urge to ignore Nurse Jenks and see for myself.

"How is that possible? He was barely conscious when I was here the other day."

"He self-discharged against doctor's orders. I can't tell you anything more, sir. There are strict rules regarding patient confidentiality."

"Can you provide a current address for him? If he's no longer your patient, you can release information to a family member or a close friend." I'm spewing bullshit, but as a famous hockey player said, you miss one hundred percent of the shots you don't take.

Chris isn't an idiot. "Sir, I'm still bound by hospital guidelines and privacy laws."

"Can you at least tell me if Detectives Keane or Romo stopped by this morning to check on him? They're not your patients."

Jenks frowns and looks around with a, "Will someone please get rid of this asshole," expression. Sarcastic condescension probably wasn't a sound strategy. "Not while I've been on duty," he says, answering the phone.

"Nurses' station, how may I help you?"

"What time did you start your shift?"

He covers the mouthpiece and spits out, "I came on at six a.m. As you can see, sir, I am terribly busy. Is there anything else?"

"Is Dr. Allen in the building?"

"He doesn't come on until this afternoon. I can leave him a message if you'd like."

I won't make headway here and don't want to burn any bridges by morphing from pushy to obnoxious jerk. Quite a few of my clients end up here, so I want to be on the good side of Nurse Jenks.

"Thanks for your help, Chris. I truly appreciate your patience and apologize for my pushiness."

Plan B is to call Doc Allen on his cell. Hopefully, he won't be as anal about patient privacy as Nurse Jenks. I head to the mercifully empty waiting room, take a seat, and dial.

"Hey, Fred, this is Jason. I'm here at the hospital, and David Chaney is gone."

"I know. He checked himself out this morning."

I'm having difficulty processing how someone with multiple fractures pops out of bed and strolls out of the intensive care unit as if he's a self-healing alien from a distant world.

"How could he even walk?" I ask.

"Beats the hell out of me. I'm as surprised as you are. Even with the pain medication, he must have an incredible discomfort tolerance. The doctor on duty called and asked me to talk sense into him, but David wouldn't come to the phone. He apparently demanded his clothes, more pain meds, crutches, signed the release forms, and left."

"Mr. Feldman, funny seeing you here again."

I flinch at the interruption and unwelcome intrusion by the familiar voice.

"Detective Keane, what brings you here," I ask, hanging up on Doc.

Keane's holding a white Styrofoam coffee cup and munching on a doughnut. She reaches into a paper bag and takes out a strawberry Danish. "You want one?" she asks politely, too much so. "One's my limit. Too many of these and the bad guys outrun me."

Romo takes a seat next to me, flipping through his cop book. "We're here to interview David Chaney. Have you spoken to him since yesterday?"

"I walked in five minutes ago, Detective. I was about to head to his room."

Keane peers toward the nurses' station where Dr. Fleming is again conversing with Nurse Jenks. "I'll be right back," she says.

Out of the corner of my eye, I watch Keane engage in a focused conversation with Jenks, who points at me. I grimace and want to kick myself. Write the words on a blackboard one hundred times, Jason, you dumb ass. Don't conjure bullshit by the seat of your pants. Keane shakes Jenks's hand and strolls back in our direction. If Jenks informed her about telling me David was gone, I'm screwed. There's only one play here—double down.

Keane is back in her alpha stance, glaring down at me, her eyes blazing with irritation and impatience. "Why didn't you tell us you knew David left the hospital?"

I have a peripheral view of Romo drilling a hole in my temple as I rise out of my chair and stand toe to toe with Keane. I'm at least four inches taller than her. The height differential will hopefully add oomph to my retort.

"First off, I don't appreciate your tone. I'm aware David is gone because you just told me."

"That's not what the nurse—"

I cut her off. "I don't care what Nurse Jenks says. Why would I hang out in the waiting room if he told me David isn't here?"

Romo fires back, "Maybe you're trolling for your next car accident client."

I ignore the dig, point to the wall clock, and say, "We'll have to continue this later."

Keane says, "I don't think David tried to kill himself." The oxygen is sucked out of the room as they both inch closer to me.

"What do you think happened?" I ask.

"This is an ongoing investigation," she says. "You're a lawyer. You should know how things work."

"I do understand, and unless you're detaining me for a bullshit reason, I'm leaving," I say.

Keane's eyebrows rise, and her right hand sweeps toward the ER entrance. "You're free to leave anytime, but we'd like you to come downtown tomorrow morning for an official sit-down."

I'm not sure what page it's on in the criminal's handbook but never ever walk into a police station for questioning without your attorney. One moment you're a witness, the next you're behind bars.

"Sit down for what? I've told you all I know."

Romo snorts and rolls his eyes. "You haven't told us dick, and I'm starting to believe you're intentionally holding back on us."

"I'm not withholding anything and have a busy day. We're done here. Best of luck with your investigation."

"That's fine," Romo says. "We know where to find you, and I'm confident we'll be speaking with David soon, assuming he's still alive."

Walking to my car, David's dire warning about messing with the wrong people echoes in my memory. Trent's dad wasn't a choirboy, but everything about Trent's present-day endeavors appears entrenched in the respectable, upper-class echelon of the Pittsburgh elite. I pull the article David gave me out of my pocket. If he figured the family history out, the cops will surely make the historical connection to Trent. The legal dominoes would fall, one of them at the feet of my ex-wife, Sonya. It's time to push that one over on my own.

"Allegheny County District Attorney's Office, how may I direct your call?"

The voice on the other end of the phone is pleasant and familiar. Mikkayla Jones has staffed the front desk for over twenty years. Sonya jokingly called her the de facto DA. Nothing happened in the building Mikki wasn't aware of, whether it was a lawyer about to get the axe or an office love affair.

"Hey, Mikki. Jason Feldman here."

"Jason, honey, your voice is a sound for sore ears. How long has it been?"

"Too long, Mikki. How have you been?"

She plays back her usual refrain. "Same old grind, snapping necks and cashing checks."

We both laugh.

"To what do we owe the honor today?" she asks.

"Is Sonya around this morning?"

"Yes, but she walked into her office for a meeting about that poor girl who never came home after a ball game all those years ago. Her remains turned up the other day."

"I read about it in the paper. Can you stick your head in and tell her I'm on the line and need to speak with her?"

My phone vibrates with a text from Kevin: *When are you coming by?*

I almost forgot I have to pick up the WarpMobile at his place for the babysitting gig and Yak rendezvous this evening.

"Jason, I'm sorry it took so long," Mikki says. "I put a sticky note in front of her. She said she will call you back as soon as she can."

"Thanks, Mikki. I appreciate your help."

"Of course, honey. Come by sometime. A lot of us miss you."

I'm still friendly with a few lawyers in the district attorney's office, but most of them despise me, and I don't blame them. Why wouldn't they hate the person who almost imploded their boss's reelection by getting himself arrested on a DWI?

I return Kevin's message: *Be there soon.*

I'm halfway to Kevin's condo when Sonya's name appears on the caller ID. Speaking with her is always a crapshoot. Lawyers are adversarial by nature, but a failed marriage and an estranged son who hates my guts is a recipe for verbal jousting.

"Hello, Jason. What's the emergency?" she asks. "You're not calling about Sam. I spoke with him yesterday, and he said he hasn't heard from you in months.

"I've been meaning to call him. How is he?"

"Here's an idea," she says, the sarcasm dripping from her voice. "Ask him."

We fall back into our combative dance like the dysfunctional version of Rogers and Astaire.

"We've had this conversation," I say. "He has my number and can dial a phone. Let's move on. Are you aware of the guy who fell from the Cathedral of Learning yesterday?"

She sighs. "Yes, I saw the story on the news. I'm swamped with work, Jason."

"His name is David Chaney, and we were childhood friends. In fact, we got together not long before he fell."

"Okay, and?" she says, impatient.

"And I went to check on him at the hospital. He's banged up but going to recover. Two PPD detectives named Keane and Romo showed up and questioned me. They treated me like a perp and want a formal interview. I have no idea why and would rather give my statement to your office."

The silence is now beyond uncomfortable.

"I'm sorry about your friend, but you don't need my office involved to give a statement and this isn't really—"

I don't let her finish. "I would prefer to speak with Mitch. I trust him. Those two cops are jagoffs, especially Romo."

More dead air. "Sonya?"

"Is his name Jeffery Romo?" she asks.

"That's the guy, and you're right about Sam. I've been an asshole dad. I'll call him tonight."

"That will make him happy," she says, her voice softening a bit. "Detective Romo and I have had dealings. An investigator will contact you. I'm late for a meeting. And, Jason—call your son."

I arrive at Kevin's place and punch in the security code to take the elevator to the underground garage. Kevin owns two vehicles. The car covered with a tarp is his Tesla, and the other is my ride, a black Mercedes SUV with the WARP logo painted on the driver's side along with the phone number and tagline, *We pick up and get you there at WARP speed*. I lift the second-row passenger seat and strip back the brown carpeting, revealing a digital safe, ingeniously built into the floorboard to appear as a normal part of the undercarriage. I'm about to open the safe so I can transfer the cocaine to its hiding place when Mitch's cell number flashes on my caller ID. I stop what I'm doing, sit in the SUV, and pull the door shut.

Mitchell Williams is a senior investigator with the district attorney's office, as well as my Alcoholics Anonymous sponsor. He's also the only person besides Sonya and Sam who has confronted me about my penchant for Single Malt Scotch and blow. If cops are human lie detectors, Mitch is a walking urinalysis. Heroin, coke, weed, booze, meth—he nails who's on what with uncanny accuracy. It's probably because he was exposed to so much of it growing up in the Hill District projects not far from where my grandfather spent his childhood before the Jews migrated eastward to Squirrel Hill. When I first stopped showing up to AA meetings, he called once a week but didn't ask if I was using or when I was coming back. He'd say, "Miss you, man. Stay on the beam and be careful out there." He eventually stopped calling.

"How goes it, Mitch?" I ask, glancing nervously at my narcotics as if his Spidey sense travels over the airwaves and through the mouthpiece of my phone.

"Jason, my man. The boss asked me to give you a call. What's new in your world?"

"Ups and downs," I say. "Sorry I haven't been to a meeting in a while. I've been super busy."

"You'll come when you're ready. I'll keep praying for you until then. Let's get down to business. Sonya tells me you know the guy who jumped from the Cathedral yesterday. Why don't you talk to the Pittsburgh cops? You don't need me for this. I'm happy to call the detectives for you and set up a sit-down."

My shirt collar is closing in around my neck. I hate lying to Mitch. I'll have to settle for a half-truth.

"Yes, he's a childhood buddy. This one detective, Romo, was a real dickhead and incredibly accusatory at the hospital. I don't have a problem giving a statement, but I want a friendly face in the room."

"Man, that's tough. Is your friend going to be okay?"

My mind whirls, searching for the right response. "I think so. The doctor said he's lucky the injuries aren't more severe."

"Nothing wrong with good old-fashioned luck. Look, I'm slammed today. I picked up the missing girl cold case that's been in the news."

"I understand the hassle, but I'd consider it a personal favor if you can be there. Why's Romo such a jagoff? Does he think I banged his wife or something?"

Mitch laughs and says, "Nothing like that. You're in the crossfire of bad blood between Romo and your ex. Remember the planted drugs case in Homewood a few years back?"

"I think so. Three cops indicted for perjury and falsifying government records over a drug raid gone bad. They batter-rammed the wrong door down and allegedly planted a gram of blow in the bedroom nightstand.

"Correct. Romo was one of them. The department canned his ass, but a grand jury no-billed him. A review board in their infinite wisdom decided to give him his job back. He hates Sonya, and I suspect by proxy despises you as well."

That's why Sonya knew his name. I don't need the added stress of dealing with a potentially dirty cop who wants to stick it to me as payback for crap I had nothing to do with.

"Thanks for the heads up. It explains a lot. Will you please do this statement with me?"

He mutters, "Fuck it. Yeah, man, I'll make a call. But they may throw a fit for pissing on their fire."

"By the way, Heather Brody and I attended the same high school. Anything about to break?" I ask.

"I'm just digging into the file. Gotta run. I'm sorry about your friend."

I punch my personal security code into the safe's digital keypad, and the lock disengages with a metallic click. The combination changes each time I drive the vehicle for deliveries. The intent is to discourage drivers from sharing the password with cohorts who can stage a carjacking and rob Kevin of his product.

At first, I thought the whole enterprise was insane, and Kevin would surely be caught. Dealers using rideshares to deliver drugs isn't a new concept, but the venture as a money laundering operation is unique, at least Kevin thinks so. I unzip the gym bag he gave me, exposing six quart-size baggies filled with varying amounts of cocaine. Each Ziploc has a preprinted label with a QR code for a specific WARP driver. There are fifty legitimate drivers around the city and ten select drivers delivering the narcotics to the end customer. Kevin's personal security detail of five linguistically challenged Ukrainians distribute the products to the select drivers. Once the kids are on the boat, I'll hand the gym bag off to Yak, a goofy, good-natured, six-foot-five, three-hundred-pound Ukrainian Jew.

I have no clue how Kevin connected with Yak, or where he finds the plethora of thuggish Russians and Ukrainians who work for him. While the regular WARP drivers are a diverse bunch, members of his personal secu-rity entourage are all heavily accented Arnold Schwarzenegger types. They all carry guns and have a former military vibe. When I inquired about their origin, Kevin shrugged and said, "Trade secret."

I stuff the gym bag inside, close the safe, and reenter the code. The lock-ing mechanism whirs and clicks back into place.

CHAPTER 8

The text message comes to meet Mitch at the district attorney's office in two hours for Keane and Romo to take my statement. I decide to grab coffee at the William Penn Hotel, which is right around the corner. As a mental health offset to Sonya's brutal eighty-hour weeks, we occasionally splurged for a babysitter and spent the weekend there. Room service and quiet, smoochy walks in Point State Park allowed her to unwind for a brief time, forgetting about the trauma of incest, sexual assault, domestic abuse, and murder that caused her to privately refer to the office as the Little Shop of Horrors. Coming out of law school, Sonya had other opportunities that would have been far less traumatic and much more financially lucrative. She rejected substantial offers from prestigious law firms around the country, opting instead for a subsistence-level wage position at the Allegheny County Public Defender's Office. Prospective employers, however, were not beating down my door to hire me. I accepted the only offer extended at an eat-what-you-kill, medium-size plaintiffs' personal injury mill, specializing in low-end auto accidents. I didn't earn big money, but being the son of a postal worker, my percentage of contingency settlements seemed like a fortune.

I push through the revolving door into the crowded hotel lobby. Guests are lounging on plush couches and seated at coffee tables. Interlocking conversations echo off the crystal chandeliers and through a cavernous space that, from vintage photos I've seen, doesn't appear much different from the early 1900s. I wonder if Sonya still spends weekends here. Our one-time love nest usurped by some rich lobbyist asshole from DC I heard she's dating. I grit my teeth and exhale. Don't do this to yourself, Jason. She's entitled to move on with her life. I spy a newspaper left on a table and take a seat.

A Heather Brody retrospective takes up the bottom half of the front page, recounting candlelight vigils, the one hundred-thousand-dollar reward offered by her parents, and her father's tragic suicide. The article closes with remembrances from her high school classmates and long-time residents of Squirrel Hill who knew her as a child. Retired bakery owner Josiah Cohen said, "She was such a sweet, young girl, coming in with her mother on Thursday evenings to buy their Sabbath challah. Our community has seen so much death and pain. I hope they catch her killer so we can begin to heal."

Buried on page five is another eye-catching blurb: "According to the University of Pittsburgh campus police, an unidentified male attempted suicide by jumping out of a fourth-floor classroom at the Cathedral of Learning around four p.m. yesterday. He was transported to Shadyside Hospital, and his current condition is unknown."

I take another glimpse around the lobby and smile at the memory of our honeymoon night. This was our hotel, but I no longer belong. I tuck the paper under my arm and leave.

Mikki smiles and motions me over when I push through the doors of the Allegheny County District Attorney's Office.

"The conference room is occupied, but Sonya's out of the building and says you are more than welcome to use her office. The detectives and Mitch are already in there."

I alternate between relieved and irritated that Sonya isn't here. I thought I might pry some information about the DC lobbyist out of her. Sonya's office doesn't appear much different from the last time I was here to pick up the signed divorce papers. Her Pitt Law diploma and license to practice in Pennsylvania hang on the wall behind her desk. An impressive addition is her admittance to argue before the U.S. Supreme Court. Romo, Keane, and Mitch are all seated, messing with their phones. Keane pockets hers and says, "Mr. Feldman, we need to stop running into each other this way."

Beware of cops bearing bad jokes.

I tap Mitch on the shoulder. He lays his phone on the table, stands, and says, "Jason Feldman, how are you, my man? How long has it been?"

I last saw him at my swan song AA meeting seven months ago yesterday. He knows that.

"It's great to see you again," I say, grasping his gargantuan hand, which is attached to a six-foot-seven body that tips the scales at around 270 pounds.

"Sorry I haven't reached out before this," he says. "The workdays here are nonstop crazy."

He's being diplomatic. He stopped reaching out when I lost interest in my sobriety.

"No worries," I say, trying to short-circuit the uncomfortable truth, which is addicts disappear from the fellowship for a reason and chasing them down rarely does any good.

"I believe we are all acquainted," he says, gesturing across the table. "The detectives graciously agreed to this so let's not waste their time."

Keane places a mini digital recorder on the conference table. I expected the interview to begin with soft background questions, but the lead is a verbal haymaker from Romo.

"This is officially an attempted murder investigation. What was David doing on the fourth floor of the Cathedral of Learning and what were you really doing at the hospital this morning?"

Mitch stares at me in abject surprise. He must have thought this was a run-of-the-mill suicide attempt. He turns his attention to Keane and says, glaring, "Why didn't you tell me this when I reached out to you? I don't appreciate being blindsided."

Keane shrugs and says, "I didn't say anything because this isn't your case, and you and Mr. Feldman have history."

I stiffen in my seat. "Exactly what history are you referring to?" I ask.

Before Keane can answer, Mitch bolts to his feet, propelling his chair backward into Sonya's desk. He leans forward across the conference table, jabs his finger at her, and says, "I'm not going to stand here and take crap from you. I've been on the job a long time, and no one has ever questioned my integrity."

Romo springs up and grabs Mitch's wrist. "Whoa, back the fuck up big guy, and get your digit out of her face. Who do you think you're talking to?"

Mitch torques his massive arm, easily breaking the grip. "Keep your hands off me."

Keane raises her hand and says, "Let's all settle down and reset. You're right. I should have filled you in, and I apologize. Let's return to the matter at hand."

Mitch takes a deep breath and sits back down. "I'm sorry. Yeah, let's chill out and finish up. I have a busy day."

He turns and stares at me, probably wondering what else I've held back from him.

"We all do. What was your friend doing on the fourth floor?" Keane asks.

"I don't have a clue," I say. "He also didn't tell me where he was going when he left our meeting, and I was simply checking on an injured friend at the hospital. Wouldn't you?"

Romo says, "Sure, I'd check on a friend, but I sure as hell wouldn't lie to the police about knowing he had checked himself out of the hospital. Why did he run, Jason?"

Sarcasm is a terrible idea, but I can't help myself. "I haven't lied about a damn thing. It's your investigation. Find the bad guys and ask them why he ran. I'd love to know."

Mitch kicks me under the table, and Romo bites back. "Do you think this is funny?"

I scowl at Mitch and shake my head. "No, I don't. If someone genuinely wants to do David harm, you need to catch them. That's your job, not mine."

Keane cocks an eyebrow and says, "You asked for this sit-down, so I assumed you wanted to assist us. So far, you've been less than cooperative to the point of obstructive. Where in the Cathedral did this get-together occur?"

"We met in the Italian room on the first floor. He texted me earlier in the day that he was in the city and asked if we could visit."

"In town from where?" Keane asks.

I shrug. "I dunno. He didn't say."

Keane jots some notes and plunks her elbows on the table. Her fingertips are pressed together, forming a tent-like space between her hands.

"Let's recap, so I'm sure I have this correct. Your childhood friend, whom you last saw thirty years ago, asks you to meet him. During this reunion, he doesn't tell you where he lives, what he's doing here, or where he's going. This is the story you're going with?"

"Pretty much," I say, averting my gaze to a photo on the wall of Sonya shaking hands with Barack Obama. "And if you're thinking I had something to do with this, you're nuts. Check the campus video. I was already out of the building."

Romo tears a page out of his notebook and pushes it in my direction. "You're not a suspect but check this timeline counselor, and please feel free to correct me if I have the math wrong. Campus video has you entering the Cathedral at two fifty p.m. You're on tape leaving at three thirty. David went Superman without a cape at about quarter to four. Your meeting with your childhood friend who you hadn't seen in thirty years couldn't have lasted more than twenty or twenty-five minutes. Your story is bullshit. Why did you really meet with him?"

"There's nothing more I can say, and I'm sorry you think I'm lying, but everything I've said is the God's truth. May I go?"

I refuse to make eye contact with Mitch who I'm sure is aggravated at my lie of omission. Keane gives me a sideways glance, sighs, and closes her notebook. "You can go, but we may have more questions as the investigation progresses. Here's my card. I'll expect a call if David contacts you or anything new comes to mind."

I'm about to press the elevator button when Mitch exits the office.

"Man, you were not smart in there, and I'm not talking about lying to me about the Chaney kid and dicking around the detectives. Your pupils resemble eight balls rolling to the corner pocket. I won't ask you if you're holding."

I puff out my chest and say, "First off, I didn't lie to you. I found out they were treating David's fall as an attempted murder the same moment you did. Second, I'm not holding, and I'm not fucking high."

Mitch frowns, but his voice softens. "I'm not going to pry, but we would be honored with your presence at the group sometime. You're missed. I pray for you."

I take a quick look toward the office we just left. Keane and Romo are at Mikki's desk, talking on their phones and probably waiting for me to leave before they exit. "I appreciate the thoughts and prayers, but I'm fine," I say. "Can I ask you something?"

"Shoot," Mitch says.

"You grew up in the Hill District, right?"

"Sure did. Lived in the Terrace Village projects. Why are you asking?"

"I'm curious how Heather ended up in that vacant lot. She definitely wasn't the Hill type."

"We haven't figured that out yet," he says. "We're tracking the ownership history of the lot. The city demolished the structure in the mid-nineties. It was one of the last existing buildings on the Hill from the early 1900s. I hate that there's so little left from the golden era of the Hill District, but the place was a haven for rats and junkies."

The elevator doors are about to shut when Mitch sticks his giant paw between them and they slide back. "And about the other thing, I'm here for you if you need me."

He withdraws his hand, and the metal doors slide shut.

CHAPTER 9

My birthday party pickup location is an old-money, upper-class enclave about nine miles south of Pittsburgh. I punch the address into Google Maps and make quick time. Mansion-style homes line both sides of the street. The horseshoe driveway winds around a meticulously manicured lawn, allowing me to pull up to the front door behind a late model Jag.

A white-haired, well-groomed guy in blue shorts is standing outside and extends his hand as I exit the car. He appears to be in his early sixties, with obvious cornrow hair plugs dyed gray, almost silver. If a bust of George Washington were stamped on his head, it could pass for a quarter.

"Roger Hambrick," he announces, trying to turn my hand into kindling with his grip. "Thank you for doing this. Kevin speaks highly of you."

"I'm glad I'm able to help you out. I'll take great care of the kids."

"I'm counting on it, and please, call me Rog." He wraps his arm around my neck and guides me through the front door and into a living room resembling a set from *Gone with the Wind*. I half expect Scarlett O'Hara to appear in a green velvet dress at the top of the winding, wooden staircase. Roger walks to a fully stocked bar and removes a bottle of Louis Treize from its perch with one hand while plucking two brandy glasses hanging upside down with the other.

"How about an evening sip before you leave?" He pauses before filling my glass. "Oops, no drinking and driving. How about an iced tea instead, or an Evian?"

"I'm fine, Rog," I say, mesmerized by the cornucopia of top-shelf booze lining the glass shelf. I've never been a brandy guy, but the bottle of Macallan Single Malt next to the Louis commands over one hundred thousand dollars and it sure as hell can't be found in Pittsburgh.

Roger checks his Rolex. "The kids are upstairs and will be down shortly. Kevin tells me you're a lawyer."

I shift the weight on my feet as my discomfort level rises. "Yes, primarily personal injury law, auto accidents and such."

He winks, slaps me on the back, and says, "An ambulance chaser, huh? No offense. I'm just pulling your chain."

What an asshole. Roger's an investor and doesn't know I'm a cocaine courier for Kevin? I guess he wouldn't mention that in mixed company. How deep in is he with WARP? Narco math is easy. The profits are in the drugs, not the superficially respectable business front. Roger walks halfway up the staircase and says, "Emmy, you and your friends hustle your butts down here. Your driver is here."

Within seconds comes the rumble of trampling feet interspersed with squeals, giggles, and unintelligible code words I suspect only sixteen-year-old girls understand. They stampede into the living room and encircle us. A cute, heavy-set girl with thick soccer legs and a blonde bob breaks ranks and bear-hugs Rog around the waist. "All set, Daddy. This will be so much fun."

Her squeaky Mouseketeer voice has me regretting not bringing earplugs.

"Emmy, this is Mr. Feldman. I've given him your cell number, and he'll give you his."

Emmy lasers a disapproving glare at her dad, undoubtedly peeved at the breach of teen protocol. Phone numbers are exchanged with friends and parents only. Handing such sensitive information over to a stranger-danger old guy is way out of bounds. Roger puts his hand on Emmy's shoulder and says in a tone of pure parental lecturing, "You are to text Mr. Feldman when the Gateway Clipper is docking."

"Yes, Daddy."

This girl has Roger wrapped around her finger. Her closet is undoubtedly lined with expensive, imported ski jackets from Vail, Aspen, Whistler, even the Alps. She doesn't come off as a bad kid, but I suspect he will bail her out of trouble multiple times before she hits twenty-one.

"Do you remember the ground rules?" Roger asks.

"Yeeees, Daddy, no drinking and no marijuana," she replies, rolling her eyes.

An elegant female voice rings down from upstairs. There's a Slavic flavor to her accent, but not like Yak, who's made an art of missing vowels and butchering the English language. "Are they leaving, Roger? I'm coming down the stairs."

A perfectly manicured Barbie doll in a red cardigan sweater and hip-hugging white jeans strides down the spiral staircase and beelines to the bar. She must be at least twenty years younger than Roger.

"Jason, this is my wife, Ulyana."

Ulyana is busy mixing herself a gin and tonic and doesn't acknowledge me. Up close, the work is obvious. The stretching of the facial features and the perfect but unnatural nose. Her collagen-engorged lips jut out from her face like overinflated pool floats. Her oversized boobs point straight out, straining the fabric of her sweater. In her teens, she was probably a beauty queen in whatever small Russian village she came from. Miss Stoli Vodka or something.

She takes a sip of her drink, holds out her hand, and wiggles her fingers. I grab them with my fingertips and wiggle back. "Roger tells me you are a lawyer and work for Kevin?"

"Yes on both counts," I say, nodding.

"Do you oversee all his legal matters?"

"Not exactly."

"The work must be remarkably interesting," she says robotically. "Thank you for chaperoning the girls. We are delighted they have someone trustworthy watching over them."

"I'm happy to help out Mrs. Hambrick," I say, tabulating the cost of all the cosmetic surgery she's had done.

"Please, call me Uly," she says, beckoning to Emmy who sprints in from the living room. "Come give your mother a kiss before you go. Listen to Mr. Feldman and don't cause trouble my malen'kaya devochka."

"Okay, Mommy."

Roger walks me through a kitchen door into a five-car garage at least as big as the entire first floor of my house, and occupied by a Mercedes, a Rolls, a Grand Prix Roadster, and a late-model, silver BMW M4 I suspect belongs to Emmy.

"Do you race this thing?" I ask, running my hand over the hood of the Roadster.

"I sure do. Every other Sunday at the racetrack in Wampum. Come out and take a spin with me sometime. It's a real adrenalin rush."

He picks up a terrycloth rag, zeroes in on the smudges I left, and massages the area in circles. Seemingly satisfied he's removed all evidence of my fingerprints and talking more to himself than to me he says, "She's a real beauty."

I'd bet he loves his cars more than his wife and kid.

We exit the garage and stroll around the front of the house to the WarpMobile. Roger pulls the screen door open and shouts, "Let's go, Emmy. You don't want to be late."

"We're coming, Daddy," she yells back from inside the house.

The girls stream outside and move en masse toward the car like a flock of ducks to breadcrumbs. I click the remote and open the rear passenger door for the little princesses. They pile in and fight for the best seat. There's a moment of sheer panic wondering if I locked the safe compartment. I assure myself I did and have fallen victim to the leaving-the-stove-on syndrome and regardless, it's too late to check. All five stuff themselves into the back while the seat next to me remains empty, as if occupying it is a Scarlet X of lameness.

"One of you is welcome to sit up here," I say, patting the leather. "You're packed back there like sardines."

No one utters a peep. No one moves. Before we hit the first traffic light, the kids are giggling. Three clicks followed by a hissing, like air escaping from a tire puncture, precede the unmistakable odor of weed flooding the vehicle. I adjust the rearview mirror and confirm they are passing around a doobie. I shake my head and mutter obscenities to myself. This is going to be a long-ass night. After veering into a 7-Eleven parking lot, I twist my body around to face the kids.

"This isn't happening, ladies. Put the joint out and toss the ganja out the window."

A rail-thin girl with blue hair, who can't weigh more than eighty pounds, asks, "What's ganja?"

"Marrriiijuaaana," I say. "Throw out the marijuana."

I want to scream, "*You self-absorbed, entitled brats will get me pulled over with thousands of dollars' worth of cocaine in my car.*"

Emmy stares daggers at me, clearly unaccustomed to being told no. "My dad blazes. We're not snorting cocaine or shooting heroin."

"I understand, but you're a minor and it's against the law."

"Lighten up, old man."

I concede defeat, shake my head and mumble, "Please finish before we get to the boat, and do this old man a solid by rolling the windows down an inch."

We're entering the Liberty Tunnels when a cellphone attached to Emmy's outstretched arm appears in the rearview mirror. Behind her, four grinning faces are cheek to cheek. "Everyone say, 'four-twenty.'"

With one hand on the wheel, I reach back and snatch the phone.

"No selfies toking weed. Take all the pictures you want when you're out of my vehicle and someone else is responsible for you, verstheht?"

"Vers what?" Emmy asks.

"It means, 'Do you understand?' It's German."

Emmy grumbles, "Whatever, speak English. Will you please give me my phone back?"

I consider holding it until we arrive at the dock but decide the potential drama eruption isn't worth the effort.

We pull into the parking lot without further incident. The girls pile out of the car, stuffing multiple sticks of gum in their mouths as if that will conceal the overpowering marijuana odor embedded in their clothing. Two thick-necked steroid monsters flank each side of the inclined gangway leading up to the deck of the open-air, paddle-wheel-style riverboat. They greet the teens with a heavily accented, "Welcome aboard." Both have gone full Versace with their outfits. The shirts are open to their nipples, exposing muscled, hairy chests and gold Stars of David. Less conspicuous are the sports jacket breast pocket bulges, undoubtedly concealing firearms. Where does Kevin find these guys? Ukrainian Thugs"R"Us? Kids exit from other cars and scurry up the gangway. The horn blasts, and the boat drifts away from the dock.

I drive my car across the street to my rendezvous with Yak and walk into the calming nostalgia of Three Rivers Bowl. Other than the new high-tech, digital score displays, these are still the old school lanes of my youth, throwing gutter balls with my dad here every Sunday morning in a B'nai B'rith league. The entertainment area consists of three rows of pool tables, two Skee-Ball machines, and a Space Invaders console. Alone in a far corner is an old Rambo pinball machine with an "out of order" sign hanging from the ball ejector. I thought they were extinct, like the Rambo series should have died after the first installment.

Yak is sitting at the bar with a drink in his hand, focused on a bowling match displayed on a sixty-inch, wide-screen, HDTV television. I take the stool next to him and motion to the bartender who appears in her early sixties with a dirty blonde beehive hairdo stuffed into a Pittsburgh Steelers ball cap.

"An Iron City, please," I say.

"Draft or bottle, honey?"

"Draft, please."

"Why do you drink shit beer?" Yak says, nudging my shoulder.

"Only a freaking Ruskie would drink rotgut, bowling alley vodka," I retort.

Without taking his eyes off the television he says, "I am Ukrainian. You know this."

"Yeah, I know. By the way, I saw you toss a gutter ball when I walked in."

He swigs his drink, then gives me a sideways glance. "No gutter balls, ever. I have a 203 average. I could be on professional tour here. I was Ukraine national champion and won many trophies. There were many women."

The thought of Yak as the bowling stud of the Eastern Bloc amuses me. I'll play along.

"Who's your favorite bowler?"

"Earl Anthony is the greatest of all time. We watch him on Wide World of Sports. He is famous in Ukraine. I have his poster. One day, I will be on a poster."

I almost laugh out loud at the visual of two smoking-hot Ukrainian women hanging all over Yak while he palms a bowling ball in each of his Bigfoot hands. "I expect to get an autographed copy. Finish your drink, and let's do our business."

He doesn't budge and stays focused on the big screen. The bowler draws the ball back above his head, bends at the knees, and swings his arm forward like a pendulum. The urethane sphere slides across the oiled wood without rotating and heads straight for the gutter. Then, like magic, it catches and veers toward dead center like a perfect baseball curveball. All ten pins scatter, mowed down like they were hit by a Mack truck. The bowler turns, smiling to the politely clapping audience and pumps his fist.

A lady walks past us with a child and enters a kids' playroom. My mom held my hand walking David and me into the same room. I held David's hand. We played cowboys and Indians on the rocking donkeys. We engaged in all-out squishy Nerf ball warfare, constructing impenetrable forts from giant plastic building blocks. I loved that room. I loved that time, and my best friend.

Yak punches my left shoulder, this time aggressively, almost knocking me off the stool.

"Match is over. Let's go."

Miss Beehive takes his glass, picks up the remote, and switches the channel to a local station. Yak grabs his bowling ball bag off the floor and heads for the exit, but now I'm the one stuck in my seat, staring at the chyron running at the bottom of the television screen.

Break in Heather Brody disappearance. The news promo plays over and over in my head like a Times Square digital ticker tape. As Yak and I exit the complex and walk to the WarpMobile, I wonder if the new development is David.

I survey the parking lot, open the rear door of the WarpMobile, and pull away the carpet to expose the safe. Yak hands me his bowling ball bag and turns his back to me, his head moving like a pendulum, oscillating left to right and back. Thirty seconds later, the cocaine is transferred from the safe to the bag. I close the lid and re-engage the lock. Yak will scan the QR codes and distribute the product to the WARP select drivers, who will deliver to the end customers.

A text from Emmy: *On our way back. We want to party!*

So soon? I planned on at least another hour.

The Clipper glides smoothly and silently toward the dock, maneuvering sideways and slamming against the rubber bumper protecting the hull from striking the concrete embankment. The Ukrainian thugs are the first out, assuming their gangway positions. The first teen off the boat bolts ten yards down the riverbank, drops to her knees, and vomits into the Monongahela river. Two of her friends run over, hold her hair back away from her face, and comfort her as she retches while I amble over to the Ukrainians.

"Howdy fellas, I hope you're having a nice evening. I thought these kids weren't supposed to drink. They're all underage."

One of the goons with arms the circumference of a California Redwood shrugs and says, "They do what they do. Girls of all ages drink in Ukraine."

I want to say, "*Don't you beef-brained Terminator wannabes understand English? These are kids,*" but I hold my tongue.

"I don't think we've been introduced," I say. "My name is Jason. I'm a friend of Roger and Kevin."

Redwood says, "We know who you are. We receive a full briefing from the boss. You're a lawyer. I am Sergei. This is my brother, Andriy."

"Nice to meet you both," I say. "Since we're now all acquainted, those girls are all hammered off their asses and puking in the river." I point to the riverbank where Emmy is now on all fours, vomiting. The skinny girl is bent over her with one hand on Emmy's shoulder. I continue, "I thought your job was to keep these kids out of trouble."

"Better in the water than they *blyuvaty* in your car," Andriy says, laughing. "We are here to protect from harm, not babysit."

Protect them from what? I think. What's happening is precisely what they should have been monitoring, especially if I risk shouldering the blame. In war movies, the guy on point always takes the first bullet.

Sergei side-eyes me. "You're a Jew, yes? Where are you from?"

I shrug and say, "Right here in Pittsburgh, born and raised."

"No, where was your grandfather born, your roots?"

Kids continue wobbling off the boat. Two topple over in the gravel parking lot, cursing in pain as they scrape their knees on dirt-covered stones and pebbles. Their parents are going to shit bricks.

"My grandfather is from a small town in Ukraine, Noua Sulita."

Sergei and Andriy nod in unison. Sergei says, "Ah, yes, small village, not many Jews now—all murdered."

I assume he's referring to the Holocaust, which no one in my family ever discussed growing up.

"You lost family, no?" Sergei says.

I shrug. "I'm not sure."

Sergei frowns disapprovingly, making me self-conscious of my ignorance. For a split-second, my father's disappointed expression is superimposed on his face. I walk over to Emmy at the riverbank. She's upright but unsteady on her feet. I worry she's about to tumble into the river and latch on to her left arm. "What happened to the stuff your dad told you about not drinking?"

Her eyes are glazed and bloodshot. Her mouth opens, but the only sounds that escape are incomprehensible drunk-speak along with awful breath, a mixture of tequila, weed, and vomit. All the gum in the world won't cover the stench. Roger will be awake and waiting for us when I get these kids home. I can shift the blame to the steroid brothers but don't like the idea of two large Ukrainians with guns upset at me for ratting them out. I yell to the group still meandering around the riverbank.

"Get your asses in gear, ladies. Time to go."

The bat phone text notification beeps.

How did things go?

I figured Kevin would check in to be sure I didn't screw up the gig. This isn't the time for true confession. I'll drive these kids home and smooth things over tomorrow.

I reply: *Driving back to Roger's place. No problems.*

The only sound in the SUV during the drive home is loud snoring. A check of the rearview mirror confirms the girls are in snooze mode. Emmy is leaning to the side, her head on skinny girl's shoulder. Another is sleeping sitting straight up, her head bouncing like a bobblehead. As I approach Roger's house, the porch light is on and the front door is open. Kevin must have alerted him when we left the dock. I had hoped I could quietly drop the kids and get the hell out of Dodge. I turn into the driveway and come to a stop well short of the front door.

"Rise and shine, kids, we're here."

Emmy yawns, stretches her arms, and says, "Why are you stopping so far away? Drive us to the door."

Roger is on the porch, circling his arm in a "come closer" motion.

"I gotta go, kids. Please exit the vehicle."

Emmy grumbles, "Fine," and gets out. The other kids follow. I wait until they are all in front of the car and, without making eye contact with Roger, back into the street. Thank God this night is over.

CHAPTER 10

Walking up the stairs to my front door, I'm tempted to drop to my knees and kiss the concrete. I crave a piping hot shower-jet massage and visualize the single malt Scotch and cocaine chaser awaiting me. I insert my key and push the door open.

My coffee table has no glass top. Shards lie scattered across the living room carpet, and my La-Z-Boy reclining lounge chair is on its side. Cans of tuna and boxes of mac 'n' cheese lie scattered on the kitchen floor among broken coffee mugs, ceramic bowls, and plates. I've been burglarized. I have a basic security system and pay the monthly monitoring fee, but as practice and out of paranoia, don't activate the alarm when I leave the house. The last thing I need is a burglary call going out and cops rummaging through my secrets. I've considered adopting a yappy dog, but the thought of my traumatized cat chased through his own castle is too much for me. I take a deep, resigned breath. There is a depressing irony to my night.

I'm on all fours picking pieces of broken china off the kitchen linoleum when a cricket hops across my path, followed by a warm night breeze. During the summer, the noisy chirpers invade the house when I forget to completely close the sliding glass door leading into the backyard. Without moving my head, I roll my eyes up as if what I know to be true won't be if I don't look directly at it. The door is wide open. That's how they entered the house.

It could be the work of either neighborhood kids looking for drugs or professional thieves. Years ago, there was a rash of what the police dubbed "porch pull" burglaries. The crooks went house to house, looking for idiots who left their back door unlocked. Sonya constantly got on me for neglecting the simple task of locking the sliding glass door to the back porch. Frustrated at my inattention, she always made sure it was secured before we went to bed or left the house.

I slide the door shut, secure the lock, and peer into the darkness. A small army might be out there, and I wouldn't see them. After taking two deep breaths, I flip the porch light switch. A rabbit scampers into the shrubs, and bugs swarm to the glow of the lights.

Where's Willie?

I rush to the master bedroom. He isn't under the bed.

"Willie. Come, Willie."

After grabbing a handful of treats from the kitchen, I begin a systematic search of the house.

"Treats, Willie, treats!"

Meow...meow...meowwwwwww.

The cry of my frightened feline echoes from upstairs. I bound three steps at a time.

"Treats, Willie." He cries out again from my bedroom, peeking his head out from under a mountainous pile of dirty clothes. God loves the slovenly. I gently place him in the cat carrier. Other than the mess downstairs and drawers pulled open, only a box of photos upended on my bedroom floor is out of place. Snapshots lie scattered across the carpet. Why would they waste time rummaging through old pictures instead of hunting for cash and pawnable items? My television still sits mounted on the living room wall, and my laptop is where I left it on the kitchen table. Someone was looking for something. This wasn't random.

I pick up the carrier and bolt out of the house to my car. I place Willie in the front passenger seat and drive a few blocks into the park before pulling into a picnic area. This is as good a place as any to sleep tonight. I shut off the engine, turn on the radio, and recline my seat.

A knock on the driver's side window startles me awake. The digital car clock has advanced to early morning. A motorcycle cop is staring in, flashlight in hand. I roll down the window.

"Is anything wrong, sir?" he asks, his eyes roving the vehicle. "Did you sleep here all night?"

"Yes, everything is fine, officer. My girlfriend kicked me out last night, and I needed a safe place to crash."

He shines his flashlight into my eyes and says, "I'm sorry, sir, but you can't sleep in the park. Have you had anything to drink? Where do you live?"

I pull out my wallet, remove my driver's license, and point in the direction of my house. "I haven't been drinking and live down the street. My girlfriend and I had a bad argument. I defused the situation by leaving and didn't think I could stay at a hotel with my cat, so sleeping here seemed the best option."

I put Willie on my lap and pick at my fingernails as the cop studies my identification. If he runs my name, he'll know I have a prior DWI, and I'm not in the mood for a field sobriety test. He hands me back my license and shines his flashlight into Willie's carrier. "I don't smell alcohol, so I'll take you at your word. Would you like me to enter your domicile with you?"

"That won't be necessary. Our disagreements are loud but never violent. I'm driving over to Denny's and ordering her blueberry pancakes with whipped cream to smooth things over."

"If I catch you sleeping in the park again, I'll have to cite you. I hope there's not a next time but if there is, please stay at a hotel. There are pet-friendly places around here."

"I will, Officer. I'm very sorry."

"Have a nice day," he says, hopping back on his motorcycle and revving away.

I glance at the clock again. Mary's spin class should be over. She'll be changing and heading to the clinic soon. I'll clean up the mess and, to be on the safe side, drop Willie at her office. I drive home, grab a broom and dustpan, and turn on the local morning news.

Erin Campanara, the *Tribune* investigative reporter, is on the scene in the Hill District.

"The county coroner has positively identified the skeletal remains found buried in a vacant lot on Wylie Avenue in the Hill District as those of then seventeen-year-old Heather Brody. Heather was a senior at Squirrel Hill High when she was reported missing by her parents after not returning home from a Pittsburgh Pirates baseball game thirty years ago. No cause of death has been announced, and the police are not disclosing if they know how she came to be buried in the lot, citing the ongoing investigation. However, according to my sources, based on the circumstances of the discovery, foul play is suspected."

I shut off the television. After a shower, I spend the next sixty minutes lying in bed. I shut my eyes but can't sleep. Where is David and who breaks into a house but doesn't take anything. The same people David was following?

I text Mary: *You out of spin class?*

She texts: *Yes, heading home, then to office.*

My place was broken into last night.

She texts: *Oh no! Are you ok?*

I'm fine.

She texts: *While you were babysitting the kiddos?*

I guess so. I'll come by in an hour. Bringing Willie with me.

She texts: *Sure, see you then.*

CHAPTER 11

Walsh Accident and Injury Center is in a low-end strip mall, four miles east of Pittsburgh in an area populated with fast food restaurants, tote the note car lots, and pawnshops.

After a quick stop for donuts and pastries, I pull into the parking lot. Willie howled the entire way. He's not a fan of either the crate or road trips. More often than not, it means a visit to the vet.

I grab the pastry box and carry Willie into her office. The customer alert buzzes. The waiting room is empty. Mary exits the exam room with an older, overweight woman wearing a whiplash neck brace.

"Mr. Feldman, to what do I owe the honor today?"

We fall into our rehearsed and flawless waltz.

"I was in the neighborhood and thought I'd drop off a box of goodies," I say.

"How thoughtful of you. Mrs. Rossi, this is Mr. Feldman. He is one of the top trial lawyers in the city and, coincidentally, handles accidents like yours."

"A pleasure to meet you, Mrs. Rossi. May I offer you a donut?" I open the box at the tip of her chin, so the sweet and sticky aroma assaults her senses. "Let's see what we have here: jelly, glazed, and apple fritters."

Mrs. Rossi contemplates the selection for a few seconds and reaches into the box, pinching a glazed.

"Can I get you anything else, Mrs. Rossi?" I ask. "I'm happy to grab you a cup of coffee from the kitchen. Was it a bad accident?"

Mary says, "Mrs. Rossi was rear-ended on the Route 28 highway after coming to a stop in heavy traffic. She sustained serious neck and back injuries and has been out of work for the last week."

Mrs. Rossi nods in agreement and pulls at her neck brace.

"That's terrible, Mrs. Rossi," I say. "I hope you feel better soon. Are you related to Edna Rossi from East Liberty?"

Mrs. Rossi takes another bite and breaks into a surprised smile. "Why, yes, I am. She's my mother. Are you acquainted with her?"

"When I was a kid, she was a regular at the post office my father worked at. I went to work with him on weekends and took the letters from the customers. There was a kind word and a smile with each letter she handed me. Such a wonderful person."

"What a small world. My mother rarely had an unkind word for anyone," she says.

I pat Mrs. Rossi on the back and take her arm. "May I walk you to the front door?"

She loops her arm inside mine and says, "Well, yes, you may, young man. You are such a gentleman."

I smile at Mrs. Rossi and wink at Mary.

"How's your mother doing?" I ask as we shuffle to the lobby.

"She's in an assisted living home in East Liberty. She turned ninety last week and doesn't move around like she used to."

"Wow, ninety. I'll bet she's had an interesting life. My dad's in assisted living as well. Please give your mother my best, and we will talk soon about your accident." I give her a hug.

"Thank you so much, Mr. Feldman," she says. "I'm so happy and relieved Dr. Mary recommends you. Knowing who to trust these days can be difficult. No one can understand the pain I'm in. I ache from head to toe."

It sure is difficult, I think.

"Of course, you can trust him, dear," Mary says, putting her hand on Mrs. Rossi's shoulder and giving her a finger massage. "I'll walk you out. Stay off your feet and wear your brace. I will see you next week."

I push open the door, and Mrs. Rossi trudges to her car.

"Mrs. Rossi was my last patient today," Mary says. "She'll retain you. Come by during her next appointment to sign her up." I follow Mary down the hallway to her office and plop Willie's crate on her desk. She locks the door and stands behind me, massaging my shoulders as she kisses the back of my head down to my neck. "I'm sorry last night didn't go well and about the break-in," she says.

"The entire evening was a shit show. Or more aptly, a puke show," I lament. "The kids got drunk on the boat and vomited into the Mononga-hela."

"It sounds god-awful," Mary says. "I wish I had been with you to help out. Did you call the police about the burglary?"

"No, and I don't plan to," I say between erratic breaths.

"Why not?"

"It doesn't appear they stole anything."

"That's odd," Mary says, continuing to plant kisses. "What do you think they wanted?"

"Probably neighborhood kids pranking. Could have also been crack-heads scrounging around for a quick score and I surprised them coming home. Do you mind if I leave Willie with you tonight?"

"Of course you can leave him with me. Will you be staying over as well?"

"I was thinking we could hole up in a hotel suite. Room service, plush robes, champagne. Scarface is even on the tube."

As Mary's hands slide over my chest heading south, last night's events melt from my memory. "The nightmare is over, and Dr. Mary is here to make things all better," she whispers.

"Don't stop," I moan.

"I won't, sweet Jason. Are you relaxing?"

"Oh, yes, please don't stop."

My body slumps back against her breasts, only her body weight keeps me from falling backward onto the floor. She kisses the top of my head while tugging my shirt out of my pants.

Mary's hand finds its way to my crotch. "Will I be able to say hello to your little friend tonight?"

I moan and thrust my hips upward. "You can say hello right now if you want."

Mary's breathing becomes more erratic. In a smooth motion, my shirt is over my head and airborne. Her hands roam around the front of my waist. My jeans and underwear are at my ankles. I lose my balance and fall back into her physician's chair. She spins me like a dreidel and drops to her knees. Oh, God. New clients are the best.

CHAPTER 12

The Law Office of Jason Feldman consists of me, my paralegal Stacy, and the ghosts of long-retired and dead sports figures. Autographed baseball photos decorate my office walls. Signed baseball cards in their sealed, rigid plastic sleeves lay on the credenza. Two of my favorites are a 1933 Goudey Babe Ruth SCG 4.5 and a 1955 Topps Roberto Clemente SCG 7 rookie card that commands over twenty grand on eBay. Ironically, my most sentimental piece of sports memorabilia in the office isn't baseball-related and is as valuable on the open market as a photo of Pee-wee Herman. An autographed snapshot of me at ten years old, sitting on the shoulders of former Heisman Trophy winner and NFL flash-in-the-pan Mark Yanzer, also known as *Hit the Hole Yanzer*, or *the Yanz*. His nickname came from his uncanny instinct to find an open hole and dart through it at lightning speed. The Yanz was the prototypical local boy made good, the son of an Edgar Thompson steelworker, and heavily recruited by major universities across the country.

Yanzer chose the University of Pittsburgh and was a first-round pick of his hometown Pittsburgh Steelers. Hit the Hole was destined to be a Pittsburgh football sports legend mentioned in the same breath as Terry Bradshaw and Franco Harris. My dad idolized him. The legend didn't come to pass, though. His generational talent went hand in hand with a gambling obsession. He couldn't satisfy his need for action on the gridiron, so he chose backdoor, high-stakes poker games.

The backdoor for local celebrity high stakes at the time was the second floor of Stodgehill Toys and Novelties, otherwise known as the Odessa Club. Owned and operated by Trent's father, Chuck Stodge, it had a colorful history as a gathering spot for low-level mobsters, crooked politicians, and professional athletes. Yanzer was a lousy poker player and no match for the seasoned gamblers who won and lost tens of thousands of dollars in one sitting without blinking an eye. His rookie signing bonus and salary quickly became the property of other card players, then the markers piled up.

My dad's ticket into the Odessa Club was his relationship with Chuck Stodge. Mr. Stodge's father and my grandfather knew each other growing up in the Hill District, where the vast majority of Eastern European Jews immigrated to Pittsburgh in the early 1900s. The upper-crust invites to the Stodge charity gatherings, which raised money for the homeless and bought political clout, didn't find their way to my dad, but the common family tie was enough to garner an occasional coveted spot at the card table. He rubbed elbows with people who didn't bother making eye contact when they tossed their letters at him or bought a roll of stamps. Sitting at the card table for a few hours, he was one of them, an equal in the elite tribe of the Odessa Club.

My dad sometimes bragged about sitting next to Hit the Hole. It was his favorite seat at the table. Stories flew back and forth about my dad's life growing up in the Hill District and Yanzer's father's struggle as a steelworker while supporting a family of eight. Now and then, when my dad went bust, Yanzer slid a twenty-five-dollar chip over to him, winked, and said, "You'll get my bill in the mail."

In a rare television interview, Yanzer spoke about threats of busted legs and kneecaps. He opted to take the physically safer route of disclosing inside game information to his loan sharks who then relayed the information to bookies. He divulged secrets about who was playing hurt, partied the night before the game, or had drug problems. Next were the bets placed on his own team. While never proven, the rumor was Chuck Stodge bought up Yanzer's debt and became the sole recipient of the inside information. The scandal rocked the sports world and ended the career of Hit the Hole. After only three years, the NFL banned him for life. Yanzer went on to modest success as a professional wrestler and after that, faded away.

Being the weekend, I'm surprised that Stacy is at her desk when I walk into the office. I'm in no mood for conversation but put on a smiling face to match hers. Stacy has a law degree, but for now, has to settle for paralegal work. After graduating from Carlow University, she met a guy and moved to California with him where she enrolled in one of those for-profit law schools churning out lawyers who fail bar exams like Ty Cobb stole bases. She moved back to Pittsburgh over $200,000 in debt and unable to sit for the Pennsylvania bar exam because her school wasn't accredited by the American Bar Association. The upside is Stacy's an excellent paralegal and manages all aspects of my practice. She drafts my pleadings, is a Westlaw wiz, and ensures I show up at morning court hearings, even when I'm hungover and sleep-deprived. I would be lost without her. She would make an outstanding lawyer.

"You're here on a Saturday? Must have been a quiet night," I say.

"The usual," she says. "Alone on the couch with a dry Cabernet Sauvignon and Netflix. A good glass of wine and my television are infinitely preferable to the Pittsburgh meat market. Did the case with Judge Steelman settle?"

"Yep, done deal," I say.

"Cool beans," she says. "You have several client messages. Jeff Stern from TriState Insurance called on the Lastig accident. He says his last settlement offer is final and you can accept or take the case to trial. He's not offering one more cent.

She hands me the file, rolls her eyes, and pistons her fist up and down. I give the pleadings a quick once over. They're all the same. The other driver was negligent. My client suffered permanent injuries, can't work, and is enduring enormous physical and psychological pain. Blah blah blah.

"This is fine," I say, handing the lawsuit back to her. "Email a courtesy copy to the adjuster. Tell him his offer is an insult, and we're filing a lawsuit next week if he doesn't accept our settlement demand."

The bell on the front door jingles, and two familiar faces enter, Keane and Romo.

These two keep flaring up like a bad case of herpes. How did they know where to find me on a Saturday?

Keane says, "Things got a bit tense the other day. Let's start over. Friends?"

I execute an exaggerated sigh. "Sure, come on back," I say, motioning down the hallway to my office.

As we pass Stacy's desk, I extend my left arm in her direction with my fingers spread apart. Her signal to call me in five minutes. My guess is, Romo and Keane are here to jolt me with a metaphorical cattle prod and watch which way I jump. I sit behind my desk, lace my fingers behind my head, and lean back in my chair.

"Have a seat," I say, gesturing to the two wooden chairs facing my desk, normally reserved for prospective and current clients. Instead, they both walk to the credenza serving as my sports memorabilia display. Romo picks up a glass cube enclosing a grimy, dirt splotched baseball. He turns it over, from side to side and front to back like he's manipulating a Rubik's Cube while trying to pry it open. I jump from my chair and snatch the case from him.

"I'd prefer you didn't do that," I say, placing the case back on the credenza. "Contaminants from the skin rub off on the ball, degrading the cowhide and its value."

Keane picks up a framed photo of my dad and I posing in front of the statue of Honus Wagner at PNC Park.

"Is your father still with us?"

"He's a resident at Rolling Groves," I say, sighing and glancing down the hallway at Stacy who is on the phone.

Keane rests the photo back on the credenza. "A lovely place but pricey. Does he have Alzheimer's?"

I edge past Keane and slide the picture frame to its proper spot. "He has vascular dementia."

She continues to probe. "How old is he?"

"He's in his eighties. I appreciate your concern, but you didn't come here to discuss my father's health or fawn over my memorabilia collection. What do you want? I've told you what I know."

"You'd be surprised how much people forget, then remember later. Let's start easy," Keane says. "Have you heard from David since he fled the hospital?"

I count the seconds until Stacy buzzes me.

"The same answer as yesterday: no."

"Let's go back to the day you first spoke with him," Keane says. "Were you surprised to hear from him?"

I peer past her into the lobby, hoping to attract Stacy's attention. *You can call me anytime now.*

"She asked you a question," Romo says.

I glare at him and fight off my urge to imitate Stacy's jerk-off motion.

"As I told you the other day, his text was unexpected. Yes, I was surprised because the last time we spoke before yesterday was in high school. You two are scratching the wrong cat post, and you're not the only ones concerned about him."

Keane flips a page in her cop book. "I understand, but we're the public servants tasked with solving an attempted murder."

"You keep referring to what happened to David as an attempted murder and not a suicide attempt. Do you have any suspects?"

"Assuming your friend is still alive, when we find him, we will. I'm going to level with you, Jason. There was evidence of an intense struggle in a fourth-floor classroom at the Cathedral of Learning. Blood on the floor was a match to David's blood type. We need your help. Would you mind if we took a glimpse at your texts and your phone records?"

How stupid do they think I am? I'm not a criminal defense lawyer, but I've been around long enough to understand the prime directive they drill into their clients. Never agree to a consensual search. Make the police obtain a warrant if they can. The cops are looking for evidence to convict you, not clear you. They're not your friends, even when they offer a Danish. I maneuver so I'm facing Keane and Romo's looking at my rear end because, screw him.

"With all due respect, Ms. Keane. You're a professional, so you won't take this personally, but not a chance in hell without a warrant."

My office phone buzzes, finally. I lift the receiver and put my hand over the mouthpiece. "I'm pressed for time. I think we're finished here."

"Thanks, counselor. We won't take any more of your valuable time," Keane says. "You have a kick-ass memorabilia collection. I hope it's insured."

I follow them down the hall to the front door. Keane stops and turns. "Why was your get- together with David so short? As my esteemed partner pointed out, it didn't last more than twenty-five minutes. After thirty-years apart from my childhood best friend, I'd be blabbering like a giddy school-girl for hours."

"Frankly, I was expecting more time with him. But then he abruptly left, not even sure why."

I walk over to Stacy's desk, pick up a blank piece of copy paper, study it for a minute, and say, "Please file this and pull the case folder for my trial tomorrow." She looks at me with a blank *I have no idea what you're talking about* expression. If only I was telepathic. This isn't brain surgery, Stacy. I want to get rid of them.

Keane runs her finger along what appears to be a transcript of yester-day's statement. "He didn't tell you why he had to leave?"

I'm not an idiot. They want discrepancies, even tiny ones. Her job is to trip me up. "You have my statement in your hand, and I have a busy day. If you call or make an appointment, I'll try to give you more time, but no promises."

Romo chuckles. "We don't call or make appointments, but you'll be seeing us again."

Keane and Romo are barely out the front door when the bat phone goes off in my pocket. I'm amazed Kevin waited this long to call. I expected immediate blowback from the Gateway Clipper debacle.

"What's up, Kev?" I ask, holding my breath for the explosion.

"What the fuck happened on the river, dude?"

"Kids happened," I say, keeping my composure. "I didn't put the booze on the boat. Did you smooth things over with Roger?"

"He's pressuring me to fire your ass."

Yeah, right. You'll find another lifelong, loyal friend willing to deliver narcotics and who won't drop a dime on you to save his tuches.

"Pressuring you? Whose business is this anyway?" I say.

"Don't be a smart ass. Roger and I have other deals going. I don't want to be on his nasty side and believe me, neither do you."

"What do you mean?"

"I mean he has a substantial investment in this company, so I need to keep him happy."

Is it bad I'm unsympathetic to Kevin's problems with Roger because I have to kiss Kevin's ring whenever he beckons? The reality is, he'll smooth things over, and I'll be delivering product as usual next week. Long standing relationships and implicit trust are platinum commodities in this trade.

"I guess now is not the best time to ask a favor," I say.

"I'm not sure you have any goodwill left in the piggy bank after last night but go ahead and hit me with it," he says with a hint of annoyance.

"I need help tracing someone, but I want to explain in person, not over the phone."

The only sound is Stacy tapping away at her computer.

"You there?" I ask.

"Yeah, I'm still here," he says, his tone agitated. "This can't be discussed by phone?

"I prefer face to face. It's important."

Kevin sighs loud enough to make the imposition clear. "This screws with my afternoon, so it had better be life or death. Meet me at the Squirrel in thirty minutes."

CHAPTER 13

During the fifteen-minute drive to the Squirrel Bar, my mind isn't on the road but the rear-view mirror. Vehicles behind me are potential threats. If someone tried to kill David, am I next? What's the saying? You're not paranoid if someone throws your childhood friend out a window?

Holy shit! I slam my right foot down on the brake pedal. Brake pads in dire need of replacement squeal in objection. The metal frame of my car shudders. My focus rips forward to an irate and screaming old woman. She has one hand on a full shopping cart and the other holding what appears to be a babushka in her fist, which she's shaking at me. I wipe the sweat from my face, relieved I didn't turn her into roadkill. I jump out of the car and rush over to her.

"I'm so sorry. You appeared out of nowhere. Are you okay, ma'am?"

Her much younger female companion tries to nudge her through the crosswalk, but she isn't budging. She continues to shake her headscarf at me, screaming in Yiddish.

"Gay kaken offen yam."

My Yiddish is a bit rusty, and I don't recognize the phrase, but I'm confident she's not telling me to have a lovely day.

I make eye contact with the younger girl who, I assume, is her daughter or caregiver.

"What did she say?"

The girl is clearly embarrassed. "I'd rather not say. No harm done. She tends to speak Yiddish when she's upset."

"I know a bit of Yiddish but mostly curse words."

She shrugs and says, "Then you should understand what she said. Please don't worry and have a pleasant day."

Now, I'm adamant.

"Please, miss, my ears can take it."

"Very well. She told you to go take a shit in the ocean."

I can't help but break out into laughter. Bad move. This enrages the old woman further.

"Schmuck!"

The young girl opens her mouth, but I hold up my hand. "I recognize that one. Is this your grandmother? Where's she from?"

"Yes," she says, her cheeks blushing. "She was born in Poland and is usually not this cranky. I'm sorry."

Despite the woman's Yiddish dress down of me for my inattention, a nostalgic warmth radiates from her. She's every Jewish grandmother from my youth, walking into the kosher butcher or the bakery on Murray Ave. They jabbered in Yiddish, Polish, or Russian, waiting for their cut of meat. Many had lost family in the Holocaust or were themselves survivors.

I smile and say, "No need to apologize. The fault is mine." I place my hand on granny's back, peck her cheek, and say, "Gay ga zinta hate. That means, 'Go in good health.'"

The cranky old woman scowls and says, "I know what it means you putz."

The Squirrel Top Bar and Grill has stood since 1918 and is the quintessential Pittsburgh dive bar. Its clientele spans multiple generations from old timers singing the Pittsburgh Steelers Polka on game days to law students with their books spread out on the table quizzing one another on the free speech case, New York Times v. Sullivan. The place is packed with only a few tables unoccupied. The bartender is a twiggy young woman with a nose ring and tats visible on both arms of her open-sleeved, Squirrel Top T-shirt. I wonder if Sal's still here. He's tended bar at the Squirrel since I was a kid. He served my dad and the countless local celebrities who stopped by. I stand at the corner of the bar and motion to attract nose ring girl's attention. Kevin announces his entrance with a slap on my back.

"Hey, chief," he says. "I ask you not to be late and guess what, you are. Grab me a cerveza. I scoped an open booth in the back."

I want to say, *"Dude, you walked in two minutes after I did, so shut up."*

Nose ring girl glances in my direction and makes her way down the bar. "What can I get for you guys?" she asks.

"An Iron City and Rolling Rock draft please. Where's Sal?"

She places a chilled mug under the beer spigot and pulls the lever. "Sal died last year. That will be six dollars."

My heart sinks. Sal was an avuncular presence behind the bar, dishing wisdom on politics, relationships, raising kids, and Pittsburgh sports. He was beloved by Squirrel regulars across generations and often lamented the "yuppifying" of the neighborhood. I hadn't thought about him in years and wallow in nostalgic depression. When I came in with my dad, he served me a free Shirley Temple. He opened a jar of cherries and, after taking one out, would hold it high above the bar, and release it. The cherry hit the ginger ale with a plop. Sal would say, "Bullseye, Yinz know I never miss."

"What happened?" I ask.

"Heart attack."

"That's sad to hear. May his memory be a blessing,"

She smiles sadly and says, "Thank you. We miss him a lot."

Everyone loved Sal. Sonya adored him. She'll be sad when I tell her.

The bartender pushes the beers in my direction. Across the inside of her right wrist is a coal-black tattoo of a semicolon. Does she teach high school English? I point to the tat and ask, "What's the significance of the semicolon?"

She raises her arm until the punctuation mark is staring me in the face, and without hesitation, says, "Addiction could have been my end, but it was only a pause."

"Nice," I say. "How long do you have?"

She beams with pride and says, "I hit two years sober yesterday."

"An outstanding accomplishment. I'm happy for you."

I'm unable to shake the semicolon image as I slide into the booth and push Kevin's beer glass across the wood table. A middle-aged waitress takes our food order. I recognize her, but the name escapes me. She's another longtime employee. "You boys need anything else?" she asks.

"I'll take a menu," I say. "Do you still serve the squirrelly fries?"

She winks. "Did Nixon go to China? Of course, we do. Been on the menu for over fifty years."

I tap on the menu and glance at Kevin. "Wanna split a plate?"

He wrinkles his nose. "I don't eat fried crap. I've been vegan for years. You should try a detox."

Like I give a shit about his diet. Is he going to brag about how much he bench presses?

The routine is, however, paying off for Kevin. I take in his toned chest and his short-sleeved shirt displaying rippled arms. My jeans are tighter against my waist than they were a month ago. I bought a treadmill after Sonya and I split and exercised fanatically for a month. The handrails are now fantastic dirty towel hangers, and Willie loves to stretch out on the belt and nap. I sigh and hand the plastic menu back to the server. "We're fine for now, thank you."

"I'm sorry I'm late," I say. "I almost ran over an old Polish grandma."

Kevin takes a sip of his beer. "What's this ask we couldn't manage over the phone?"

I tip my glass toward my dry lips. The ice-cold beer hitting the back of my throat, combined with air conditioning on over-blast, ignites goose-bumps. "I need help tracking down an old friend of mine. His name is David Chaney."

"I haven't heard his name in a long time. I recall you two were pretty tight as kids."

"We were through high school, but he and his dad moved our senior year. We lost contact and didn't have any interaction until he texted me a couple of days ago."

Kevin sticks his index finger into his beer glass, penetrating the foam. Within seconds, the froth dissipates.

"What did he want?"

I'm torn about how much I should reveal. Kevin and I have known each other a long time, but despite his religious pronouncements and Torah sayings, he's still a drug dealer. Playing my cards close to the vest seems the best route for now. Bringing Trent into the equation is foolish without knowing who my allies are.

"He wanted to catch up, so we got together on the Pitt campus. Fifteen minutes later, he took a dive out a fourth-floor window at the Cathedral of Learning."

Kevin jerks his head back. "Whoa, I saw it on the news. The anchor said it was an apparent suicide attempt but didn't give a name. So, he survived?"

"He survived. I visited him at the hospital right after. When I went back to check on him the next morning, he was gone, and two police detectives showed up and questioned me. The cops are looking for him. They don't believe he jumped, and I think he's in trouble."

Kevin's interest piques. "What kind of trouble? The law, psycho girlfriend? Drugs, gambling?"

"Take your pick. I need this done quietly and without a lot of questions asked."

Kevin leans back against the wall and clasps his arms behind his head. "I have the perfect guy. His name is Zev, former Israeli IDF. He was in their intelligence service. He's not cheap, though. Kevin's phone dances on the wooden table and his eyebrows raise.

"Speak of the devil," he says, taking the call. "Hi, Zev. Shalom Aleichem. Ma nishma?"

The next few minutes of conversation are primarily in Hebrew. I dropped out of Hebrew school in fourth grade.

Kevin periodically nods with an "uh huh" and "I see."

"L'hitraot," he says and hangs up, grinning. "Done deal. You two will work out the overall finances, but to start with he wants a ten-grand cash retainer plus expenses."

My jaw drops. Talk about sticker shock. "You're kidding me," I say. "I don't have a big enough cash reserve. Does he take credit cards?"

Kevin shakes his head. "Sorry, dude, this would be off the books and cash only. You can't manage with the extra shekels coming your way? You should have serious bank squirreled away, pardon the pun."

I let out a resigned sigh. "Most of the money goes to Rolling Hills."

I decide not to mention my memorabilia collection. Kevin signals the waitress for our check.

"You're a good son. I'll advance Zev's retainer against future compensation. We'll keep a running tab."

Kevin's not throwing out the first offer of a negotiation. This isn't a car accident. I have no choice but to accept. Kevin's motto is business is business. He uses his foot to slide a gym bag across the floor to me. I know what's in it. The bag is why he agreed to come. The bag is business.

I look down at the bag and back at Kevin. "Dude, I'm not driving the WarpMobile. I'm in my personal vehicle, and I'm not putting that shit in my trunk."

Kevin's eyes scrunch, and he appears confused. "What do you mean you're not driving it. Didn't you pick it up to take the kids to the boat, and for the meeting with Yak at the bowling alley?"

"Yea I did, and I returned it after I dropped the brats off. It's parked in your garage where it should be."

Kevin looks at his watch and says, "Well shit, that really screws things up. We can't have you driving around Pittsburgh with product in your trunk. It messes up my afternoon a bit, but I'll take the bag home and put it in the WarpMobile safe myself."

I use my foot to push the bag back over to him.

"Yak will contact you to arrange delivery," Kevin says.

"How do I contact Zev?"

"He'll reach out to you on his timetable."

Timetable? Did I not sufficiently impress the urgency of this?

"Out of curiosity, what do you want Zev to do for you when he finds David?" Kevin says.

"Report back where he is and how he's doing. I'll tell him if I need anything more."

"Okey-dokey," Kevin says, sliding himself out from the table.

"I wait for him to contact me?"

"Yep. Zev has his own way of working," Kevin says, tapping his watch. "Gotta roll. I have a date with a nice Jewess I met on J-Swipe, and I'll be cutting it close after taking the bag back home. I have nothing else for you this weekend. Go get laid with your pretty girlfriend."

What a mind reader.

He guzzles the rest of his beer, slams the glass on the table, and says, "Brews are on you for inconveniencing me."

I pay our bill and am at the exit when I do an about-face and head back to the bar, motioning to the nose ring girl.

"Can I pour you another draft?" she asks.

I shake my head and say, "Nah, but I want you to have this." I pull a twenty out of my wallet and place it on the bar. "Congrats again on two years sober."

She blushes and says, "Thank you, but you don't need to give me this."

"I insist. One day at a time."

CHAPTER 14

After picking up the WarpMobile and confirming Kevin secured the gym bag full of cocaine in the safe, I check into the Hotel Monaco and text Mary.

I'm here and waiting for you. Ordering room service.
She texts back: *Can't wait. Be there soon. :o)*

I'm looking forward to champagne, gangster movies, and sex, but also can't shake a nagging reminder: the inevitability of confronting Trent, which I have to do sooner rather than later. I don't want looking over my shoulder to become a lifestyle.

I ring room service for an order of chocolate-covered strawberries and a bottle of Moët, then power on my laptop, scanning the Internet again for mentions of Heather and David. Three light raps on the door interrupt my frustrating and futile search for the latest information. The cops are usually a sieve of intel leaks but not in this case.

"Guess who, sweetie?"

I peer through the peephole and open the door. Mary has an overnight bag strapped around her shoulder and is wearing jeans ripped at the knee-caps and a white blouse. A white baseball cap funnels her long, blonde hair into a ponytail.

"You are absolutely stunning," I say.

She drops her overnight bag on the bed. "You're so sweet. This room is amazing,"

Mary takes off her cap and says, "My current scent is hand sanitizer and peppermint oil. Do you mind if I take a quick shower?"

"You smell like a candy cane, and I've loved candy canes since I was a kid," I say. "Of course you can. Mi casa es su casa."

Mary's eyes drop to my groin, and she presses her body to mine.

"Mmm, someone's ready for an exciting night. I won't be long."

She runs her fingernails up the inside of my thigh and walks into the bathroom. The shower jets have begun their pulsating rhythm when there are two thumps on the door.

"Room service."

The attendant rolls the table to the end of the bed. As soon as he's out the door, I strip naked, pop a chocolate strawberry in my mouth, grab one for Mary, and saunter to the bathroom. She inches the door open and pokes her head out. The water drips from her hair and earlobes, soaking the bathmat. Her hand stretches toward me and takes the strawberry with two fingers. In slow motion, she inserts it in her mouth and leaves her index finger between her lips, licking off the excess chocolate.

"Mmm, delicious."

The finger slowly withdraws from her mouth and beckons me into her lair. I open the door, and her hands drop below my waist, wrapping around my erection, pulling me into the steam, and into her.

The room phone rings and keeps ringing. I don't remember setting a wake-up call. What time is it? The morning sun blasts through the open curtains, causing me to drape my elbow over my eyes. I reach across the bed, pick up the receiver, and set it back in the cradle. My head rages with a Moët hangover. We should have stopped at one bottle. A painfully familiar morning after thought.

Mary exits the bathroom with a turban over her head, wearing a plush white bathrobe with the hotel logo. She unwraps the head towel, allowing her locks to fall free. She strokes them with her brush, wearing a relaxed and contented smile as the individual bristles grab hold of each strand and stretch it out to its full length.

"Did you sleep well?" She asks. "You were quite the energizer bunny last night. As a reward, I decided to let you sleep in."

"Do you have any aspirin?" I ask. "My head is raging."

"I'm fairly sure I put a bottle in my overnight bag. Help yourself."

I pop two and collapse back onto the mattress. The bat phone vibrates as I fire up my laptop.

I'm downstairs at the bar -Zev.

Has he been following me? It creeps me out a bit. He's either good at what he does or I'm an easy mark.

I text back: *Give me 20. Wasn't expecting you.*

He responds with a thumbs-up emoji.

Mary stands in front of the vanity mirror, fully dressed. She purses her lips and uses a tissue to wipe the edges of her mouth. I risk a quick scan of the *Tribune* website. An Erin Campanara byline captures my attention.

"A community planned for the worst but held out hope for the best. For thirty years, the loved ones and former classmates of Heather Brody prayed for the miracle of her safe return. She will return to Squirrel Hill, but the sad reunion signifies the end of hope and the beginning of even more questions about her disappearance. Next week, she will be laid to rest next to her father, walking distance from her childhood home.

Mary's hand is on my shoulder. "Are you reading about that poor girl?"

I power down my laptop and close the cover. "Yes, her funeral is next week."

"Are you going?" she says.

"I'm not sure yet, but probably."

Will I go? I don't think I can face her mother and all the other people who will be there mourning her loss. They will see right through me. I suspect the cops will also be there taking notes. Don't arsonists return to watch their fires burn?

"I'm ready to head downstairs," Mary says. "Do you have a few dollars for the valet, and should I wait for you?"

"My wallet's in my pants pocket," I say. "You go ahead without me."

Mary frowns, walks over to my pants draped over the back of the desk chair, and removes the wallet. "I'd hoped we could walk out together like a couple," she says.

I grab her around the waist from behind, planting a kiss on her nape. "I need to shower and return emails. I don't want you to be late for work waiting on me." Mary is one of the few chiropractors in town who sees patients on Sundays.

Her body stiffens, and she pulls away, her arms crossed flush against her chest.

"How do you think it makes me feel to do a walk of shame from the Monaco?"

A serious question demands a thoughtful answer. I don't give it.

"We're at a hotel—people walk in and out all the time."

I regret the response within milliseconds of it leaving my mouth.

Mary escalates from irritated to indignant. "I wish you wouldn't patronize me. I'm aware of where we are. The point is, I don't flit around, weekend hotel-hopping with men. I came because we're a couple. At least I think we are. I hope you think so too. Couples leave hotels together after spending a romantic night making love."

I wince at the truth of her scolding, "You're absolutely right," I say, doing my best to come off as contrite as possible. "If you wait for me to dress, I'll walk out with you."

Mary checks her phone. "I'm running late. In the future, let's leave together the way couples should."

She unexpectedly flips my wallet to me. It hits my outstretched hand and falls onto the carpet. Cash and credit cards spill out onto the rug, along with a baggie. The blow Kevin gave me for babysitting the brats. Fuck.

My heart pounds, and time slows to a crawl as we both gape at the incontrovertible evidence that I'm not the person I pretend to be.

"Mary, this isn't what you think."

She's funeral quiet, but her mouth is open as she stares at a gram of Columbia's finest.

She finally asks, "Is that heroin?"

I snatch the baggie off the carpet and sit on the edge of the bed with my head bowed and my hands folded in my lap. A litany of potential explanations cycle through my mind. I carry my coffee sweetener with me or powdered Vitamins? None of it will fly. Other than Sonya, Mary is the smartest person I've dated and certainly the smartest in this room. I'm not sure whether I should laugh or cry at the tragic irony of the situation. I regularly transport enough blow to send me to prison for decades, but my relationship may end over less than a gram.

I set the baggie on the mattress. "It's only cocaine, and I'm not an addict. I know a lot of lawyers who dabble recreationally. It's no worse than a joint."

The explanation is a winner as the words cross my lips, like I hit a home run with my closing argument to a jury. The war on drugs is ending. Marijuana is legal in many states. Occasional personal use doesn't hurt anyone. Who am I kidding, though? I stepped way over the occasional line a long time ago.

Mary sighs and sits on the bed next to me.

"First off, we both know there's a difference. I care about you a lot, and you're a grown adult but..."

I raise my hand to wipe at the tear running down her cheek, but she pushes it away.

"My father severely injured his back in a work accident ten years ago. His doctor prescribed Oxycontin. When the prescriptions ran out, he turned to the streets to score. The further down he spiraled, the more he took his physical pain and frustration with the system out on my mom."

"Mary, cocaine isn't Oxy."

"Just...quiet. Let me get through this. I've never told anyone."

I nod and bow my head, unable to look her in the eyes.

"When Oxy wasn't available on the street, my dad turned to the next best thing, heroin. Jason, my father died of an overdose three years ago.

He unknowingly snorted heroin laced with carafentanil. The police told us it's used to tranquilize elephants, and even a tiny amount can be fatal to humans. My dad died hopeless and angry. My mom lives hopeless and angry. I won't live that way. I'm sorry. I can't."

Did I want this to happen so she could cut her losses early and run? My shrink and I talk about my sabotaging relationships. I wrap my arms around her neck and snuggle my cheek against hers.

"I am so sorry, Mary. May his memory be a blessing. I didn't mean for this…"

In a courtroom, I'm never at a loss for words. In the here and now, I can't think of one coherent argument.

She stands and straightens her skirt. "I'm sorry, too, Jason, for both of us."

I pick up the baggie and plead. "I'll stop. I'll flush this down the toilet right now. Sit down and let's talk this through."

The tears stream down her face, falling onto the carpet like a faucet left dripping so the pipes don't freeze. "Then stop, Jason, but I've been down this road. I will not go through it again. I'm sorry."

Without another word, she opens the hotel room door, walks into the hallway, and pulls it shut behind her. Her sobs fade as I bend over to pick up the contents of my wallet. I'll call her later to smooth things over, but right now, Zev is waiting on me. I change, put the baggie back in my wallet, and head for the elevator. The only person sitting at the lobby bar is messing with an iPad. He's dark-complexioned and bald, with a closely shaven beard. I put him in his early to mid-thirties.

"Zev?"

He lifts his right hand in a shushing gesture and closes the iPad case with the state flag of Israel on the cover.

"Let's walk, my friend," he says in a heavy but understandable Israeli accent.

"Lead the way," I respond. "How did you find me?"

I realize the absurdity of the question but can't pull it back.

"Do you like to read?" he asks.

I hesitate, wondering where this is going. I'm also trying to remember the last thing I read other than a legal journal, court filing, or case law. Does *Sports Illustrated* count?

"Ahh, sure, love the Grisham novels, being a lawyer and all," I say.

"I don't read Grisham," he replies. "I like the classics. Read *Man's Search for Meaning* by Viktor Frankl."

"I'll check it out," I say. "Where are we going?"

I fall in lockstep behind his right shoulder with Mary's sobs still echoing in my head. We almost collide when Zev comes to an abrupt stop. "Stay one step in front, my friend. We are almost there," he says.

A little dramatic for my taste, but I long-stride past him while also checking my phone for an apologetic text from Mary telling me she overreacted and wants to see me tonight. Focus Jason. She'll cool off, and everything will be back to normal, I hope.

"Kevin says you're formerly with the Israeli intelligence. Is that like Mossad?" I ask, resisting the urge to twist my head around so passersby don't think I'm a nutcase babbling to myself.

He doesn't answer and shouldn't. It was an idiotic question. The guy probably thinks I'm another diasporic American Jew who hasn't been to Israel and doesn't know the difference between Mossad and Mickey Mouse.

"How long have you known Kevin?" I ask.

"Here we are," Zev says, stopping in front of Hemingway's Boat Book Emporium and Coffee Shop, the only decent book-browsing hangout in the downtown area. Sonya and I attended a book launch here after a lawyer in the public defender's office authored a true-crime novel. I'm a bit shocked someone hasn't turned Heather's story into a best-selling book or a Netflix documentary, though I'd prefer it not occur anytime soon. The last thing I need is to have a starring role.

As one might guess from the name, the interior is adorned with decorative lamps, posters, and knickknacks associated with the store's namesake. The only Hemmingway novel I've read was in my high school fiction class, the ponderous and nap-inducing *For Whom the Bell Tolls*. The aroma of mocha lattes and fresh-baked pastries tugs at my empty stomach as I follow Zev in a casual loop around the perimeter of the store. He smiles at each customer we pass and says, "I hope you are having a fabulous morning."

We come up on a brown-haired, college-aged girl who's lounging in one of the many brightly colored beanbag chairs scattered around the store. Her T-shirt reads, *Do Yoga, Drink Coffee, Eat Tacos.*

Cute, though I don't consider Pittsburgh the taco capital of the world. Zev stops and kneels in front of her. This guy has balls. Is he going to hit on her?

"You are enjoying your book, miss?"

She responds with a silent, cursory smile and returns to her reading. She probably thinks he's a bookstore lothario. Her dismissal doesn't dissuade Zev.

"What are you reading today, miss?" he asks.

She raises the book until the cover blocks her face. It's a meditation self-help book.

"Very nice," he says. "May I recommend?"

"Sure," she says, lowering the book. Her head doesn't move, but her eyeballs shift upward.

He gives her the title of one of those trendy mindfulness books written by a yogi with a familiar-sounding Indian name.

"You must read the book," he says. "It will change your paradigm of wellness. Shalom."

He moves on. Her eyes track him, not with uneasiness but an unmistakable gaze of intrigue and attraction. It must be the accent. Zev zigzags through book sections with no discernible pattern or destination. We hit sports, philosophy, self-help, and memoir. With each stop, Zev pulls out a title, thumbs through the pages, and returns the book to its slot.

"Are you after a particular book?" I ask.

"Yes," he says, stopping in front of a row of books about California getaways. "Do you like to travel?"

"When I have time," I reply.

Where is he going with this? I hope he doesn't have a side hustle as a tour guide and is going to pitch me a cruise. Zev pulls a book from the shelf: *Fifty Great Places to Live Off the Grid*. "Many people want to vanish, even when no one is chasing them," he says, opening the book and flipping multiple pages at a time. "Others are running and have reason to be afraid. Which is your friend?"

"I think he's running," I say. "The police believe someone is trying to hurt him."

Zev seems to gauge my words, tone, and inflection. Of course, he would be trained in lie detection if he's Israeli intelligence, Mossad, or whatever. Those guys are the best. They kidnapped Adolph Eichmann in Argentina and spirited him back to Israel where he was tried and hanged for masterminding the Holocaust. This is a guy I don't want to mess with.

"Kevin tells me he's a childhood friend," Zev says.

"Yes, he was. At one time, we were close."

"Now you want to make sure your old friend is well. I understand. Friends are important."

"Yes, they are. Can you find him?" I ask. Zev continues to turn the pages of the book, seemingly absentmindedly.

"This should not be a problem," he says, closing the book. "People think they can't be found, but they are mistaken. There is always a trail of digital and physical breadcrumbs."

"Where do we start?" I ask, checking out a book on traveling to Tahiti, wishing I were on a deserted island right about now.

"You should read this," he says, handing me the *Fifty Great Places* paperback. He turns to page thirty and taps the caption three times with his right index finger. "The fifteenth best place to vanish. Fort Bragg, California."

"Never heard of the place," I say, flipping through the pages while also scanning for an open beanbag chair. "Do you have an exact address? I thought the only Fort Bragg was the military base in North Carolina."

No response.

"Zev, do you have the address?"

"Zev?" I turn, and he's gone. My head swivels 360 degrees. How can I find David without an address? This James Bond secret agent nonsense is more than a bit over the top.

I find an unoccupied beanbag and plop down, my lower back and knees aching in protest. The beans crunch and shift under my butt as I attempt to find a comfortable seating position.

Fort Bragg, California. I thumb through photos of rocky beaches, cliff-side picnics, and tourists hiking by huge waterfalls. The closest we get to falling water in Pittsburgh is the fountain at Point State Park and the iconic home designed by Frank Lloyd Wright. I grab a caramel latte with whipped cream at the coffee counter, then head to the cash register to pay for the book. The yoga, taco girl is gone. I wonder if Zev left with her.

CHAPTER 15

Yak texts me to deliver the gym bag full of blow to him at the Mt. Everest Cabaret on the North Side, the most popular high-end strip club in Pittsburgh. The fliers and cab advertisements boast the finest business executive's lunch buffet, the stiffest drinks, and the hottest dancers in the city. Yak loves strip clubs, but I'd rather be anywhere else. My body has been in a constant state of tension since David's first text, and insufficient REM sleep is frying my cerebral hard drive. Nights are spent on the edge of consciousness with a parade of characters from the past invading my present.

As a former fixture on the recently divorced, lonely guy club circuit, I'm intimately familiar with Everest. I was a regular following my split with Sonya but eventually tired of it. Like the next line of blow, the next fantasy girl was always alluring if you ignored the harsh reality of why they took an interest in you, which was money. For a while, I was on a first-name basis with at least half the dancers, some of whom were deep into the drug scene and selling their bodies in the VIP room. In appreciation for my many lap dances and generous tips, they occasionally tipped me off to the identities of vice cops rotating through the club. Loyal customers were always appreciated.

I spy an open table in the far corner of the club, away from the stage and the main traffic area of strippers conga dancing their way through the lunch crowd and trolling for twenty-dollar lap dances. An overbearing mixture of perfume and over-applied men's cologne saturates the air; bass-heavy, brain-pounding stripper music makes me wish I had brought Mary's aspirin with me.

I spot Yak wandering the club. He's moving through the crowd, swiveling his head like he's the Terminator searching for Sarah Connor. I stand and raise my hand to get his attention.

"Why did you sit here in corner? We should sit by stage where the action is," he says, yelling above the music.

As if they heard his booming bellows, two dancers are at our table within seconds. Each plants her butt on one of his massive thighs and begins grinding while also starting a head and chest massage straight out of a stripper dance manual. These two exude a hardened-by-life vibe but still carry the traces of once drop-dead gorgeous young women.

Yak eyeballs each dancer from head to breasts to toes. Appearing satisfied with the quality, he says, "Do the girls want drinks?"

The dancer on his right leg, who is in dire need of a roots refresh, hugs him tighter and kisses him on the cheek. "We'd love a bottle of Grey Goose."

A bottle girl hovering nearby needs no other signal and hustles to the table. Yak wrinkles his nose and says, "We need real vodka. Bring us Absolut."

I chuckle to myself. Yak's disdain for anything Russian clearly doesn't extend to top-shelf vodka. Bad Roots plants another kiss on Yak's cheek and squeezes his bulging bicep concealed beneath his Armani sports jacket.

"We love Russian vodka, baby. We especially love hard, handsome Russians. What's your name?"

Yak tosses his Amex Black on the tray and corrects her. "My name is Yakov, I am not Russian. I am from Ukraine."

We pass the time waiting for the server to return with a lap dance for Yak. I gawk in awe as both girls manage to squeeze between his spread knees, gyrating their hips in unison with their arms raised high, like they have imaginary hula hoops orbiting each waist.

Yak punches my shoulder and says, "We will party first, do business after."

The server returns with a bottle of Absolut, decanters of juice mixers, and four cans of sugar-free Red Bull.

"What type of mixer, baby?"

"Mixers are for women," Yak says.

The waitress repeats the process for the two lap dancers, but they mix their drinks with cranberry instead of vodka straight up. I fill my glass three-quarters full of orange juice and cover the rim with my hand when she tries to top it off with vodka.

"No vodka for you, baby?" she asks.

"None for me, thank you." I turn to Yak and say, "They rip you off by jacking up prices on Vodka bottles at least two hundred dollars."

"I piss two hundred dollars. Two hundred is nothing. Let's drink and toast." He extends his drink toward the center of the table. The girls follow suit. "Za druzba!"

We all clink glasses and repeat, "Za druzba!"

The girls chug their iced-tea-sized glasses. I don't blame them. I couldn't do this job day in and out without consuming massive amounts of vodka.

Bad Roots wastes no time in refilling her glass, this time not bothering with the cranberry. She says, "Zadruga is such a cute saying. Is it Russian? What does it mean?"

Yak responds, "Not zadruga, it is Za druzba. It is not Russian, but Ukrainian. It is a toast to happiness."

"Ukrainian?" Ms. Roots says. "You talk like you're Russian. I adore your name. Yakov, it sounds Russian."

Yak jumps to his feet, ejecting Bad Roots off his lap. She screams, "What the fuck," as she sprawls to the floor.

"Yakov is my name, and it is Ukrainian."

His voice is seething with an anger way out of proportion to the innocent faux pas. The last thing I need is an international incident because a stripper got his accent wrong. A bouncer as substantial as Yak appears at our table within seconds. I immediately recognize him as a backup defensive lineman for the Steelers a few years ago. He didn't play much after shredding his knee in a preseason game, eventually retiring.

"What's the problem here?" he asks.

I position myself between Yak and the bouncer. "This is an innocent miscommunication. Didn't you play ball for the Steelers?"

He helps Bad Roots to her feet. She glares at Yak. "I asked him if he's Russian, and he flipped out. He hit me and threw me to the floor."

Her version is bullshit, but this is her house. We won't receive any benefit of the doubt. At a minimum, they will toss us out. At a maximum, they will kick our asses and call the cops.

"This is a simple misunderstanding," I say. "He's Ukrainian and doesn't have a solid grasp of our language." I turn to Yak and beg, "Please apologize and give the young ladies some money for their trouble."

I'm eye level with the barrel chest of the former lineman. He would give Yak a run for his money in a bar brawl and would squash me like a hammer smashing a watermelon. "Will a cash settlement for your injuries smooth things out?" I ask, praying she says yes.

Yak isn't letting go. "This is an insult. I am Ukrainian. Russians killed my friends in the war."

What war is he yammering about? He must be out of his mind causing a scene when we have very illegal business. Yak is one or two more broken English phrases from starting World War III. The former backup lineman says nothing but continues to stare him down. I hope Yak's not strapped. Who knows what a crazy, worked-up Ukrainian with a gun is capable of? They are nipple to nipple, neither backing down. This is a hair's breadth from becoming a shitstorm.

I rest my hand on Yak's shoulder, gently pulling him back from the bouncer.

"Calm down," I whisper. "We don't need this attention. Give her some cash for her injuries, and let's bolt. We have business to transact."

Yak's expression goes blank. "What is bolt? Like a thunderbolt?"

"Let's leave, Yak, as in go. Give her money, so this doesn't turn into a disaster."

Yak doesn't walk into a strip club without a few thousand dollars to spread around to the dancers before heading up to the VIP room.

Without breaking off the dick-measuring stare down, he says, "You are my lawyer now? How much should I give her?"

I glance at Roots. "How much to smooth this over?"

She presses her right index finger to her top lip, squints, and scratches. "Five hundred dollars."

I tap Yak on the shoulder. "Do you have five hundred on you?"

He reaches into his pocket and withdraws a hippo-choking roll of bills.

Bad Roots's eyes go double wide. She probably wishes she had asked for a grand. Yak peels off five one-hundred-dollar bills and hands them over. Her expression miraculously changes from frowning at having suffered grievous and permanent bodily harm to ecstatic at having made a night's income by falling on her ass. International crisis averted. I turn to the bouncer. "Are we chill now? I'm sure you played for the Steelers. Blew your knee out?"

He's in no mood for memory lane. "We're chill but control your Russian—sorry, I mean Ukrainian—friend."

Roots appears satisfied with her haul and has no further interest in hula hooping with the mad Ukrainian. There is, however, no shortage of women waiting to claim her spot.

"Are these chairs available? Mind if I sit?"

A thirtyish, soccer-mom type with a cute Dorothy Hamill haircut takes Bad Roots's chair. She winks at me and selects one of the sugar-free Red Bulls from the tray, pulling the tab and sipping. Yak is back to being Yak. He presses his hand out to me, which I correctly assume is an invitation to a high five. We slap and sit. Within minutes, one of Yak's legs is again occupied, this time by Dorothy. I walk away from the table and motion to him with my middle finger. He takes Dorothy by the waist with both hands and gently lifts her off his quadriceps.

"Don't go away. I'll be back," he says.

"I'll be here, sweetie," she says, taking another sip of the Red Bull.

Yak punches me on the shoulder and says, "You are a damn smart lawyer. I will call you next time there is trouble."

Out of the corner of my eye, I see the former Steelers lineman talking to Bad Roots and glowering at us. "Let's hope this is the last time you need me, and while I'd like nothing more than to stay and party, we need to finish our business. I have lawyer shit to do.

We exit the club to the WarpMobile. Yak gets in the passenger side, and we roll over to his bright yellow Range Rover with a gigantic set of deer antlers attached to the front grill. What is it with these guys needing to be as loud as possible? Does he think we're in Texas? Yak scans the parking lot while I unzip the gym bag holding a kilo of blow with a street value of about twenty grand. He opens the rear of his truck, lifts the carpet, and punches a code into a safe identical to the one in my car.

"You should head back inside. Dorothy Hamill is waiting," I say.

Yak secures the safe, now full of cocaine, and closes the door to his car. "I know Dorothy. Ice skater. Ukraine has first-rate Olympic skaters."

He turns and heads back to the club. I think about it. I shouldn't say anything. It would serve him right if he's busted for solicitation, but I happen to like this goofy guy, and more importantly, Kevin depends on him, which means I do too.

"Yak, hold on," I say, jogging up behind him. "Do you think I'm a smart lawyer?"

Yak punches me on the shoulder and says, "You are a smart lawyer."

"You bet your ass I am, and I'll prove it by saving yours."

Yak scratches his head, pulling up his sports jacket and exposing the butt of his Sig Sauer tucked into a shoulder holster. This knucklehead walked into a strip club strapped. I didn't know how close we were to a clusterfuck.

"How will you save my ass?" he asks.

"We both know you're going to eventually head upstairs to the Everest VIP Club with Dorothy where she will offer to suck little Yak for two hundred bucks and sell you cocaine."

"Yak never pays," he says, his chest puffed out.

"Whatever, dude. Are you ready for my big-time smart lawyer moment?"

"Yak is ready," he says.

"Here it comes," I say.

"Don't be a shithead," he says.

"She's Pittsburgh PD Vice. Enjoy your evening."

I put the WarpMobile in reverse and pull out of my spot. As I turn onto the street, I check the rearview mirror. Yak has his hands on his hips. He hasn't moved.

CHAPTER 16

I drop off the WarpMobile at Kevin's and decide to take the rest of the afternoon off. My mind is batting options back and forth like a ping-pong ball. The most obvious choices are go to the cops and spill thirty years of guilt or do nothing and let the shit fall where it wants to fall. I can also call Sonya and put an end to this, but will it end? I'll accuse Trent Stodge, one of the more respected and wealthy residents of Pittsburgh, of a thirty-year-old murder but with what evidence? The passage of so much time is like pouring sulfuric acid over the facts. There's nothing left but the word of an ambulance-chasing, cokehead lawyer and a onetime Billy Joel prodigy in hiding. Even if I find David, why would he return voluntarily, giving Trent another opportunity to take him out? I wouldn't come back either. Still, I have no choice. I can't put an end to this madness alone, and I refuse to live the rest of my life waiting to be tossed out a window.

It occurs to me, though, there may be a door number three. A direct appeal to my childhood friendship with Trent and our shared family history. Can he feel empathy or pity? The catch is, I have to confront him to make it work. As if the number will miraculously function again, I dial David. Same result—invalid number. I can't sit on my ass, hoping he reaches out and wondering what either of them will do next.

After one last check-in with the office, I'll head home to de-stress and map out my Trent game plan.

"The Law Office of Jason Feldman, how may I help you?" The words roll off Stacy's tongue as if we are the most prominent personal injury firm in Pittsburgh.

"It's Jason. I'm heading home and taking the rest of the day to myself. Anything new going on?"

"Your girlfriend Mary stopped by and dropped Willie off. She said you knew she was coming and seemed pretty upset."

"Did she say anything else?"

"Nope, she plopped the cat carrier down on the desk, turned around, and left."

I merge onto the highway and put my phone on speaker. "I'm driving your way to pick Willie up. Anything else going on?"

"Not a thing. Enjoy your afternoon off."

"I plan to. The weather is perfect for a run."

She laughs. "Since when do you run?"

I have no desire to explain that my newfound interest in fitness is the result of a squirrelly fry food shaming by my drug dealer.

"Since later this afternoon. See you in a few minutes."

I pick up Willie, and driving home, I still can't get Mary's hallway sobs out of my head. I dial her cell.

"Jason, did you get your cat? I'm not in the office," she says.

"Yes, I wanted to call and thank you for dropping him off."

"What did you think I was going to do, cat-nap Willie and hold him for ransom?"

I wish she could see the smile on my face. I love her sense of humor when she has every reason to be less than cordial.

"No, I didn't think you would abduct Willie. He loves you, though. Are you doing okay?"

The silence tells me how much I hurt her.

"I guess it depends on how you define okay. This morning made me face long-suppressed emotions about my father. I needed to confront them and should thank you for that. I saw signs in our relationship and told myself I was imagining things or being hypersensitive because of him."

What signs? I thought I had done well in showing only what I wanted her to see.

"My family went bankrupt trying to help my father. There was rehab after rehab, and nothing seemed to work. In the process, however, I became an expert in the treatment industry, and I'm happy to share what I've learned if you ever want help."

"So, we are over?"

This time she doesn't hesitate. "Yes, romantically we are, but I'm not angry. I'm concerned. Keep my number in your phone and call me if you want my help."

I swallow to keep the tears down while both my hands crush the steering wheel.

"Take care of yourself, Jason."

"I will. You too," I say, my voice choking.

I maneuver through a steady stream of Schenley Park joggers and bike traffic to pull in my driveway. A run through the park will take my mind off the phone conversation with Mary. I let Willie out of his carrier and head up to my closet. For my first jog in ages, it seems appropriate to break out the Pittsburgh Marathon T-shirt that belonged to Sonya. I might as well at least look the part. When Sonya left me, she was in the same competitive shape as when we met. She was a runner, a real runner. She was a regular, top twenty-five percent finisher in the Pittsburgh Marathon and won the law school Res Judicata 5k through the back trails of Schenley Park three years straight.

I'm lacing up my running shoes when the doorbell chimes. The bedroom window gives me an unobstructed view of Detective Keane standing in my driveway, peering into my car. What is she looking for? As she approaches the front door, the skin on my arms prickle like I stepped out of a sweltering desert heat into an air-conditioned room. Has she been following me? As she walks up the stairs, the little voice in my head is screaming not to let her in. I wish she'd stop nosing around my life, although I might as well ask water not to be wet. I open the door but stay inside the house.

"This borders on harassment. Do I need a restraining order?"

Keane ignores my empty threat. "Your office said you left for the day, so I thought I'd take a shot coming here and bingo, here you are." She peers over my shoulder into the living room. "May I come in?"

Never let cops in the house and don't step outside when being questioned.

"Do you have a warrant?"

Keane frowns. "Do I need one? Let's not make this adversarial."

What is she blabbering about, adversarial? My profession is about confrontation. The practice of law is referred to as an adversarial process for good reason.

"I'm actually not here about David," she says. Your name came up in another investigation. Are you aware the remains of Heather Brody were discovered in the Hill District?"

"I read about it and remember when it happened. I'm glad the family will finally have closure."

"Closure is when I catch the person or persons responsible for her death. I'm one of the detectives working the case and came across your interview at the high school."

"Yeah, the cops interviewed all the kids."

"Yes, they did. I'm following up on all the statements and reinterviewing everyone we can find. Can I please come in? I'll play nice." She holds up two fingers and says, "Girl Scout's honor."

"Were you a scout?" I ask.

"No, but my sister was. Close enough?"

The only items in plain sight are my laptop, magazines, empty bottles of water, and a dirty soup bowl. I see no harm in a controlled kitchen sit-down and unlock the screen door.

"I'll give you fifteen minutes. No offense, but this is my day off. I don't want to spend it hanging out with a police officer."

Keane chuckles and breezes past me. "I wouldn't want you to waste such a beautiful day on me either. You look like you're headed out for a run. It's perfect weather for it."

I motion to the kitchen. Keane pulls out her notebook, shielding the pages with her forearm. She flips a page, studies it, and noisily flips to the next one. I crane my head to steal a glimpse of her notes and ensure the pages are not blank. I watched a *Law & Order* episode where the cop pretended she had damning information in her notebook when it was empty pages. She made up a bunch of bullshit, convincing the defendant to confess. Keane snaps the notebook cover shut.

"In your interview after she went missing, you stated you didn't know Heather well and, I quote, 'just to say hello around the hallway and lunchroom.'"

"That's correct. She hung out in different social circles."

Keane appears startled, and her knees jerk upward. She glances at the floor, where my tabby is circling her right ankle. "Your kitty caught me off guard. She's a cutie."

"She's a he," I correct her. "His name is Willie."

Keane reaches down and scratches Willie behind the ears. He preens his head and flops on his side. She brushes her fingernails across his stomach.

"Such a sweetie. I'm glad my partner is off today. He's allergic."

The revelation makes me wish Romo were here and sneezing his brains out.

"Reflecting back, do you have any idea on why Heather would have been in the Hill District? It wasn't a place where you'd expect a well-off young girl to be hanging out as it was extremely dangerous in those days."

"Yeah, not a place I hung out either, but I have no idea why she'd be up there."

"Do you know if Heather used crack cocaine?"

The question doesn't catch me off guard. Why else would a privileged, young white girl visit the Hill District in the 1980s?

"I said I didn't know her well, but if someone wanted crack or powder, they didn't have to go up to the Hill to buy it."

Keane cocks an eyebrow. "Where would they go?"

Fuck, I veered onto a road I didn't want to go down. A lot of kids in school knew who had the good drugs: Trent.

"You heard kids talk about scoring, but there were never specifics. It was a long time ago." I stand in the hope she takes the hint. "I can't add anything more to what I told the detective thirty years ago. We didn't hang out. You'd be better off talking to the kids she ran with if you can locate them."

"We are in the process of tracking them down. One more question and please don't get upset. I have to ask about David Chaney."

Of course she does. David was in my class and my best friend.

"Did David have any kind of relationship with Heather? I've been unable to track down interview notes, so I can't account for his whereabouts either the day she disappeared or in the days following."

"Do you mean dating? I don't recall David ever having a girlfriend. We were best friends. If he knew her, I'd be aware of it. I don't believe he did."

Keane reaches down, picks up Willie, and places him on her lap. He doesn't squirm or fight.

"He's taken with you," I say. "He isn't friendly with everyone. Not to be rude, but I would like to continue with my day off. I hope you solve her murder. I'm sure all of Squirrel Hill hopes so. It's been an open wound."

Keane sets Willie back on the floor. "Oh, I will, you can count on it. What happened to David after her disappearance? From what I can gather, he and his father picked up and moved in the days following."

"I'm not sure. It was sudden, and we didn't speak after he left. I don't even remember him saying goodbye."

Keane nods her head, scribbles in her notebook, and says, "His leaving that way must have hurt your feelings. Your best friend packs up and hits the road without a phone call, or even a note."

"It hurt a lot, but time heals."

Keane closes her notebook. "One more thing. We performed a deed history on the lot her remains turned up in, and the information we dug up is quite interesting. Ownership goes all the way back to the early 1900s. It was owned by an organization named the Odessa Social Society. That's Odessa over in Ukraine, not Texas. It appears to have been a hotbed of bootlegging and illegal gambling over the decades. You're of Ukrainian descent, right?"

I side-eye her in disapproval. "Yeah, my grandfather immigrated with millions of others. How did you know about that, and why are you asking?"

Keane shrugs and walks to the front door. "Things you learn in an investigation. Enjoy your afternoon off. Don't hurt yourself running. Ease into it."

CHAPTER 17

Keane hasn't been gone thirty minutes, and I'm pacing a small circle around an imaginary sun on the carpet. David knew about the Odessa Society. Keane's digging into it. It's only a matter of time before they question Trent.

I walk outside, bracing my arms against my porch railing to stretch. My right knee flexes too far, and my hamstring screams. The toe touch is an utter failure with my fingertips barely reaching my ankles before my calves beg for mercy. One more stretch, and I'll injure myself before my first stride. A young couple passes by, pushing a stroller with an infant. The mother stops, bends over, and reaches in. She kisses the baby, adjusts the blanket, and pecks her male companion on the lips. Two female joggers, who must be competitive runners, pass them at a speedy clip. Their calves and quads explode outward with each stride, reminding me of Sonya's legs when she ran hard or wore shorts when we walked the park with Sam.

I can still see us. The trees were shedding, and it seemed to be snowing leaves. Sam laughed with awe and joy as a leaf settled on his face. Sonya picked it off and adjusted the Steelers baby blanket to cover his hands and feet. She bent over and kissed him on the forehead.

The stroller couple executes a leisurely U-turn in my direction, still the lovebirds. The dad is wearing a ball cap and a backpack, though the logo on the cap isn't the usual I see in the park. On any given day, the vast majority are college or Pittsburgh professional sports teams. His is neither, but I can't place it. I raise my hand in a waist-high half-wave.

"A beautiful day for an outing. If you don't mind me asking, what team does your hat represent?"

He smiles but doesn't answer as they stroll past me.

I start uphill in the opposite direction of the couple. After a few painful strides, a white van drifts into the pedestrian lane and blocks my path. What the hell? Stay in your assigned lane, asshole. Is this idiot going to run me over? I stop jogging and walk toward the van, which comes to a complete stop. The side door slides open, and a guy in work overalls gets out.

I glare at him and grumble, "This lane is for runners, walkers, and bikers only."

He appears apologetic and speaks with a heavy Eastern European accent. "I'm deeply sorry, sir, we have appliance delivery in this area. Can I impose to check our address and point in the right direction? He shoves the clipboard in my face. I recognize the address and point. "You need to head down Schenley Park Drive and—"

I slap at a sharp, piercing pain on the right side of my neck. A wasp? Joggers, walkers, trees, and the clipboard guy spin around me. Why am I on my back? A bird flies across my field of vision. Voices call out to me from the other side of a fog-covered bridge.

"Sir. Sir! Are you all right?"

The fog thickens. A euphoric blanket of calm sweeps through my body, from my toenails to eyeballs. Oh Jesus. I love this. Oh wow.

Dreams of pushing Sam's stroller on a cool fall afternoon give way to blindfold darkness, cold, wet air, and the stench of urine, vomit, and stale beer. My first thought is that I must be dead, and while Jews don't believe in going to hell, an exception has been made for me.

My involuntary gag reflex engages. I call out to anyone within earshot: "I'm going to be sick!"

My voice echoes like shouting in an empty sports arena. Other than my words bouncing back, the answer is the shuffle of tiny feet. Where the fuck am I, and why are my hands tied behind me? I push down with my feet and rock back and forth. The legs of the chair smack the concrete floor and send shock waves of pain up my leg into my scrotum, like my entire body is a funny bone. I twist my head to the right as far as I can, and vomit.

Voices from behind me. "He's coming around. Hit him with the bucket and clean the puke off him." An ice-cold drenching soaks my back.

I cry out, "Oh shit."

My torso quivers as my body temperature plummets. The blindfold is ripped off me.

"Wake up, Jason."

"Someone grab a towel and wipe that shit off him."

"No fucking way. You clean it up if you want to. Let's hit him with the water again."

"Great idea."

The sound of a faucet, and liquid hitting metal. They're filling a bucket. Here we go again. I close my eyes and hold my breath. This time, the drenching comes from the side, but out of my peripheral vision.

"I...I don't understand. What happened? Where am I?"

With every syllable, water sputters from my mouth like an outdoor spigot turned on for the first time in a year.

A gravelly male voice responds, "The Reader's Digest version is you overdosed on heroin, and as miserable as you think you are, this is as good as it gets for you if we don't get the information we need."

I strain my head to the left and the right, but whoever is behind the voice is outside of my peripheral vision. My eyes adjust to the darkness. There are countless syringes scattered across the concrete floor among old candy wrappers, half-eaten sandwiches, and empty cans of tuna and baked beans. The scurrying comes from rats. They are everywhere, sniffing, nibbling, and nosing through the decay and rot.

"Let me the fuck up!" I scream, contorting my body and rocking the chair from one side to the other until I tip over. I'm now eye to eye with the biggest motherfucking rat I've ever seen in my life. Is this a drug-induced nightmare? The rat sniffs at my nose and lips and squeaks. I don't understand rodent-speak, but I have the distinct impression he's ringing the dinner bell.

"Jesus H. Christ. Help me up. Help me up."

A pair of arms grabs the chair while another pair wraps around my shoulders from behind. "One, two, three, up."

The chair is reoriented upright, taking me with it.

"If you tip the chair again, we're going to leave you on the floor. I'm not going to drag this out or bullshit you. I need a simple question answered, and then you can go. If you don't give us the answer we want, see all the rats and needles on the floor?"

I nod.

"Do you see them, Jason?"

"Yes, I see them."

"There were a lot of dead junkies attached to those needles. Do you want to end up a dead junkie found three weeks later with half his face eaten off?"

I shake my head.

"I asked a question. Do you want to be one of those dead junkies?"

"No, I want to go home."

"Answer one question, and you can leave. If you lie to me, I'll know. Once I decide you've lied, nothing else you say will matter. Do you know what fentanyl is? I'll shove a needle full of it so deep into your neck, it will come out the other side. Your heart will stop in seconds. Where is David Chaney?"

I'm still not convinced this isn't a bizarre, acute, cocaine-fueled nightmare.

"I don't know!" I shout. "What have I done to you? I don't understand why I'm here." I clench my teeth and strain against the ropes until the pressure in my head and neck is unbearable. "Let me the fuck up, now."

"You met with David last week. What did you talk about?" he asks, ignoring me.

"The weather and the lousy year the Pirates are having. If you let me walk out of here right now, we'll forget about this unfortunate misunderstanding."

"Lying to us is a mistake. We know you met with David. You both witnessed something you shouldn't have."

Mr. Gravel Voice confirms my worst fears.

"I will ask again," he says. "If you give me the right answer, you can go home."

I sense a presence behind me. A beefy stomach presses against the back of my head. The menthol odor of Aqua Velva is suffocating. After he shaved, my dad often handed me the bottle. I poured a tiny amount into my palm, rubbed my hands together, and patted his cheeks. He let me pretend I was shaving and dabbed my face with the stinging liquid. I was suddenly a grown up. When he came to kiss me good night, Aqua Velva announced his entry into my room. I loved the smell, but not here, not this. Will I see him again? A hand runs up the back of my neck and over my scalp. Fingers gather a thick tuft of hair and snap my head backward with such violent force I'm surprised my cervical spine doesn't fracture.

I cry out, "Stop, please. You're going to break my neck."

"Smart boy. You have the general idea. Where is Chaney?"

"The last time I saw him was in the hospital. You have to believe me."

He releases his grip on my hair. "Give me a hand here."

He's talking to someone else. A pair of hands clamp down on my shoulders. A latex-gloved hand with a syringe filled with milky white liquid reaches around my head.

"If I inject this fentanyl solution, you're a corpse. Where is he?"

Who the fuck is this guy? Dr. Kevorkian?

"Please, don't. I have a son. If you kill me, you will never find David."

I jerk forward as the needle pierces my skin. I sense the pressure of the plunger inching forward. The burning liquid pulses into my vein.

"Did Trent send you? Tell my son I'm sorry."

My bladder opens, soaking my running shorts. The haze rolls in again and again. I'm repeatedly doused with ice water. The same question. I lose track of time and answers.

CHAPTER 18

My senses reengage to the sound of heavy raindrops thumping against a window. A bright flash followed by a thunderclap rattles the glass. The brain fog is lifting, and my synapses speak to each other as they should, but the nausea and cramps churn my stomach like a blender. I breathe deep and swallow hard to keep from vomiting again. The blindfold is gone, my feet unrestrained, but my arms are still tied behind me with thick, scratchy rope. My wrists and ankles throb. Painful reminders this isn't psychosis or a simple nightmare. Another thunderclap. The sky lights up through a square window. The only other sound is the driving rain against the glass. They moved me, but to where? Three syringes catch my attention. They are on a small wooden table by the door, neatly lined up next to each other like pencils.

I push up from my feet, but the wooden chair rises with me. I sit back down and grimace when a metallic object presses into my stomach. My keys are still in the hidden pocket I put them in before I left the house. The chair is old and wobbly. With enough force, I may be able to break off pieces and free myself. Another lightning strike. The thunder will come. Boom. The window glass shakes again. More lightning, and I can briefly make out the tops of buildings at eye level. I'm nauseous and exhausted, but can't take my eyes off the needles of death. They are not done with me, but why decide the blindfold and feet bindings are no longer necessary? The answer hits me like a Nolan Ryan 100-mile-per-hour fastball to the head. I'm not leaving here alive, no matter what I tell them.

The cracked and dirty window has no latch and appears painted shut. I jerk it upwards, pushing at the knees the best I can with a chair on my back, but it doesn't budge. My aching kneecaps are warm Jell-O supporting a brick structure.

I can ram the chair against the wall until the wood fractures, but the racket will alert anyone who may be here. Whatever I do, I have one shot. I'm not going to make it downstairs and out the front door tied to this chair. The neighborhood lights up again with a lightning strike so close it resembles an electric spear. The wind has picked up and roars like a locomotive. The racket is probably as loud downstairs. A Pittsburgh summer night monsoon may save my life.

I estimate three running strides across the room from door to window. The glass is thin, single pane, so I should be able to shatter it with enough force. The next flash gives me a distance to the ground below, a good fifteen to twenty feet. I may fracture my skull leading with my head or end up paralyzed from the fall, but in the grand scheme of things, it's a better risk than ending up a rotting corpse. I wobble toward my starting point, terrified a creaking sound from a rotting floorboard will give me away. God, I hope I generate enough force and don't bounce off the window. I position my head so there's an acceptable margin of error, like a bull taking aim before goring his cape-waving tormentor. Wait, Jason. Wait. Wait. The sky lights up. Another thunder clap.

My head crashes into the window, shattering the glass. My body is thrown backward, and the chair crashes to the floor taking me with it. Pieces of broken window lie scattered about the room, which is moving in waves. Voices echo through the floor.

"Get the fuck upstairs."

I stagger to my feet, still attached to the chair and unable to orient myself. The window fades in and out and appears to slide to different sides of the room. Feet stomp up the stairs. I fill my lungs with air, angle my head forward, and hunch my shoulders, praying I pick the right spot. Bull rush number two. This time my head barrels through the hole in the glass. My feet catch on the window, tipping me forward headfirst. I drop straight down the side of the building like a sack of wet cement and into thick shrubbery. Ooof. The chair shatters and the force snaps the rope. A jagged wood splinter impales my right calf. I close my eyes, cover my mouth, and let out a silent scream as I yank it out.

Another lightning flash illuminates my surroundings. The neighborhood resembles a set from a zombie apocalypse movie. Boarded up buildings and overgrown lots line the street. I half run, half hobble down the middle of the road, my impaled leg throbbing in pain and gushing blood with each foot strike.

I make a hard right between two houses and into an alley. I glance back, but the downpour is torrential. Visibility isn't more than ten feet, but the storm is my salvation. Please keep pouring.

I crisscross streets, backyards, and alleyways, trying to make it as difficult as possible for my former captors to pursue me. Nothing about my surroundings rings familiar. I stub my toe on the uneven sidewalk and grab a pole to restore my balance. The sign at the top reads Bedford Ave. I'm in the Hill District. Across the street is the housing project my father lived in with my grandparents. I'm also not far from the lot where Heather's remains were discovered.

I spend the next two hours cutting between houses and walking in alleys trying to make my way home while worrying about being pursued by Dr. Kevorkian or stopped by a police officer. A white guy hobbling through the Hill District in the middle of the night wearing running shorts is bound to attract attention. Darkness is transitioning into dawn as I finally trudge up to my front porch. A bicyclist speeds past and waves. He probably thinks I'm squeezing in a few miles before work, which I could be other than the cuts, bruises, and blood running down my leg. The puncture throbs with each beat of my heart, but the bleeding has thankfully slowed. I take three deep breaths, turn my key, and inch the door open. The house is silent, and Willie is in the kitchen sitting like an Egyptian Sphinx in front of his empty food bowl.

Despite my legs wailing in pain and fatigue, I inspect the house top to bottom. Satisfied my only company is Willie, I sit on the edge of my bed and inspect the damage. The first to go are my waterlogged, blood-soaked socks and running shoes. The wound is oozing blood, but I can't chance a trip to the emergency room. A hand towel is the best bandaging I can come up with. I fold it up like gauze and use a larger towel as a tourniquet, holding the smaller one in place. I open the bedroom window and embrace the now light rain as it blows in along with leaves. Willie bounds off the bed and pounces on one. The water against my face, and the park fragrance of oak trees, dandelions, and freshly cut grass are home. My brain fights to access fragments of corrupted data, but one thing is clear: this was well planned.

A noise downstairs stops my breathing. There it is again. It's like a swarm of bees found their way inside. Willie's head swivels and rotates, transfixed on raindrops and leaves finding their way inside and swirling around him. It comes again, more like the electric static from rain hitting a transformer. Someone is in my house.

My first thought is to text Yak to race over here with his Sig Sauer, but I might be dead before he even makes it to his car. I return to my bedroom closet and wrap my hand around the grip of my Babe Ruth autographed Louisville Slugger. Each step forward is painful and unsteady. It takes an agonizing three minutes to reach the staircase. I'm now convinced the noise is a timer on an explosive device. My house will explode like the Odessa Society did. There won't be any pieces of Willie or me to find. The thought of him suffering saddens me more than my impending demise. If we are going to die, please God, let it be quick and painless.

I hobble down the staircase like a tractor tire is chained to each ankle. What will my obit say? Will Kevin's dad recite the Mourner's Kaddish at my service? I hope Sonya says a few words about the person I was before it all. She and Sam will sit shiva. I wonder if Mary will come. I think she and Sonya would get along, maybe even become friends after I'm in the ground.

My first instinct is to bolt out the front door and across the street, but I can't without Willie. I raise the bat above my head and let loose a guttural war scream as I sprint into the kitchen.

The time bomb is my personal cellphone, which is lying on the glass breakfast table and vibrating with a text notification. I remember; I didn't have it with me when I left the house to jog. The message is from Mary.

> I really want to help. I'm here if you decide to deal with your problem.

Is it an olive branch or closure? I'm wrestling with returning the text when a phone number I don't recognize pops up on my caller ID. It could be David, so I can't risk not answering it.

"This is Jason Feldman."

"Hello, Jason Feldman, do you know who this is?"

The last time I heard his voice was the night Heather disappeared.

All I manage to croak out is his name: "Trent."

"Yep, long time no talk. Don't you think it's time we got together?"

I think back to what my dad told me after I was challenged to a fight by an antisemitic kid who repeatedly called me a kike and a Christ killer. Dad had been through much worse growing up in the Hill District projects. He said, "When a bully tries to stare you down, don't blink and don't retreat." I fought the kid. He beat me black and blue, but I got my licks in. He didn't bother me again. I'm done retreating.

"I agree, this is getting out of hand," I say, keeping my eyes on the sliding glass door and backyard for Dr. Kevorkian and crew.

"Why don't you come up to my place on Mt. Washington," he says. You will meet the family, and we can have a nice dinner and catch up. I'll text you the address. Come by this evening at six."

My first inclination is to demand a neutral location, but I don't predict him offing me in front of his family in the living room of his five-million-dollar condo. At least I hope not.

"I'll be there." I disconnect without waiting for his response.

As the adrenaline of my ordeal winds down, fatigue sweeps in. I recline my La-Z-Boy and shut my eyes, trying to clear the mechanism, but I'm unable to shake the phantom pressure of needles piercing my neck. I press on the tiny bumps left by multiple injections. It wasn't a cocaine delusion, and no one will believe me.

CHAPTER 19

I n the three decades since I last laid eyes on him, Trent Stodge has sky-rocketed to the pinnacle of the Pittsburgh business and philanthropic community. A *Post-Gazette* business section story last year covered the rise of Stodgehill Enterprises from the small toy and novelty store owned by Trent's dad, Chuck Stodge, to a multinational supplier of novelty promotional products found in goody bags at conferences and symposiums around the world. I recently attended a personal injury law conference in Vegas. The gift bag coffee mugs were emblazoned with the Stodgehill logo and contact information.

The story also noted the unrelenting, charitable contributions from both Trent and his wife, Lana, to causes ranging from breast cancer research to animal rights and the arts.

Stodgehill has offices in London, Madrid, Kiev, and Los Angeles. Its corporate office, however, is based where it all began, right here in Pittsburgh. The company remains at its operational core a closely held family business with Trent at the top as CEO. His two kids, Trent Jr. and Kayla, control international and U.S. sales and distribution.

The Duquesne Incline will transport me to the top of Mt. Washington and Trent's home. It's one of the few working inclines in the United States, cited by *USA Today* as one of the ten most beautiful views in America. The mechanics are simple. One car goes up the mountain while the other simultaneously goes down. I buy my ticket and wait for the 140-year-old gondola to inch its way back down the mountain for the ten-minute reverse ride. I take my seat facing the city with my back to the mountain. Sitting here, I'm slightly bummed about missing the incline sex with Mary, although it would be almost sacrilegious to copulate where Sonya and I sat with Sam in our laps.

Stepping out of the gondola, I stare out over the city of Pittsburgh and assess the past. I see the courthouse where Sonya handed me the divorce petition. In the distance is the Cathedral of Learning that spit out David.

The gatekeeper in the lobby of Trent's building is an elderly security guard sitting behind a large, semicircle reception desk. He's not going to thwart any terrorist plots. He's the Walmart greeter or the peanuts and beer vendor at Heinz Field. To his right is a bank of video cameras. As I walk up, he's absorbed in a thick paperback, Tom Clancy's, *The Hunt for Red October*. He ignores me for thirty seconds before I cough.

"How may I help you?"

"I'm here to see Trent Stodge. My name is Jason Feldman."

He puts down his book and picks up the phone. There are no buttons or dial. It's a direct line to Trent's penthouse.

"I have a Mr. Jason Feldman here to see you." He nods. "You may go up, Mr. Feldman. He's the only resident on thirty."

The floors tick off. The higher I go, the more my gut twists. I'm unsure whether Trent will take a full-court press or subtle bully tact. He didn't rise to the top by backing down. I can't back down either, but I don't want to provoke a violent response. I think I understand what Nik Wallenda—King of the High Wire—must have felt walking a tightrope twenty-five stories above Times Square.

The elevator opens to the thirtieth floor and a white marble flooring stretching down a long hallway, ending at a decorative dark wood door. As if he sensed my presence, two equal sides of the door slide away from each other to reveal Trent standing against the backdrop of an expansive living room and a massive, rectangular floor-to-ceiling window. My heart beats like a jackhammer as I step inside and extend my hand. His fingers squash inward with such force my knuckles crackle. I grimace and shift my gaze to the floor. I'm standing on an inlay of a crest resembling something I'd expect to see on a crusading knight's shield. At the center are two calligraphic letters, "OS." The Odessa Society?

"Let me look at you. You haven't changed a bit," he says.

Why do people who haven't seen each other in ages say things like, you haven't changed or aged? We both have. He has the same salt-and-pepper blonde hair, but the lean build of his youth is gone. His white, button-down Polo shirt is tucked into his jeans, exposing the third greatest fear of the vain, aging male after impotence and hair loss: love handles. Unless I'm in court, I never tuck my shirt in, keeping the mountains hidden. Problem solved.

"What do the letters on the floor stand for?"

"Nothing really, just a family crest of sorts, goes back to the old country."

"I never knew you descended from royalty."

Trent chuckles. "Nothing like that. Come meet the Stodgehill clan." Trent leads the way through a marble foyer and into his living room, which probably has as much square footage as the entire first floor of my house. There are two people seated on a gray sectional couch long enough to accommodate the starting lineups of two baseball teams.

"Your place is beautiful."

"I wish I could take the credit; my wife's hobby is interior design. Kids, come say hello to an old friend."

His son stands and says, "Sure, Dad."

My heart palpitates, and a drop of sweat ebbs its way from under my earlobe to my jaw, followed by another and another. I'm not ready for this.

"Do you mind if I use your bathroom?" I ask, tensing my entire body to suppress outward signs of distress.

Trent points down a hallway. "The guest bathroom is the last door on the right. I noticed you're limping and the cuts to your forehead. Did you have an accident?"

Yea right. He knows exactly what happened. "Of sorts, not a big deal."

My right leg buckles on my first step. If Trent saw it, he doesn't let on and walks over to an enormous globe on a wooden stand in the far corner of the room. He opens the top, exposing a bar.

His voice booms from the globe, "Can I pour you a drink?"

I don't answer and take another step, regaining my balance, my wind, and my sanity for the moment.

CHAPTER 20

The bathroom is at least as nice as what I've seen at four-star hotels. The oversized jetted tub. A brass rainfall water head enclosed in a glass shower large enough to lie down in. I tug on the bathroom door handle to confirm it's locked, open my wallet, and pull out the baggie that ended my relationship with Mary.

The paradox of this moment doesn't escape me. Everything is 360 degrees from New Year's Eve 1988. Trent was obsessed with showing off and acting the alpha dog. Bullying me into a life-changing decision.

From that rolled up ten-dollar bill in Trent's living room, to this bathroom and a rolled Andrew Jackson inserted in my nose. All I have to do is inhale. Nose ring girl's semicolon is dancing the jig in my head. Her smile was ear to ear, so proud of herself. I was proud of her as well, a total stranger. She could be about Sam's age. I want him to be proud of me. I want my son back. For those things to happen, tough choices must be made, decisions I might not make in other circumstances.

I place my right hand underneath the marble edge of the countertop, palm cupped upward. Using the side of my other hand, I slide the powder over the edge into my palm and place it into the water stream gushing from the gold-plated faucet. The cocaine instantly dissolves and the whitish solution circles down the drain. The baggie is next, flushed down the toilet. For this one moment, I'm in control. I pull two tissues from a decorative holder box and wipe the residue from the marble top.

I walk back down the hallway to find Trent, his wife, and his kids all seated on the couch.

"Sorry I was gone so long," I say.

"You appeared rather pale when you came in," Trent says. "I hope you feel better now."

Trent stands up, walks behind the couch, puts his hand on her shoulder and says, "This is my incredible wife, Lana."

CHAPTER 21

Lana is striking in a classic sense. Mid-length black hair with sophisticated streaks of gray. She exudes a Kate Middleton, philanthropic grace. Unlike Roger's overstretched and overly botoxed spouse, there are no signs of surgical attempts to turn back the clock.

"How about that drink?" Trent asks. "What's your poison?"

I take longer than I can remember to contemplate my response.

"Do you have any sparkling water? If not, a diet soda is fine."

"I think we can handle bottled water," Lana says and walks into the kitchen while Trent turns his attention to the kids.

"Jason, I'm sure you've never met my two kids before. Kids, this is one of my oldest friends, Jason Feldman." Trent places his right hand on Junior's shoulder. "Both are in the family business," he says. "Kayla is Vice President of U.S. merchandising, and Trent Jr. oversees all our overseas business. He flew in from a sales conference in Dubai yesterday. They are fraternal twins, by the way."

"A pleasure to meet you both," I say, extending my hand to Junior. He tilts his palm downward and tries to rotate our grip, so he has the upper hand. Last year, I attended a continuing education seminar on body language. A good portion was spent on the psychology of handshakes. Trent Jr. is going for the dominant clasp. I subtly adjust our squeeze, so our palms are vertical to the floor.

"My dad has told us wonderful things about you," he says. "I've also heard wild stories."

I glance over at Trent with a *what have you told them* grimace.

He smiles and says, "Don't worry. I didn't tell them any of our top-secret stuff."

Kayla says, "Ooooh, are there juicer tidbits than underage drinking at my grandfather's club while the big shots played cards?"

Trent winks at me and says, "We could tell you kids, but we'd have to kill you."

Lana reappears from the kitchen with a Perrier in hand. "I hope this works for you," she says. "By the way, everyone, dinner is served."

I follow the clan to a dining room adorned with multiple paintings. The memory of the baggie swooshing into the sewer system is fresh in my mind as I inspect the signature at the bottom right of a landscape: Claude Monet.

"Is this real?"

Trent puts his hand on my shoulder. "Yep, they all are. We were the top bidder on this when we summered in Nantucket last year. Lana fell in love with it and had to have it."

My tongue is dry and thick as if I showed up fresh from an all-night cocaine bender. I take a swig of my Perrier.

"You've done well for yourself," I say.

Trent waves his arm in an expansive arc and says, "Yes, not bad for a guy whose grandfather didn't have a pot to piss in when he came to this country. You know how it is. We have a shared struggle. Our grandparents came here from shtetls. They worked their asses off so their children would have a better life than they did. We work our asses off for the same reason. It's the Jewish way. Don't you agree?"

Yes, it is, but murdering a young girl isn't. Even Bugsy Siegel had his limits.

Trent Jr. enters the room and says, "What's on the menu, Mother?"

Lana walks out of the kitchen and says, "Chef Donatello has outdone himself. Prepare yourself for a gastronomic delight. Please sit and make yourself at home, Jason. The appetizers will be served momentarily."

Trent takes his seat at the head of the long, conference-like dining room table. I can't help but think of scenes from movies where the husband is at one end and the wife is at the other, screaming at each other to be heard.

Trent Jr. sits mid-table and says, "Please sit next to me, Mr. Feldman. I'm looking forward to more stories about you and my dad."

"Please, call me Jason. Your dad scooped you on all the good stuff, but I'm sure you have your own stories. How do you like working in the family business?"

He's silent for a bit, seeming to choose his words carefully. "I love it. I've learned a lot, and I'm still learning. I hope one day, God willing, I will take the reins, like my dad took them from my grandfather. I also hope to buy into a professional soccer team. Living in London half the year has converted me into a huge fan. Do you enjoy soccer, Mr. Feldman?"

"Jason, please," I repeat. My son lives in London. I wonder if you two have ever run into each other. "Can't say I am a major soccer fan, but I do know Cristiano Ronaldo. He's from Portugal, right?"

Junior nods in approval. "You are correct. He's one of the all-time soccer greats. What's your son's name?"

"His name is Sam, works at a hedge fund. He hates soccer though; the Steelers is still his team. Are you still a fan of the black and gold?" I ask. "Please don't say no."

Junior chuckles and says, "I guess I still am, but I've become addicted to soccer. In the UK, a real football is round."

Trent jumps in. "When all is said and done, he'll be able to buy a team on his own. This kid is talented and driven. They both are, and make me proud."

"Kayla, how about you?" I ask.

She sips her wine, and her eyes dart toward Trent. "Well, I'm happy right now and love living in New York City. I'm recently engaged."

I raise my Perrier and say, "Mazel tov, I wish you both much happiness."

She blushes and raises her glass. "Thank you so much, Mr. Feldman."

"Please, call me Jason. Mr. Feldman is my dad."

Trent stands and raises his glass. "Her fiancé is one of you, a partner at a white-shoe law firm in New York City. A toast to my daughter and to our guest. It's been too long, my friend. I have no doubt we will stay in close touch after today."

One of me? Her fiancé is pulling in four or five times what my practice generates on an annual basis.

I raise my glass and say, "You can count on it."

I wolf down my meal and take the last bite of my lasagna. "Lana, this was incredible. It's the best meal I've ever eaten."

I don't mention that for me, four-star Italian cuisine is anything above quick-casual.

"Thank you so much, but all the credit goes to Chef Donatello. I hope you left room for dessert and coffee. He's prepared a scrumptious vanilla and walnut spumoni. We also have café Americano, latte espresso, and cappuccino."

"Do we have any soy milk, Mom?" Kayla asks.

"Of course, dear. I bought it for your visit."

"Wonderful," Kayla says. "I'll have a soy latte."

"I'll have the same, Mom," Junior says.

It figures, I think to myself. It won't be long before this conversation steers to yoga and Peloton scores. They would get along well with Kevin.

"I'm going with a brandy," Trent says, walking back over to the globe.

"If it's not an imposition, Lana, I'll have another Perrier."

I've come this far. I might as well ride out a sober evening.

"No trouble at all," she says.

Lana presses a button on the wall, and the curtains part like the Red Sea to reveal a sensational view of the city of Pittsburgh by night.

"Honey, Jason and I are going to take our ice cream on the balcony," Trent says.

"Trenton," Lana corrects him, "ice cream is Ben and Jerry's. This is authentic Italian spumoni."

Trent rolls his eyes. "I stand corrected. Kids, I'm sure you have other stuff to do, don't feel obligated to hang out with the old folks."

Junior picks up a ball cap from the coffee table. He extends it in my direction and says, "This is from my favorite soccer team. I want you to have it. We'll make a fan of you."

My breathing quickens, and goosebumps raise like a million ant hills. Where have I seen it before?

"I don't think it will ever replace the Steelers, but if you buy a team, I'll be sure to watch," I say, taking the cap from him.

We exit the living room onto the balcony. The fireflies are electric, like neon, pulsating snowflakes against the backdrop of an illuminated City of Champions.

Pausing at the door, Trent says, "Lana, would you mind hitting the button to close the curtain?"

The motor hums again as the curtains move across the window. Before it blocks my view of the living room, I glimpse Junior and Kayla. They are on the couch, drinking their lattes, eating spumoni, and chatting with Chef Donatello. Trent raises his arm and sweeps it from left to right across the view with the bravado of an orchestra conductor.

"This is the greatest city in the world. Standing here, I know it's mine for the taking. Doesn't everyone want this?"

He's right. The city is beautiful, and the vista is intoxicating. PNC Park is ablaze in lights as the Pirates take on the Cardinals. The Point Park Fountain is blasting high, the water cresting and free-falling back into the surrounding pond. Even this late, the fountain steps are crowded with kids, lovers, and tourists. Across the rivers, a bit farther to the northeast and shrouded in darkness is where they found Heather's remains. It occurs to me this didn't start when Heather was killed. It started at the Odessa Society in the Hill District two generations before I was born.

"When did you start going by Trenton?" I ask, taking a seat at the wrought iron patio table that probably costs as much as my car.

"It's the name on my birth certificate," he says. "I use it in more formal environments, particularly business. Lana prefers it to Trent."

"I never knew that was your real name," I say with mild surprise.

One of the more innocuous secrets of our childhood. I wish they were all so harmless.

Trent leans back against the railing and sips his drink.

"What are we going to do about our problem?" he asks, staring down at me.

Which problem? What happened thirty years ago? Someone abducting me in front of my house the other day? Or your thugs throwing David out of a window?

"What problem are you referring to, Trent?"

Trent glances into the living room. I don't have a view inside from my angle, but the voices of Lana talking to the kids penetrate the glass. She's planning a charity event to raise money for a local women's shelter for domestic violence victims. The incline rumbles its way up Mt. Washington. A firefly flashes inches from my face. I drop my voice to a notch above a whisper.

"You want me to say it aloud about what happened in the stockroom? Yeah, I ran. I was a coward. I should have stopped you and gone to the cops."

Trent finishes his drink, crosses his arms, and steps away from the railing. His eyes drill a hole through me without expression. "Why didn't you go to the police? You still can."

I reciprocate his stare. "Because I was scared, plain and simple. What's your excuse, Trent?"

"Let me ask you a question," he says. "Do you see a difference between a reason and an excuse? I certainly don't, so what's the point of moral time travel? What happened thirty years ago is unchangeable. It's the present we both have to deal with."

The night air is more stifling than when we walked out here. I wipe the sweat from my forehead.

"Were you in love with Heather?" I ask.

Trent sighs and stares out over the city. "Does an eighteen-year-old understand what love is? I liked her, and she liked me, but we weren't exactly from the same side of the tracks. Her parents didn't approve of me."

"And the drug dealing? All the kids knew. I also know about the Odessa Society and your dad. Is he where the cocaine came from?"

Trent turns to face me and shrugs. "You mean the Odessa Club above the toy store? It's no secret my dad was involved in the gambling rackets. He went to prison. So what? Your father was at a lot of those card games."

I stand and shake my head. "I'm not talking about the Odessa Club. The lot where she was found was once owned by the Odessa Society. It formed back in early 1900 as a gathering spot for immigrants from the Ukraine. Later it became the center of Jewish organized crime in this city. The authorities will eventually figure out that lot was in your family. I don't believe in coincidences, and the cops won't either when they make the connection."

Trent's stare is blank as he rubs his chin. He finally says, "Been doing a bit of research, have we? There will be no connection to me, Jason." He steps toward me. I fight the urge to back up. "You told me I have a great family. Did you mean it?" He doesn't wait for my answer. "They are my world. I would do anything for them to keep them out of harm's way. Wouldn't you go to the mat for your family? Wouldn't you lay yourself down to shield your ex-wife, your son, and your ailing father, even your pretty doctor girlfriend?"

His composure is unsettling. How does he know about Mary? He obviously hasn't found out she dumped me. My stomach feels like an ice cream scooper is scraping it hollow.

"What happened after the storeroom?" I ask.

"Life happened, like it's happening now. What are your intentions, and where is David?"

"My intentions are for my life to proceed without looking over my shoulder. Why is David a threat to you? Let's call it a wash and everyone goes on with their lives. I'll keep my mouth shut, so will David."

Lana appears at the door. "Anyone need a refill?"

I hand her my empty bottle. "I should be heading home."

"Leaving so soon?" she asks.

"Yeah, busy day tomorrow. Thank you for the wonderful meal."

"It was our pleasure."

Trent hovers a step behind me as I head for the front door. "I'll walk you out so we can finish our conversation," he says.

I say goodbye to the kids, thanking Junior again for the cap, which is still setting off my déjà vu. The moment the elevator doors open, I take a position in the far corner and fix my gaze on the floor indicator lights. Trent enters right behind me with his back to the doors, and never taking his eyes off me, reaches behind his back and hits the lobby button. The uncomfortably familiar force of his glare bends my head toward the carpeted floor.

"It's ninety seconds to the lobby," he announces like an elevator attendant.

I nod my head and switch to staring at the floor lights clicking off, focusing on the metallic hum of the machinery lowering us toward what, I assume, will be an ultimatum. I've never been claustrophobic, but the four walls seem to be closing in and touching me.

"It's sixty seconds to the lobby, Jason."

What's with the countdown? Is he expecting me to break like a suspect beaten with a rubber hose? Without looking at the panel, Trent slaps the red emergency stop button with the back of his hand. The elevator shudders to a jarring halt, jolting me off my feet. I slam against the side and grab the handrail as the alarm shrieks. What the fuck? Is he going to off me here in this box?

"Mr. Stodge, is everything okay? Do you need assistance?"

It's the voice of the peanut and beer guy blaring through the speaker.

Trent doesn't answer. He says nothing at all and is just staring at me.

"Mr. Stodge, someone will be there momentarily to assist you."

Trent tilts his head one way, then the other, smiles and says, "No need, Monte. We're good."

The elevator jerks and resumes its journey to the lobby. The doors slide open. I rush past the security guard, and out the front door. I'm standing on the sidewalk with my hands on my hips and gasping for air when Trent steps outside.

"Are we on the same page, Jason? Old friends need to stick together. We need to talk to David."

Who is we? I think to myself.

"Here's a truth I should have hit you with thirty years ago. We were never friends. You were a prick and bully when we were kids, and you're a prick and a bully now."

"I can live with that," Trent says, pulling a handkerchief out of his pocket and mopping his forehead. "I still need to know if we're aligned. Your family and mine connect back over one hundred years. In the old country, it's as good as blood and certain obligations come with it. One is loyalty. You're loyal to your father and your son, and I'm loyal to my family. I want you to be here for your family. This is bigger than the two of us, and David is a loose end that needs to be resolved."

"What do mean by that?"

"David is not family, and we need to speak with him."

"Who is we, Trent?"

He's looking at me as if he's a concerned father. I have the distinct impression he's pitying me.

"What are you going to do, Jason?"

I shrug and walk into the street.

"Find him."

CHAPTER 22

The gondola lurches downward toward the city and an uncertain future. I'm relieved to be the only passenger. Sam's number is on speed dial, but the last time I pressed his baby photo icon was six months ago. He told me I was an embarrassment and that he had no interest in a father-son relationship until I checked myself into a rehab program. I can't blame him, and being told to go away, even by my son, was a relief. It was easier to crawl back into a bottle and glassine envelope than face my problems.

How far ahead is London time? If people watched us fight, they wouldn't know it, but Sam has a gentle, non-confrontational nature. Sonya fiercely defended him, taking on school officials, when his mixed-race looks subjected him to relentless high school bullying. Not only was he a Jew, but a half-Asian Jew. We finally pulled him out of public high school and sent him to a private school in Fox Chapel.

"Dad, is anything wrong?" Sam's tone is concerned but comforting. At least he's not snapping at me for calling in the middle of the night. The same apprehension I'd have if he woke me up at three in the morning.

"Did something happen to Mom?"

"Mom's fine," I say. "I'm fine. I...I wanted to hear your voice."

How do I bridge the gap? A relationship steeped in lies, my lies, will never be real.

"It's three in the morning here, Dad. Can this wait until later?" I worry he's going to hang up on me, a behavior at which we both excel.

"Don't hang up, Sam, please." Painful silence.

"It's my dad. Go back to sleep."

My son has a girlfriend? Maybe a one-night stand? I don't know a thing about his personal life.

The gondola jolts to a stop.

"I'm back, Dad."

"I heard you talking to someone, a girlfriend?"

"My partner, yes. Are you sure nothing's wrong?"

I didn't prepare a speech. My heart is pounding against my chest. I press my hand to it and push in as if the compression will slow the breakneck rhythm.

"I just want to tell you I love you and miss you."

Only his breathing breaks the quiet. Maybe leading with my heart was a bad idea. Too much, too soon, but as Kevin once said to me, the easiest thing to say no to is nothing, although he was referring to jacking up the price of his product.

"I love you, too, Dad. Ah, has Mom told you I'm flying in tomorrow?"

She didn't tell me, and I'm wondering if he would have if I hadn't called. It doesn't matter. His words envelop me with a more powerful high than the best cocaine I've ever snorted. Like the next line, I need to hear them again.

"When do you arrive, and where are you staying?" Part of me wants him to tell me he's staying at Sonya's, so I can start the drama. "Why don't you stay in your old bedroom at my place?"

"Sam?"

Did he hang up? I shouldn't have pushed.

"I arrive mid-afternoon but promised Mom I'd stay with her," he says.

What did my shrink say about these moments? Draw a full breath, hold it, and count to five. Let it go, Jason.

"I'd love to see you," I say. "We can have dinner and catch up. You can tell me about your girlfriend, and what else you've been up to. Is she coming with you?"

He corrects me again with a hint of annoyance. "Amelia is my partner, not my girlfriend. No, she won't be with me. I have an early flight, Dad."

"I hope to meet her sometime," I say. "I'll let you go back to sleep."

"Goodnight, Dad."

The next call is no easier, but this time, I have my opening argument. Our son. What I don't have is an uncomplicated explanation for why I stayed silent for over thirty years while a family, high school, and community grieved. Trent is right about one thing. There is no difference between a reason and an excuse. I'm out of excuses to keep pretending I had no part in it. I'm all in regardless of whether I want to be or not.

I text Sonya.

Need to talk. Calling you.

She texts back: *It's late, not tonight.*

It's urgent.

She texts: *What's so urgent?*

Can I come over?

She texts: *What? Why?*

Can't explain over phone, please, begging you.

I'm ten minutes into the twenty-minute drive to her condominium in the Mexican War Streets area before the answer comes.

You can't stay long.

On my way.

I haven't been inside Sonya's home, but I've spent a lot of time parked in front of it. During the separation, and for a month following the divorce, I stalked her from across the street, down the street, and driving up and down the street too many times to count. I even occasionally rented a car, so I could park close without arousing suspicions. I was occasionally drunk and coked up, driving myself batty, wondering if she were making love with someone in the bed we shared. My half-assed surveillance came to an ignominious end when a neighbor called the cops to report a suspicious person parked in the same spot night after night. A patrol officer found me passed out in the front seat.

Sonya got me off the hook, explaining our situation and pulling an executive favor, so they didn't bust me for DWI, which they had the legal right to do because I was behind the wheel, intoxicated, with the engine running. She made sure to remind me the favor came with substantial risk to her reputation and career if it leaked to the press.

As I pull up in front of her building, a car drives past, slows, and drives on. About twenty yards down the street, it does a three-point turn and stops, facing me. It could be a rideshare pickup. After five minutes pass without activity, I exit my car and take a casual stride up the sidewalk. As I draw closer, I make out two males. The glow of the tip of a cigarette illuminates the driver's face, but not to a degree that I can discern any facial details. The car is a late-model Cadillac with no front license plate. I'm almost at the heavily tinted front passenger-side window when the car pulls away. I turn and head back.

My right hand is shaking as I stand at Sonya's door. I let it drop to my side, balling a fist and pushing it against my right leg. I shut my eyes, again raise my hand, and ring the doorbell. The left sidelight curtain moves a bit. Two seconds later, the door opens. Sonya's hair is pulled into a ponytail, and she's wearing a Pitt Law sweatshirt and gray sweatpants. She is still every bit the stunning law student I confessed my Valentine's Day sins to, although not the most important ones.

"I'm sorry to bother you so late," I say. "Thanks for letting me come over."

I can tell she's contemplating a range of responses as she steps aside to create a pathway into her home.

"Let's talk in the living room," she says.

Sonya's condo is modest by major elected official standards. She's not pretentious or materialistic. She drives a ten-year-old beige Volvo and still wears the same washable suits she purchased working long hours at the public defender's office.

"I was about to have some tea. Can I make you coffee?" she asks, taking a ceramic teapot handed down by her mother off the stove and filling her cup. Sonya had always been a tea person and tried in vain to convert me from my five mug a day coffee habit.

"No thanks. Your place is nice. It has your decorative touch."

I sit on the heirloom Korean couch bequeathed by her grandparents as was most of her furniture. The walls are crowded with ancestral family photos. I almost fall off the couch when my eyes pan to a picture of her, Sam, and me at Kennywood Amusement Park. I blink twice to ensure I'm not hallucinating. The memory floods in. Sam couldn't wait to ride the Jack Rabbit and threw his hands in the air, yelling, "Daaaaddy," when the coaster crested the top of the climb and rocketed down the other side.

"My goodness, were you in a fight?" she asks. Those cuts on your forehead look painful."

"I'm sorry. I was lost in thought," I say, turning my attention from the photo to the problems of the moment. "Not a fight, two left feet. I tripped and fell face first on the porch stairs. It looks worse than it feels."

"You were always the clumsy one," she says, taking a seat on the couch next to me. "What were you thinking about?"

"All the crap I put you through."

"Water under the bridge," she says, taking a sip of her tea. "Why did you need to see me tonight? Is this about Sam? Are you in trouble?"

Am I in trouble? How should I answer? How can I tell her we lived a lie, and the lie was all mine?

"I spoke with Sam," I say.

Sonya's face softens, and her posture relaxes.

"I'm so glad you did," she says. "How did it go?" She takes another sip of her tea. The ginseng triggers summer evening memories on the back porch of our new home—Sam in his bassinet, rocked by Sonya with one hand, her tea in the other.

"It started out rocky, but when we hung up, I thought we took a step forward. We agreed to have dinner when he comes into town."

"This makes me so happy," she says. "It's important that you two have a real father-son relationship."

I decide that this isn't the time or place to ask why she didn't tell me he is flying in tomorrow.

Sonya walks into the kitchen, returning with her teacup refilled, and sits next to me at an angle so our knees touch at the caps.

"There is something I've never told you. When I was seventeen years old, rebellious, and confused, my parents wanted me to stay in LA, but I was ready to see what the world had to offer me," she says. "Against their wishes, I decided on college at NYU. We fought. We argued. We cried. I was sure they would disown me, but my father said, 'My sweet angel, we will fight, we will argue, we may be separated by a continent or an ocean. We will love you when we fight. We will love you while we argue. We will love you across the world. We are always with you.' I want to see the same love with you and Sam," she says, putting her hand on my knee.

Sam and I argue. We fight. We're separated by an ocean and more. My breathing is deep and erratic. I tighten my eyes to hold it back. I can't. The tears come. Sonya moves up next to me and puts both arms around my neck. Her head leans against mine as my body shakes and convulses with decades of shame, guilt, and loneliness. She kisses me on the cheek and wipes my tears from her face.

"I miss you so much," I whisper.

She doesn't respond but pulls my head around to face her and places a light but firm kiss on my lips. I press back and put my hand on the back of her head.

"Jason, I can't," she says, pulling away. "I have to tell you…"

I kiss her harder, and my hands roam her body. She reaches down, pulling my shirt up over my head. I have her sweatshirt off in less than a second. We explore each other's bodies for the first time in years. I'm gratefully reacquainted with the softness, the color, the warmth. She stands and takes my hand, leading me into the bedroom.

CHAPTER 23

Fragmented sunlight reflecting from the bedroom window is my alarm clock. Sonya's side of the bed is empty. Still, I revel in her familiar and comforting fragrance embedded in the sheets and pillows. I close my eyes and, for a few seconds, fantasize about waking up in the same spot tomorrow morning. A rustling in the kitchen interrupts my make-believe. I sigh and roll out of bed. Sonya's seated at the breakfast table, drinking a cup of tea and reading the newspaper.

"Sleep well?" she asks. It's as if we are still married and merely waking up after a three-year nap. "I made coffee," she adds. "Black with Equal."

"Bingo," I say, basking in the warmth of that remembered detail.

She sets my cup in front of me and rolls her eyes. "It hasn't been that long. We do, however, need to talk about last night."

I hoped it was real as we made love, but I also contemplated the possibility of this, a reality check over morning coffee. I reach my hand across the table toward her, hoping she reciprocates. She doesn't.

"Okay. Let's talk about last night."

She takes a deep breath, exhales, and says, "I've been trying to find time to talk to you about this, but with everything going on with the Heather Brody case, well, you understand how it gets. I've been seeing someone for over a year. His name is Alan. He's a lobbyist and lives in DC."

I take a sip of my coffee, contemplating the liquid darkness while absorbing the stomach-churning truth. She's moving on with her life much better than I am. "I heard about it through the grapevine," I say, sticking my index finger into my coffee and stirring.

"We've tried hard to keep it out of the papers and the rumor mill," she says. "He's asked me not to run for another term and to move to DC. I love my job but can't take any more of the political drama."

"Are you going to marry him?" I ask, my stomach in knots, waiting on the words I dread.

"We're discussing it," she says, taking another sip. "We agreed to live separately for a while after I move and see how things develop. I'm ready for a change."

"And after last night?" I ask, the knot twisting even tighter. My stomach's an interstellar black hole about to collapse on itself. She sighs and bites her lower lip as her head tilts up to the ceiling.

"I'm confused and still processing. I'm not sure last night changes anything. We were both, well, vulnerable. It happened. I don't regret it. It was wonderful, familiar, and comforting. Your reconciliation with Sam triggered feelings I thought were gone."

Her explanation for last night isn't verbatim what I had hoped to hear, but for now, I'll take it. "I understand," I say. "I'm not going to pressure you about this. I'm working hard on changing. I'm not using, and I'm not drinking."

"I'm thrilled you're making strides, but I'm not sure it changes anything."

Her voice fades, and she again stares into her cup as if the ginseng will supply magical insight.

"Are you going to tell him about this?"

Her back stiffens, and the familiarity is gone. "Sam?" she says.

"No, the lobbyist."

"That's none of your business."

She's right—lousy question.

"What was so urgent you needed to come over last night?" she asks. "Neither of us could have predicted the ex-sex, so I know it wasn't for that."

"No, of course I didn't come expecting we'd sleep together." I clear my throat and tug at my collar. This went easier when I played it out in my head. It's like skydiving. Edging yourself up to the door is easy. Pushing off into the weightless point of no return is a different story. If the parachute doesn't open, nothing you did in your life to that point matters.

"Do you know a guy named Trent Stodge? He's CEO of Stodgehill, Inc." I open my phone browser and pull up a news story about one of his charity donations. "We grew up together. His dad owned a game and novelty shop in Squirrel Hill. Trent's turned his novelty business into an international corporate conglomerate. His kids are in the family business as well."

"Stodgehill," she says, handing the phone back. "I know about it, but why are you asking?"

Now, I'm silent and searching. Where do I begin? No matter how I slice it, I'll have to admit I covered up a murder and lied to her by omission since the first day we met. Not the breakfast conversation I hoped for the morning after.

"I had dinner last night at his place."

Sonya's right eyebrow arches and wrinkle lines materialize on her otherwise flawless forehead. "You had dinner with Trent Stodge last night at his place. Why?"

"Yes, with his wife and two kids as well."

"Why?"

I see the concern and confusion on her face.

"It's what I want to discuss with you," I say. "Trent isn't what he appears to be. I've known it all my life and said nothing to you or anyone else until now. He's evil, and I think I can provide helpful information about him."

Sonya's stare and silence slows time to a crawl. She finally stands and disappears into another room, returning with a bulging file folder, slowly unwinding the string as if she's afraid of what's inside. She pulls a document out and places it on the table. She leans forward in her chair, looking at me while her fingers nervously strum the paper. Her familiar, judging stare of disapproval shrinks me in my seat.

"Trent's novelty business is a front for what we believe is a narcotics-trafficking and money-laundering operation stretching from here to Odessa, Ukraine. This is an ongoing investigation involving my office, the DEA, the FBI, and authorities in at least four different countries."

She slides the paper to my side of the table. "It's a shot in the dark, but do any of the businesses or names on this list ring a bell? We believe they are all an integral part of his distribution and money-laundering scheme to bring in profits from his overseas enterprises."

The question reveals the painful truth. She isn't sure if I'm involved but suspects I may be. She must sense my reluctance and says, "I'm not suggesting you're in bed with any of these people, but Trent may have said something you didn't think important at the time."

I use my index finger to slowly run down the list. It covers a variety of business and real- estate holdings in London, Madrid, and Odessa. There are lots of Russian-looking names. Nothing jumps out at me. I push the document back to her.

"Nope, I don't recognize anything here. Did you expect me to? I swear on my father I am not involved in this. Last night was the first time I've seen him in thirty years."

Sonya slides a press release to me. "Trent is also killing people right here in our city."

I slump in my seat as I read: "A joint task force comprised of the Pittsburgh Bureau of Police, the Allegheny County District Attorney Narcotics Enforcement Team, and federal law enforcement officials arrested a man in connection with fentanyl-tainted cocaine overdoses at a Carson Street apartment complex that left five teens dead."

I push the release back to her and say, "If I remember the details correctly, they met the dealer at a rave, went back to his place to buy drugs, and were all dead before they made it to the elevator.

Sonya nods, affirming my recollection.

"The dealer was stupid enough to allow someone to video record the kids snorting. The videographer became a confidential informant, but the dealer had a smart lawyer," she says.

"Yeah, I remember, Cal Langdon, we called him—"

"Cut-a-deal Cal," Sonya says.

Sonya takes a sip of her tea. "Cal went to the feds with a deal to shave some time off the sentence and allow his client to enjoy the immeasurably superior federal prison chow instead of the state prison slop. His client offered up the supplier."

"Trent," I whisper.

My pained expression reflects off the surface of my coffee like a mirror into my soul. The lies must end.

"Why haven't you arrested him?" I ask.

"All we have is the word of a snitch facing prison. We're building a case with the other agencies. It takes time."

She has no clue how complicated her case is about to become. I close my eyes, edge myself to the plane door, and jump.

"Thirty years ago, I walked in on Trent raping an unconscious girl in the stockroom of Stodgehill Toys. It was Heather Brody. I'm sure he murdered her afterward and took part in disposing of her body."

Sonya's face is blank. What's going through her head? "Were you part of it?" she asks.

"Absolutely not," I say. "I've made a lot of shitty decisions in my life, but I was not involved in her murder or disposing of the body."

"How do you know he killed her?" she asks.

"It's the only thing that makes sense," I say. I want to tell her about David and the abduction as well, but she'll think I'm unhinged more than she already does. "I think you're in danger. Last night, I saw a suspicious vehicle parked across the street."

Sonya stands, crosses her arms, and stares down at me. I look away and focus my attention on the photo. Why is it on full display for lobby man? I know I'd throw a jealous fit if Mary had a smiling photo of her ex hanging in her living room.

"A lot of cars park on this street," Sonya says. "Why are you coming to me now? You knew about this when we dated. You knew about this when we made love for the first time and when our son was born. Now you're telling me that our time together was defined by a lie that ruined so many lives."

Her glare is eviscerating. She's leaving out the one wonderful thing that came out of it: Sam.

"We did produce an incredible son. Are you saying I'm responsible for all the stuff in your file? You can't be serious."

"A son you never speak with and no, of course I'm not, but holding him accountable may have certainly changed the course of history and saved countless other lives lost to his product."

Once again, she's apart from me, as if last night was a mirage. She raises her arm and jabs it toward the front door. "You lied to me for years. I'd like you to leave."

Her furious tone slices through me.

"I did not lie to you. I stayed silent for us, for Sam," I say.

"Don't you dare lay this on me, or our son, Jason. This wasn't about protecting Sam and me. You were protecting only one person—you. Each second of every day you didn't go to the authorities and bring peace to Heather's family, you lied. Please leave my house."

Nothing more I say will matter. I nod, walk to the door, and let myself out. The suspicious car is gone. I cratered my chances with Sonya, and I'm no closer to finding David than I was two days ago. My body is screaming for powder. I vow to push forward even if it means checking myself into detox. At least there, I'll be safe. Why haven't I heard from Zev? Is he out west in Fort Bragg?

CHAPTER 24

The loneliest thirty minutes of my life pass by as I drive home from Sonya's. I'm pulling into my driveway when Mitch's number pops up on my phone. I don't want to answer, as if ignoring it will change what is coming. Sonya was probably on the phone to him the moment I left her place. She had no choice.

"What's up, Mitch?"

"We need you to come down to the office this morning to talk about Heather Brody." His voice is monotone and businesslike, as if he's speaking to a witness or a suspect.

"What time?"

"Please be here at nine a.m. sharp. I shouldn't say this, but you may want to bring your lawyer."

"Why do I need a lawyer?"

"I can't say more. Consider it friendly advice, and I'll deny I gave it to you. See you at nine."

I paw through my closet for the least-wrinkled suit. A blinding headache rages as I continue fighting through the physical and psychological urges to use. Withdrawals come and go with no rhyme or reason. I read on one of those luxury rehab websites that twenty-five percent of heavy cocaine users use again within a year. At this moment, I'd be more than happy to relapse if I had any product. Willie's purring nonstop as he preens his head into my hand for a neck rub. It calms me a bit. I remind myself that I really am innocent.

I force the corners of my mouth into a smile as I walk through the door of the district attorney's office.

"What's the word this morning, Mikki?" I ask. "Snapping necks and cashing checks?"

Instead of her usual witty retort, she shifts in her chair and looks away. I sense a deep sadness. Did someone die? My gut instinct is to do an about-face, head back down the elevator, pick up Willie, and drive north into Canada. Whatever I may or may not have been proficient at in my life, running was at the top of the list.

"They're waiting for me, huh?" I say, scanning the area for Sonya. There is no getting around it. I'm here because she made calls after I left her place. That's her job."

She nods and motions to the conference area. Her voice drops to a whisper. She doesn't make eye contact. "Please take care of yourself, Jason."

I put my hand on her shoulder as I walk by. Mikki places her hand on top of mine and squeezes.

Seated around the oblong conference table are Keane, Romo, and Pennsylvania Attorney General Sean Fogler. A short female in blue jeans stands in the corner of the room with her back to me. She's speaking to a shabbily dressed guy with a gold DEA shield hanging from his neck. A shudder of nervous familiarity jolts me. I brush past Romo and Keane, giving them a curt, fuck- you nod. "Wow, the gang's all here," I say, extending my hand to Fogler. "To what do I owe the honor of a visit from our AG?"

"It's certainly been a while," he says. "Because of your involvement and former relationship with Sonya, the district attorney's office has conflicted out of the Heather Brody matter. The attorney general's office will handle it from here on out."

His use of *former* stings. What doesn't compute is his presence and not one of the Deputy AGs. The king doesn't show unless the razor-sharp metal plate on the guillotine is about to drop. Sonya's seated behind her desk. Her eyes are dull and hollow, with heavy bags and dark circles. I'm sure she's been crying.

She says, "I think you're acquainted with most of the people here."

"Everyone but these two," I say, pointing at the lady who still has her back to me. She turns and has the same gold badge hanging from her neck. My heart sinks, and the already musty air becomes noxious. It's Dorothy Hamill from Mt. Everest. She's not local vice; she's DEA.

Mitch does the introductions. "This is Special Agent Denise Webber of the DEA and her partner, Evan McNamara. They're with the Joint Narcotics Task Force."

Webber reaches for my hand and pulls it toward her while I try to bite my lower lip off.

"Wow, your hand is an iceberg. Maybe we should turn down the AC a bit. Haven't we met before?" she asks.

Mitch gives me a cockeyed stare. "You two know each other?"

I pry my hand from her grip and wait for it. Webber will announce to Sonya and the room that I'm a strip club hound. I don't even go anymore. It was business. She knows the business. She has to. Why else would she be here? Sonya said the DEA was involved.

"I can't place you at the moment, but it will come to me. I never forget a face," Webber says, winking.

"Before we start," Keane interrupts, "Detective Romo is going to read you your rights."

My inner voice screams at me not to be the idiot who has himself for a client. Clam up, walk out, and call your lawyer like Mitch said. Another voice is a lecture from David, and it's saying my crime is cowardice. The third voice is telling me to sit down because only guilty people refuse to speak to the cops.

"I have nothing to hide," I say. "I told Sonya what happened. Since you consider it necessary to read me my rights, maybe I should retain counsel."

"You're welcome to call your lawyer," Keane says. "My understanding is this was supposed to be a friendly chat.

"If it's so friendly, why are you Mirandizing me?" I ask, fidgeting in my seat.

"You've professed to Detective Romo and me repeatedly that you want to help us. We're simply following procedure."

I glance over at Mitch, but he averts his eyes. Walking out right now is the most prudent course, but my butt is glued to the chair. They won't get any information they don't already know or will learn regardless of what I tell them. Romo finishes informing me of what any cop show fan can recite by heart. I have the right to remain silent. Anything I say can and will be used against me in a court of law. I have a right to legal counsel. If I can't afford a lawyer, one will be appointed for me. I sign the waiver, and Keane leads off.

"We've recently received DNA results back from items buried with the remains of Heather Brody. I'd like you to clarify some of the evidence and put your version of what happened thirty years ago on the record."

I point at McNamara who's glaring at Sonya.

"Why are they here?"

McNamara thrusts his finger in Sonya's direction and barks, "Because your ex jeopardized a two-year-long ongoing federal investigation with pillow talk, and we need to figure out how much damage she's done with her big mouth."

Sonya bolts up from behind her desk and yells, "How dare you speak about me in the third person. I'm right here, and I have a title. Speak to me."

The agent cracks under his breath, "You won't have the title much longer, honey."

The wisecrack infuriates me. I'm about to lunge across the table when Mitch jumps to his feet and raises his hand. His deep baritone drops a blanket over the room.

"Let's all calm down and take a step back. We were talking about Jason's version of events. Jason, tell us what happened the evening Heather disappeared. Take your time."

"I don't need to take any time. I was at home watching television when Trent called about eight p.m. and asked me to come over and hang out at Stodgehill Toys. I'd done it before, gone over at night. We'd drink beer and watch television or play cards."

"Were you home alone when he called?" Keane says.

The lie flows effortlessly through my lips like fine single malt scotch: "Yeah, my dad worked a double shift at the post office distribution center. He didn't get home until about eight the next morning."

"Did he often leave you at home by yourself?" Romo asks.

Anger boils from my stomach at the innuendo my dad was a bad father.

"My mom died when I was young. We did the best we could."

"What happened next?" Keane asks.

I haven't visited my dad nearly as much as I should. My concentration and confidence in my story are slipping away. They will trip me up on details if I have to tell it again. Too many lies and too little truth. My throat is so dry it feels like a porcupine exploded in it.

"May I have a glass of water?"

"Sure," Mitch says. "Let's take ten."

He opens the door and calls to Mikki for a pitcher of water and glasses. Keane turns off the tape recorder. I rush into the hallway and fight for composure. After a few moments, my breathing and body temperature return to normal, and I return to my seat.

Keane repositions the tape recorder closer to me and says, "Before we start Jason, can I ask you to not cover your mouth while talking? It makes it difficult to understand what you say."

I jerk my hand away from my face and place them both on my lap. "I apologize. I was unaware I was doing it."

"No need to apologize. It happens all the time during statements. Ready to start again?"

I shrug, "Fire away."

She hits record and says, "After a ten-minute break, we are back with the statement from Jason Feldman. What time was it when you left your house for Stodgehill Toys the night Heather Brody disappeared?"

I take a sip of my water wishing it was a shot of whiskey. "I honestly don't remember. I thought about not going because Trent sounded drunk. He was a different person when he was drinking. He became a bully. I finished the show I was watching and went over."

My gaze roves from Keane, to Romo, to Mitch and then the DEA agents to gauge their reactions. They're all stone. I twist my head around to Sonya. She's slouched in her chair and like Mikki, avoids eye contact.

Keane scribbles notes and says, "What were you watching?"

I shrug and say, "Who knows. Do you remember what show you watched on a random night thirty years ago?"

"Go on."

"I walked over to the toy store and entered through the alley using the rear door at the loading dock. Trent often left it unlocked when he invited me over, and he told me it would be open. I entered and walked down the hallway to the storeroom door. I pushed it open and saw Heather Brody on a cot in the back of the room. Trent was, well, on top of her with his jeans and underwear around his ankles."

Agent McNamara stops taking notes and says, "Were they having sex?"

I want to say no, he was doing push-ups, you moron, but the exasperated gazes at him from even Keane and Romo do the job for me.

"Yes, they appeared to be having intercourse. Trent got up off her and pulled up his pants. Heather appeared unconscious and seemed to be having difficulty breathing. She gagged and vomited all over herself. I expressed concern and suggested we call 911. There was a white substance on a table. I assumed it was cocaine."

Romo tosses his pen onto the table and shakes his head like he can't believe what he's hearing. "Did it occur to you she might be choking on her own vomit? Did you call anyone at all or try to get her out of there?"

I calmly push the pen back to him. "I told Trent we had to take her to the hospital. He was unsteady on his feet and seemed surprised to see me. Maybe he thought I wasn't coming or forgot he asked me to come over. He became enraged and said we weren't taking her anywhere. I walked over to the telephone on a desk and told him I was calling an ambulance. He pulled a revolver out of a metal toolbox sitting on the floor and pointed it at me. He said if I told anyone what happened, he would kill me. I panicked and ran home."

Romo leans over and whispers to Keane who nods and says, "Do you recall seeing a hammer in the toolbox?"

I shake my head. "I was preoccupied with the gun barrel pointed at my nose."

"You ran like a coward and left Heather for dead," Romo says, his contempt washing over the conference table.

"Why haven't you brought Trent in for questioning? He's the one responsible. He's a rapist and a murderer," I say, my voice two octaves higher.

Keane pushes a piece of paper over to me. "This is a statement from Trent's father, Frank Stodge, taken the week after Heather went missing: Trent was in Florida at an exclusive rehab center the night Heather disappeared. He flew down on Frank's private plane that morning. We have the paperwork from the treatment center. How could he have done what you said if he was somewhere else?"

Agent Webber taps Keane on the shoulder and says, "May I have a word in private?"

Keane nods and says, "Let's take a few seconds while I confer with our DEA colleagues."

They move to a corner of the room, speaking too softly for me to listen in. Webber pulls two glossy five-by-seven photos from a manila folder and hands them to Keane, who lays one in front of me. It's Yak and I standing in the parking lot of Three Rivers Bowl.

"I think you recognize this gentleman," Webber says. "He's your gregarious Russian friend who almost started the bar brawl."

"He's Ukrainian," I say. "So what."

"So, his name is Yakov Yaponchik. He's a former mercenary, now connected to organized crime. Interesting friends you have." She lays another photo on the table. This one is Kevin and Yak together.

I have an epiphany. I've become all idiotic defendants who thought they were the smartest people in the room. Kevin must work for Trent. I'm the bridge to both of them. Webber wants to flip me.

I'm rigid in my chair. "At this time, I'm invoking my right to be silent, and I'd like to speak to my lawyer."

"That's fine," Romo says. "You can observe and listen."

He reaches down to the floor and sets a brown paper bag on the conference table. He then puts his hand inside and withdraws a tagged, transparent evidence bag, pushing it in my direction.

"Do you recognize the contents?" Keane asks.

Inside the bag is an old locket without the chain and stained with rust. I can barely read the inscription, but I don't need to. I was eight years old when my mom gave me the jewelry after she and my dad returned from Israel. A silver pendant with an inset of the Tree of Life. Below the tree are the Hebrew words, Tikkun Olam. I turn the evidence bag over. Inscribed on the back of the locket is, "To our son, Jason. Always be kind."

My mind is reeling as I struggle to reconcile a forgotten past. I'm a child searching for words to explain the unexplainable. My mom called me into her bedroom and extended the locket to me. The front had a tree with little blue shiny stones on each branch.

"Do you know what this means?" she asked, as I took the locket from her hand.

"No, Mommy, what does it mean?"

She put her finger to her lips, struggling to explain it so an eight-year-old could understand.

"The tree is the Tree of Life. The words below it are in Hebrew. Tikkun Olam."

"Tikkun what?" I asked.

"Tikkun Olam," she repeated, enunciating each word slowly.

"What does that mean, Mommy?"

Her finger went to her upper lip again. She said, "Let's see how I can explain this. Tikkun Olam means, as you grow through life, treat everyone you meet with kindness."

When I ran from the storeroom, I didn't notice the locket wasn't around my neck. I told my dad I lost it. He was furious, and the guilt of losing what my mom had gifted me before she died was unbearable. What was I supposed to do, go back to Stodgehill Toys and ask Trent to give the locket back to me?

Keane rips me out of my reverie. She says, "I understand. I'd be at a loss for words. I'm Irish Catholic and had to look up the term. Repairing the world with acts of kindness is a beautiful concept. You can help repair our little corner by telling me what really happened to Heather and giving her family closure."

It occurs to me Sonya hasn't said a word during the interview. I turn and wonder what she's thinking. She makes brief eye contact and looks away, probably trying to figure out what's she's going to tell our son.

"See the dark, rust-like substance on the back?" Keane continues. "That's blood, Jason, your blood. Crime lab forensics matches it to your DNA."

In a pool of confusion, one thing is clear. Keane and Romo sandbagged me. I snap back at her, disregarding my invocation of silence. "Bullshit, you don't have my DNA, and you're not swabbing me without a warrant."

Romo takes a document out of his briefcase and pushes it across the table toward me. "Trash warrant," he says, grinning. "We obtained all the DNA we need, and we will be swabbing you counselor."

My eyes plead with Sonya for help. The favors have ended.

"We're not done yet," Keane says, producing another evidence bag.

"Have you ever seen this hammer before?"

Check the room for the sucker. If you don't see him, you're the mark. I reach for the hammer in disbelief and confusion, stopping short of touching the translucent plastic.

Keane squeezes the bag which allows her to grip the handle. "This hammer was also found with Heather's remains. We have your prints from your DWI arrest. The base of this hammer has your thumbprint on it. Why did you kill her, Jason? Did she spurn your advances? Did a lover's quarrel spiral out of control? Help us understand so we can help you. If you cooperate with us and the DEA in their investigation, we can make a deal, and keep you out of prison. You might even get witness protection from the Feds."

Webber chimes in. "If you give us information that helps convict Trent Stodge in our case, that is certainly on the table."

Sonya is grimacing. What will she tell our son? What will I tell him? Romo's wearing a smug, we-got-you expression. I want to pick up the hammer and pound the smirk off his face.

"Why did you take her to the Hill District? What's your connection to the lot she was found in?" Keane asks.

I explode. "There is no fucking connection, and I'm done here."

Romo positions himself behind me. "Yeah, you are done. Stand up. You're under arrest for the murder of Heather Brody."

McNamara bolts to his feet and says, "Whoa, hold on. We have questions about his relationship with Kevin Goldman, and Goldman's connection to Yaponchik and Trent Stodge."

I narrow my eyes and sneer. "Fuck you is my relationship. Talk to my lawyer."

The words I should have uttered from the start. Romo sweeps the inside of my right leg with such force that my groin flares in pain. He barks, "You know the drill. Spread your legs and place your hands on the table. Anything sharp in your pockets?"

I shake my head, partially relieved I flushed my stash at Trent's place. "Only my wallet, keys, and phone."

Romo digs them out of my pockets and yanks me upright. I place my arms behind my back so he doesn't have a chance to rip my shoulders out of their sockets while cuffing me.

"At least take me out the back," I plead.

Romo chuckles. "You're going out the front door counselor."

They are about to escort me into the lobby. The perp walk is happening, and I can't stop it. McNamara is irate and berating Sonya.

"This is not what we agreed to. You said we'd have the opportunity—"

Keane interrupts, "Don't blame her. This is our show. You'll have your at-bat."

Keane grabs my arm and pulls me toward the conference room door. "Let's go, Jason."

Mikki is at her desk, transfixed on the handcuffs.

"Wait," I say.

I plant my feet and won't budge when Romo tries to shove me forward.

"Mikki, call Dr. Fred Allen at Shadyside Hospital. If you can't reach him, ask for Nurse Sarah Adelman, she can find him. Tell Fred I need him to take care of my cat until I can resolve this. He has a key to my house."

"I will," she says. "I promise you, I will." I manage a weak smile and mouth the words, "Thank you," as Romo shoves me past her desk.

Assistant DAs, defense lawyers, and members of the general public gawk as we move toward the stairwell leading down to the first floor. I recognize Erin Campanara sitting on a wooden bench. She jumps up and jogs over to us. I bet Romo tipped her off.

"Hey, Erin," Romo says. "Funny seeing you here. Mr. Feldman, the ex-husband of district attorney Sonya Chang-Feldman, is under arrest for the murder of Heather Brody. He's being taken to the Allegheny County Jail for processing and arraignment."

Campanara sticks her phone in my face and says, "Mr. Feldman, Erin Campanara with the *Tribune*. Do you have anything to say to the family of Heather Brody?"

I glance at the stunned faces in the lobby. "I'm sorry for their loss, but I'm innocent."

Her phone camera flashes. Romo shoves me toward the exit. I concentrate on my toes, so I don't trip or make eye contact with anyone. The lobby is alive with the buzz of recognition and shocked utterances.

"Is that Jason Feldman?"

"Oh man, it's Jason."

"That's the district attorney's ex-husband."

Romo jerks me backward by the shoulder, halting my forward progress. He kicks open the stairwell door and shoves me through. After exiting the building, he drags me to the rear, driver-side door of the car, opens it, and pile drives me into the door frame. The cuffs prevent me from protecting myself, and pain sears down my neck.

"I guess I misjudged it. My bad," Romo says.

Keane barks. "Damn it, be more careful. We both have to file reports."

Romo shoves me into the back and stretches the seat belt across my body.

"No worries, detectives," I say. "I won't claim you tuned me up, and I'll be out in a few hours. You have nothing solid tying me to her murder."

Romo laughs and says, "Listen to this guy with his *tune me up*. He must watch a lot of cop shows."

Keane checks for traffic, hits the gas, and pulls out.

Romo keys the car mic, "38111 to channel one operator. We are transporting one arrest to the ACJ from the district attorney's office."

The Allegheny County Jail gate opens, allowing Keane to enter the sally port. If I had any doubts about the difference between nightmare and reality, the sound of the metal gate creaking shut behind us erases them all. Romo and Keane exit the vehicle, putting their weapons in a lockbox. Romo opens the passenger door, takes my arm, and says, "Let's go—and watch your head exiting the vehicle."

Keane hits a buzzer, and a voice on the intercom blasts, "Are weapons secure?"

Keane waves at the surveillance camera. "Hey, Lorenzo, our weapons are secure."

The door lock disengages, and they lead me inside.

"What do we have here?" a correctional officer, who I assume is Lorenzo, says.

"Remember Heather Brody, the dead girl they found in the Hill District?" Romo asks.

"He's the guy?" the guard says.

"We think so," Romo says, uncuffing me.

"I'm not," I announce defiantly. "You have the wrong guy. I'm suing all of you, the police department, and the city for wrongful arrest, malicious prosecution, and false imprisonment."

Lorenzo sneers and eyes me up and down with disdain. "Did anyone ask your opinion? Raise your arms."

I place both arms above my head and he pats me down.

Romo signs papers and whispers to Lorenzo, who appears to nod in agreement to whatever was said. "He's all yours," he says. "We're out of here."

"Be sure to treat Mr. Feldman right," Romo says. "He's an ambulance chaser."

I don't expect the intake process to differ greatly from my DWI arrest. They will take my medical history and conduct a pretrial risk assessment. There will be a non-invasive search for contraband, and I'll be taken to a basement holding cell until my arraignment.

Lorenzo barks, "Strip naked, bend over, and spread your legs. We're going to inspect you for illegal contraband and weapons."

I freak out. "You're going to cavity-search me? On what basis?" My panicked voice is now falsetto.

"I don't need a basis," Lorenzo says. "You're in my house."

I shoot back, "You damn well need a reason for a cavity search, and it's unconstitutional to strip search me without an individualized suspicion that I may be in possession of a weapon or contraband."

Lorenzo responds with unsettling confidence. "Counselor, I don't know what law school you went to, but that's not the law and not the way we do things here. We do have the right to both strip search you for weapons and conduct a cavity search for contraband."

I stand motionless with my arms crossed. "I want to speak to my lawyer first, and I'm not taking off shit until I do."

"Not happening, counselor," Lorenzo says. "You can make a phone call after processing. Please don't make me help you disrobe. It won't be a love session."

I've known humiliation but never gave a thought to the other side of the criminal justice tracks. As my cheeks are spread, I close my eyes and clench my teeth to stop tears from leaking out. Even one drop is a weakness the hacks and inmates will be made aware of. Lorenzo touches the puncture area on my right calf. The pain of yanking out the chair splinter is still fresh in my memory.

"How did you get the wound on your leg?"

"Bit by a dog."

Lorenzo hands me my pants. "I'll bet. Did you sue the owner and the dog? You can put your clothes on."

As expected, I'm denied bail at the arraignment, but to my horror, placed into the general population on the sixth floor. These people are out to screw me in every way possible. As the ex-husband of the district attorney, I should be in protective custody. I finally make my jailhouse phone call to the only lawyer I want representing me.

Shelly Kowalczyk—or Give Them Hell Shel, as she's known to the Pittsburgh legal community—is part of a small pantheon of local criminal defense lawyers. She made her bones fresh out of Duquesne Law School, representing street-level drug dealers, graduating to drug-dealer distributor defense, then branching out to high-profile, hard-to-win homicide cases.

Her pinnacle of achievement to date is winning an acquittal for white police officer, Cameron Hansen, who shot and killed Graham Waters, a black man, during a routine traffic stop in Beltzhoover. In his official report, Hansen claimed Waters was aggressive and threatening when asked for his license and registration. Waters bent over and picked up what Officer Hansen thought was a weapon. Hansen fired three shots through the open window. It turned out a pair of sunglasses had fallen from the glove compartment, and Waters was simply picking them up.

The jury deliberated five days before returning a not-guilty verdict. Hansen walked. The riots afterward lasted three days, causing close to a million dollars in city-wide property damage and the death of two protesters. The acquittal and violent aftermath also served as the springboard to Sonya's upset election victory for district attorney. Shel needed a personal security entourage for the next six months but also became a fixture on the legal pundit circuit for officer-involved shootings when an unarmed minority citizen was on the other end of a bullet, a knee to the neck, or a banned choke hold.

In addition to her off-the-chart courtroom skills, Shelly is one of the more colorful members of the local bar. She's a mid-fifties, bleached blonde with silicone implants that have to date back to the early days of plastic surgery. She drives around town in a white Porsche Cayenne with a license plate that reads, "GTYUOFF."

Married and divorced three times, Shel accumulated substantial wealth from two of her now-deceased husbands, one of whom, lore has it, died in the throes of an orgasm with Shel riding him in a hot tub at a swinger's resort in Mexico.

I exhale a sigh of relief when she answers.

"Law Office of Shelly Kowalczyk."

"Shel, Jason here, I'm in the—"

"You're in the ACJ," she interrupts. "Your mug is all over the news, but the real surprise is who called to alert me."

"Who?" I ask.

"Three guesses, and the first two don't count."

I'm exasperated. "I'm in fucking jail and don't have time for this, Shel."

"I'm sorry," she says. "Bad time for shtick. Your ex reached out."

Sonya handed me one final favor. "How is the media playing this?"

"As you might expect," she says. "In the current news cycle, you're the most hated person in the city of Pittsburgh, maybe in the country. You're better off in jail."

I survey the sixth-floor pod. Inmates are passing time watching the tube, playing cards, and eyeing me, the new meat on the block. They will be sharpening their shivs in their cell when they inevitably learn who I am.

"I'm going to end up a slice of ground round on a slab at the morgue if you don't spring me."

"Let's not be dramatic," she says. "This isn't a Sly Stallone prison movie. I've made calls to have you placed in protective custody. I'll be there tomorrow and we'll strategize bail. Gotta go, walking into a restaurant, hot date."

"Don't hang up. Call Dr. Fred Allen at Shadyside hospital and make sure he's taking care of my cat."

"What if I can't reach him?" she says.

My thought process is racing and chaotic. "Call Mikki at the DA's office and ask if she's spoken with him. If you can't reach Mikki, enter my home by any means possible and take care of Willie. Also, call my paralegal Stacy and tell her what's happened. She's going to have to run things for a bit."

"Will do," she says. "I'll add the pet-sitting to my hourly rate. Stay cool. Stay calm. I'll start working on our motion for bail modification."

CHAPTER 25

The attorney meeting room on the sixth floor of the Allegheny County Jail reminds me of the waiting room at Shadyside Hospital, except that room is sterile and drab, and this one is dirty and drab with six tables bolted to the floor. One other inmate is in deep conversation with his lawyer. Neither acknowledges my intrusion as the guard escorts me in. Shel is already seated at a table, scribbling notes on her legal pad.

"Quite the mess, huh?" she says. "How are they treating you?"

I'm irate. "What the hell am I doing still sitting in the general population? I should have been transferred to protective custody immediately after arraignment. I haven't left my cell other than meals."

I'm keenly aware that if Trent is the drug kingpin Sonya and the feds think he is, he'll have no trouble reaching me in here.

"I'm not sure what happened," she says. "I'll call the deputy warden and threaten a news conference if he doesn't transfer you today." She puts down her pen and pushes the notepad away. "Try to relax. No one is going to stick a shiv in you. You're not a cop, a drug cartel snitch, or a former wise guy informing on the mob. I've filed a motion for bail reconsideration. It will be heard in two days. You'll need to surrender your passport and give me a list of people who will testify on your behalf. If we crap out, I'll raise bail again at the preliminary hearing. By the way, I printed out this morning's front-page headline." She pulls a piece of paper out of her briefcase and slides it across the table. "I like the photo. Campanara always gets the money shots," she says.

The headline reads, "I'M INNOCENT." I'm not sure I agree with Shel. With my surprised eyes, and mouth open, I look like a celebrity arrested for getting a blow job in a public restroom.

"What's the news saying about this?" I ask with apprehension.

"Do you know what being social media canceled is?" she asks.

"Yeah, when someone is videoed saying or doing something racist or otherwise idiotic. The internet mob descends. The unlucky SOB loses his job and his wife. He also has to change his name and move to another state."

Shel nods and says, "I couldn't have said it better. I'm sorry to break this you, honey, but you're canceled. You don't want to see the reviews for your law office."

Of course, she shows me anyway, removing a copy of my Yelp page from her briefcase and handing it to me.

> Feldman sold me down the river and kept my settlement money.
>
> If you want to be murdered and buried in a vacant lot, call Jason Feldman.
>
> Feldman sexually assaulted me in his office.
>
> Feldman's a pedophile.
>
> Hang the kike.

I sigh and push the paper back to her. "I've read enough."

"You even made the *Five Fast Facts* website, although you probably don't want to brag about it," she says. "A few of my other clients have been on their radar. I'm amazed how they dig up stuff no one else finds."

"Did they dig up anything on me?" I ask.

"Well, let's see," she says, putting on her gaudy, gold-trimmed, Gucci glasses and studying the printout.

"You were once married to our current district attorney and have a grown child together. You were also arrested for DWI and found not guilty because of my stellar trial skills."

I spin my index finger. "Anything we both don't already know?"

"Fast fact number five took me by surprise," she says. "You drive ride-share part-time for an Uber competitor called WARP, and you're close friends with its founder, Kevin Goldman? When did that come about? Is money tight? He's a fox."

"It's a long story and unless you're planning to convert to Judaism, you have a zero shot."

She hands me the charging document. "We can cut through all the legal mumbo jumbo. You're charged with hitting Heather Brody over the head with a blunt instrument, namely a hammer, causing her death."

"Other than not having hit her over the head with anything or laid a hand on her ever, it sounds about right."

The door opens and a stodgy guy with tussled brown hair, sporting an ill-fitting, overly wrinkled blue suit and a pink tie strolls in. Like Shel, Cal Langdon is a fixture on the criminal defense circuit for high profile cases. He pulls up a chair next to her.

"No one invited you to sit, Cal. I'm advising my client. Go advise yours."

"I heard you picked up the Feldman case and here you are. Wish I had nabbed that one," he says in a wistful tone.

Shel pushes the chair away with her foot. "Better luck next time. Please excuse us."

He pats me on the shoulder and says, "You ended up with second best, but Shel will do you right. By the way, your ex is a bitch on wheels. I hate dealing with her. I thought Asian broads were docile."

My neck muscles tighten and my right hand clenches into a fist. I'm about to bolt to my feet and lunge at him when Shel grabs my wrist and whispers, "If you do it, you can kiss bail goodbye."

Cal takes a pack of chewing gum out of his pocket and plods to the back of the room, whistling Zip-a-Dee-Doo-Dah. A hack enters the room and escorts a handcuffed and shackled inmate to Langdon's table.

"Forget about that douchebag and pay attention," Shel says. "The Commonwealth's primary pieces of physical evidence tying you to the alleged crime are your print on the hammer that also has Heather's blood and DNA on it, and the crusty piece of jewelry found with Heather's remains. The print is a twelve-point match with the ones taken after your DWI arrest. The blood on the locket has been matched to you through DNA analysis. The good news is it ties you to the locket, not to Heather, and we won't deny it belonged to you. I'll have my own forensics people analyze both."

"Obviously," I say. "Work harder for your fee I can't afford please."

"What they don't have is motive. The cops have been pouring over the original investigation with a fine-tooth comb, trying to link you to Heather. Is there anything I should be aware of? I hate surprises that don't come in a Louis Vuitton box."

I shake my head. "Nope, I didn't know her well."

"Define *well*. Did you date?"

"Nope."

"Sit with her in school or pass love notes?"

"Nope."

"Did you have a crush on her? Unrequited love?"

"Unrequited what? I knew her to say hello, Shel. That's it. We may have sat next to each other in study hall. She was out of my league and ran in different circles. How much is this going to cost me?"

"Excellent question," she says. "Let's talk about my fee. One hundred grand to take this to verdict. A ten-thousand-dollar retainer to start us off."

I do a double take and lean back in my seat, shoulders slumped. I'm not sure what I expected, but a prior client discount would have been nice. My prized Babe Ruth baseball doesn't mean as much to me as my freedom. I will have it listed on eBay as soon as I'm out of here.

"I may need to sell my sports memorabilia and take a second mortgage, but I'll make it happen," I say. "Take down this number, 412-747-WARP. Tell Kevin Goldman I asked him to advance you the retainer. He'll probably give you cash. I'll square it with him when I make bail."

"Cash is a plus, and bail is no cakewalk," she says. "You're not charged with jaywalking."

I sigh, "Thanks for reminding me. You're the queen of tasteful under-statement."

She puts the printout back in her briefcase and closes it. "I have to run to a preliminary hearing on a great case I just picked up. My client's accused of strangling his wife to death, but I can prove it was a sex game gone wrong. She loved to be choked during climax. Right up my alley. A bonus is that unlike you, he kept his mouth shut and called me immedi-ately. We'll discuss the idiocy of your meeting with the cops and DEA with-out counsel another time."

Shel stands, puts her hands on her hips, and scolds me like she's talking to a child. "I don't understand what on God's green earth possessed you to speak to them without me present. You're a lawyer for Chrissake."

I snap at her, "My ass is on the line here, not yours."

She rolls her eyes and retorts, "You've done well so far."

She's right, of course. Love and arrogance are both blind and stupid.

"Wait, how's my cat?" I ask.

"I've confirmed your doctor neighbor has Willie. He's also a hottie. I'm adding in a fee-rider requiring you to set us up."

"If you finagle me out of this mess, I'll pay for a cruise for both of you to a swinger's getaway in the Caribbean."

"Promises, promises," she says. "I almost forgot. My assistant deposited one hundred dollars in your commissary account, so you won't have to eat tray crap three times a day. Don't thank me, though. I added it to the bill."

I lean across the table. "I need you to do something else."

"What's that?" she says, inching her head closer to me.

"When you speak to Kevin, tell him I need a new bat phone. He'll understand. Tell him I'll explain when I see him."

Shel makes a note on her pad. "No problemo." She sighs and closes her briefcase. "Going to be a busy day. I guess this means no afternoon nookie with my new beau, Andre. I'll reach out to Kevin after my next hearing."

I'm lying on my bunk when a hack the inmates call Jarhead comes to my door. His sobriquet is related to his buzz cut, use of military time, and penchant for screaming orders at the top of his lungs. He was either a drill sergeant prior to being a CO or has watched one too many episodes of *Oz*.

"Feldman, get your ass out of your bunk and grab your gear. We're moving you to protective custody."

It's about time. I'm tired of being a self-imposed inmate pariah. At least in solitary, I can see the shiv coming. Administrative protective custody is a more humane term for solitary confinement. The reality is that I'll spend twenty-three hours a day in my cell, and there will be no phone calls or visitation other than Shel. I can also kiss the commissary food upgrade goodbye, but if Shel does her job, it will be a brief stay.

Shel doesn't think much of my paranoia, but she isn't familiar with my kidnap and torture. I don't intend to hold those details back forever, but I can't spring a thirty-year conspiracy on her out of the box. This isn't *Infowars*. It's real as hell. We must build this Lego house together, one tiny plastic brick at a time, or it will collapse.

CHAPTER 26

The morning of the bail modification hearing arrives. After a jailhouse strategy meeting with Shel, she heads to the courthouse, and a CO escorts me to a room converted to a control center of sorts for inmates to appear for hearings by video.

Judge Atticus Busby takes the bench and announces, "We are on the record in the case of the Commonwealth of Pennsylvania versus Jason Morris Feldman. This is a motion for bail modification. I note the dapper Sean Fogler of the Pennsylvania AG present for the Commonwealth, and the defendant is represented by the venerable Shelly Kowalczyk."

Sean Fogler rises and announces, "The Commonwealth calls Detective Jeannette Keane."

I watch through the monitor as Keane takes Busby through their case against me. She testifies that the name on the locket focused their investigation on graduates of Squirrel Hill High named Jason, and they assumed from the inscription the person it belonged to was Jewish. With that information, they researched high school yearbooks and found three potential matches. One is dead, and the other has an airtight alibi for the night in question, leaving only me.

Keane obtained a search warrant for my trash, which turned up two cut straws with my saliva, as well as two glassine baggies with a white powder residue identified by the crime lab as cocaine.

Romo takes the stand. Three sentences into his testimony, and I want to emulate real bad guys and pop a cap in him.

"I took the locket to the Rolling Hills Senior Living facility. With the permission of staff, I briefly visited with Norton Feldman, the defendant's father. He has been a resident of the facility for the last five years. Mr. Feldman confirmed his wife bought the locket during a trip to Israel, but he doesn't remember the exact time frame."

Shel and I bolt to our feet in almost perfect synchronization.

"Objection, Your Honor. Detective Romo harassed an elderly and frail dementia patient. This is outrageous," she says.

I'm blind with rage and bolt up from my seat. "You had no right. Leave my dad alone."

Two hacks are on me in an instant, forcing my butt into the chair. They keep intense pressure on my shoulders to lock me down.

Busby holds up a hand and admonishes Romo.

"This isn't happening, detective. This court did not authorize such a visit. You're excused."

I swear Romo is grinning into the closed-circuit camera as he exits the witness box.

Sean Fogler concludes the prosecution's case to keep me behind bars without bail. "Mr. Feldman concealed his involvement in this crime for more than thirty years. The evidence clearly connects him to the homicide. He's a liar, a murderer, and facing a substantial prison sentence. He's also an alcoholic and cocaine addict who will be both a danger to the community and a flight risk if released."

Shel objects to the alcoholic and addict part and calls Doc Allen to the stand. He testifies that I'm a quiet neighbor and check on his house when he's out of town. We grab a beer once a month at the Squirrel, but he hasn't witnessed any illicit drug use. The owner of Rolling Hills Senior Living testifies that I visit my dad at least once a week. I bring him brownies and read the news to him. Shel closes with the standard bail argument. I'm an established member of the community, have lived in Allegheny County my entire life, and my thriving law practice needs to be maintained. The evidence connecting me to the deceased's murder is purely circumstantial.

The minutes creep by as I wait for Busby to render his decision from the bench. My jail reds are soaked in sweat as I stare unblinking at the monitor. After a half hour of twiddling my thumbs, he finally emerges from chambers.

"The crime charged here is serious, and we all hope justice is served for Heather Brody. The purpose of bail, however, is not supposed to be punitive. The defendant has long and substantial ties to the community. He is a practicing lawyer before this bar and the sole source of support for his ailing father. I have heard no testimony that convinces me he is a flight risk or danger to the community."

I want to jump up and pump my fist but restrain myself as Busby continues with his ruling.

"While I see enough evidence to sustain a prima facie case, I see no reason non-monetary alternatives to bail will not secure his presence at trial. The defendant's bail is hereby modified to home confinement, along with other conditions to be set by pretrial services, including, but not limited to, an ankle monitor, mandatory drug testing, and surrender of his passport. This hearing is concluded."

Fogler jumps to his feet with both arms raised.

"Your Honor, this man is potentially facing a life sentence. This is highly inappropriate and contrary to the law."

Busby glowers at Fogler, bangs his gavel, and says, "Mr. Fogler, you are out of order and dangerously close to contempt of court. My ruling is final."

Shel turns toward the video camera, winks, and gives me a thumbs up.

CHAPTER 27

Three more days in solitary pass before I'm fitted with a HomeConfine ankle monitor, processed, and released. I used the time to brainstorm my plan to skip bail and find David. There are multiple moving parts. If any one of them fails, I'm back in a cell until my trial, or worse.

Shel drives me home and follows me inside. Drawers are open in the kitchen. Sofa cushions are not on the sofa. Shel doesn't wait for me to ask.

"The local po-po and the feds executed search warrants for your home and office while you were in custody. They have both your cell phones, laptop, and office computers. We can expect them to grab your phone records and texts as well."

Did I leave any blow in the house? I once found a full baggie I'd hidden in a jacket pocket and forgotten about. When they conduct forensics on my computer, the hundreds of searches for mentions of Heather will catch their attention and be difficult to explain away. I can posture the searches for David as concern for his well-being. If Kevin's bat phone encrypted messaging app doesn't function as advertised, we're both screwed.

"Did Kevin give you the new phone?"

Shel reaches into her purse and pulls it out. "Yep, here you go. Your pal, Kevin, is smoking hot. When this is all over, a personal introduction is mandatory. I'd convert for him."

Romo is still under my skin from his visit to my father.

"Romo almost blew this up for us. He's such an asshole."

Shel cocks an eyebrow. "Are you kidding? I'm sending him flowers for his moronic stunt. You couldn't see, but Busby was on the verge of reaching over the bench and bitch-slapping him upside the head. It might have been what tipped the scales in your favor." She glances at her Cartier watch. "Let's finish this up. I'm already late for a client meet."

Shel hands me my paperwork with my bail conditions. I'm required to piss in a cup at random requests and attend weekly AA meetings. I'm allowed to meet with Shel and engage in other activities necessary to assist in my defense. Attendance at work-related court hearings is allowed as is visiting my dad once a week. Pretrial services must approve each activity twenty-four hours in advance.

"I'll let you reacclimate in peace," she says. "As a reminder, your monitor isn't satellite GPS enabled but has a two-hundred-foot range out the front door. Don't go on any long walks, or you'll be back in the hoosgow. We'll talk tomorrow."

No satellite GPS? I wasn't expecting that and may have caught a huge break.

"I thought all ankle monitors were GPS enabled, so they can find you anywhere in the country."

"Not all. Budget issues, I guess. These are less expensive. By the way, I let your hottie doctor neighbor know you were coming home. Your furry feline should be around here somewhere."

"Thanks, Shel. You're worth every penny. I'll text you so you have my new phone number."

I open the curtain and chuckle at Shel wedging her Rubenesque figure into her white Porsche. The engine guns, the wheels screech, and she's gone. I'm finally alone. No hacks, no cons, no inmate counts. I estimate forty-eight to seventy-two hours is a reasonable window to put my plan into action. The first step is to speak with Kevin. I text him on my new bat phone.

I'm out and need to see you.

I know. Headed your way.

Thirty seconds pass and poof, the texts disappear from the screen. I spend the next sixty minutes swigging a warm Diet Coke and picking at microwaved popcorn. Why haven't I heard from Zev? How will I cut off or disable this contraption on my ankle? If nine out of ten things go right with my scheme, I'm still screwed.

Pulling into your driveway.

I open the door, and Kevin, the first moving part in my plan, sticks out his fist for the bro bump. "How was the gray bar Hilton?" he asks.

I've zero desire to reminisce. There are more urgent things to discuss.

"Who told you I was out?"

"No one had to tell me. You're all over the news. Your lawyer Shelly called, and I fronted your retainer," he says.

"Thanks. I'll pay you back, but you have a much bigger problem."

Kevin follows me into the living room, picks up a sofa cushion off the floor, tosses it back on the couch, and sits down.

"Dude, this place resembles a war zone."

"No shit," I say, taking a seat next to him. "The cops and the Feds executed search warrants. They also have the bat phone. I hope it works as advertised."

Kevin shrugs. "No worries on that front. The messages are not stored on a server. There is nothing for them to find."

Kevin starts to speak again, stops, and looks around the room like he's worried someone is listening in on our conversation. "I have to ask, and what you tell me won't leave this room."

"Ask away."

"Did you kill her?"

I raise my right hand. "I swear on my mother's grave I did not kill her. I'm being framed, and you're about to be in a world of shit. When I gave my statement, two DEA agents were in the room. They have a photo of Yakov and me together. They've obviously been watching, one of us or both.

Kevin is silent, staring at me, contemplating, as the seconds tick off into eternity. "What did you tell them?"

"Nada about you. I asked for my lawyer. I'm not telling them a goddam thing, but there's more. They also have a photo of you with Yak, and they are on to your operation. The hammer is coming down, probably sooner rather than later."

He pounds his fist on the sofa cushion. "I don't believe this."

What doesn't he believe? Most high-level drug suppliers always get caught while talking about the one last big score before they go straight. The rest die a violent death. Hasn't he seen Scarface or heard of Pablo Escobar? "I need your help, Kevin. We have to work together to get through this, or we are both toast."

Kevin stares at the ceiling; his lips are moving like he's talking to himself.

"Did you listen to what I said?" I ask.

This is the first time I've seen fear on his face.

"Yeah, I heard you. I was calculating how long it will take me to shut my operation down. What do you need?"

I pull up my pants leg, exposing my ankle monitor. "First off, we need to cut this contraption off my ankle. After that, I need to blow town and locate David."

Kevin leans over and touches the thick casing enclosing the electronics. "I've never seen one of these up close. How does David know what happened?"

"I hope you never have to get up close and intimate with one. David was there the night she was killed. He knows I'm innocent. That's why I have to find him."

"Who, Heather?"

I roll my eyes. "No, the Lindbergh baby. I think David saw the whole thing, and Trent is trying to kill him and frighten me into silence. Trent had me kidnapped off the street. They tortured me for information."

Kevin sinks back against the cushion. "Whoa, when did this happen?"

"Over a week ago. They took me to a crack house in the Hill District and injected me with heroin. A gravel-voiced guy threatened to give me a hot shot if I didn't tell them where David was. I was lucky to escape alive."

Kevin fidgets in his seat. I'm not sure I've ever seen him so nervous and uncomfortable.

"Why the hell didn't you tell me about any of this?" he says.

How do I explain to him I wasn't sure at the time if he was involved? I shrug. "I didn't know who to trust. I still don't."

I reach down to Willie, who is sniffing at my ankle monitor, grab him under the stomach, and lift him onto my lap. "David is off the grid and probably going under a different name. He may already be dead, but I have to try."

Kevin tugs at his shirt collar. "Do you have any booze around here? I need a drink."

"I don't," I say. "My lawyer got rid of it for pretrial services, and that's a blessing for both of us. You have two choices, soda or bottled water."

"I'll take the water."

I grab a bottle for each of us and sit back down next to him. "It's my turn for a question. You've always known about Trent, haven't you? Don't play me for an idiot. You're in the business."

Kevin jumps to his feet. "What are you implying?"

"Who supplies you?"

He glares down at me. "You're crazy if you think I'm telling you. It could get both of us killed."

"Sit down, Kevin. I'm not trying to put anyone in the jackpot, least of all me or you. I'm trying to stay alive, out of prison, and keep my family safe."

Kevin sits and leans forward with his head in his hands. He doesn't need to say the words. He is in bed with Trent Stodge.

"How long have you worked for Trent?"

"Since day one," Kevin says, breathing hard. "He's the biggest cocaine and heroin supplier in the city. His tentacles also reach into Ohio and West Virginia."

"Who supplies his product?"

"Roger Hambrick. He brokered the deal with Trent," he says. "Rumor has it he's the Odessa mob and connected to the top rungs in London, Madrid, and New York City. When you screwed up his daughter's party, I was honestly worried you'd turn up as a floater in the Allegheny River."

"The river fiasco wasn't my fault," I say.

"You don't understand. They'll kill us, Jason. They'll kill our families, and they will even kill Trent if he doesn't solve this problem. This isn't one of your gangster movies."

Maybe Kevin finally understands he's not an enlightened swami, nor is he operating on a higher moral plane. He's a mid-level drug dealer, answerable to people who will take him out with any hint of a threat to their business interests, the same as they would David or me.

"If we can find David and put Trent in the international spotlight with Heather Brody, the attendant publicity may not sit well with his mob pals. Let's view this from their perspective. They want to keep a low profile. The feds are on to them. Trent is the linchpin to their mess. You cut the cancer out at the source instead of all the limbs it may spread to."

Kevin sits quietly for at least a minute while I sip on my water and contemplate the valuable seconds ticking away. He's probably wondering the same thing I am. Why wouldn't they simply kill us all and wipe the slate clean? They may try, but I'm hoping, as Virgil Sollozzo said in *The Godfather*, blood is a big expense. They are about business.

"What about the feds?" Kevin finally asks. His eyes are closed and his shoulders slumped, as if he's playing out the closing credits of his life.

"The feds aren't going to firebomb our homes or kneel us in front of a ditch. We'll deal with them as needed."

I tap on the ankle bracelet. "The trick is to fool this thing long enough for me to blow town. Zev acts like the Israeli James Bond. I need him to be MacGyver. Can he bypass it without alerting anyone?"

Kevin drops his head into his hands, covering his face. "I think so. I don't know."

"Getting this thing off my ankle is only the start. I need your help to execute my plan. Are you in or out?"

Kevin eyes me in silence, probably trying to figure out how things went bad so quickly. The other day, he was JSwiping and working out. Today, he's a few steps from being on the bad side of the Odessa mob and possibly prison. A text notification comes through on the bat phone. It's Shel.

New developments. Can you talk?

As if he has a sixth sense, Kevin asks, "Is your lawyer in on this?"

"No. If I tell her I'm going to skip bail and she doesn't alert the authorities, not only will she never practice law again, but she can be charged with obstruction and as an accessory after the fact. Have you seen *The Fugitive*? The scene where Richard Kimball calls his lawyer and asks him for money? The lawyer says he can't give him any. It's like that."

"Yeah, I've seen the movie. Let's travel back to the real world. You were talking about trust. Can I trust you with something? I may have a way out for both of us."

Kevin hands me a business card. It reads Geraldo Picazo, President, Emerald Leaf Enterprises, Mendocino, California.

"For the last six months, I've been putting things in motion to break with Trent and, for lack of a better word, legitimize—going all legal marijuana. I'm sure you've noticed a significant drop-off in your deliveries."

"I've noticed, and so did my bank account. I attributed it to supply issues," I say.

"You're right, but the problem isn't access to supply but a contaminated one. Do you know what fentanyl is?"

I study the card and Kevin's face. It's not the face of a drug kingpin. The flawless skin and smooth forehead with a feminine, narrow nose. A face people trust is a plus in the narcotics trade. Kevin has that.

"Yeah, I know what it is," I say, reaching up and touching my neck where Dr. Kevorkian jabbed me.

"Trent has been mixing his heroin with fentanyl that he's importing from Mexico and India. I may be a drug dealer, but I'm not a murderer. I can no longer trust that his cocaine isn't contaminated either.

I hand him back the card, so livid I want to roundhouse him. "You didn't seem concerned about that when you supplied me for personal use."

"That was from another supplier and tested. It was always clean."

"Does Trent know you're out? I can't imagine either he or Roger are going to throw you a going-away party on the Gateway Clipper and wish you luck. Do they allow people like you to leave the business? I thought it was like the mafia: once you are in, you're in for life."

"People like me?"

"Drug dealers."

"I'm not a drug dealer, I'm a distributor, and I'm still working on those details. Believe me, you don't need or want to know anything about them." He stands and hands me his empty water bottle. "I'll put things in motion on my end."

I shake my head. For a guy with a PhD, he has no problem with intellectual dishonesty, but if he needs to make that distinction for his moral piece of mind, so be it.

"This is all kind of bad timing for you, huh," I say.

"The understatement of the century," he says.

Kevin's bad timing is my gift from God. He might not have helped me otherwise. Shel will unhinge when I cut this thing off my ankle and skip town. Oh well. I can't think of a better example of the ends justifying the means.

Kevin opens the front door and says, "I read online they found a locket with a Hebrew inscription. What did it say?"

"Tikkun Olam," I say.

Kevin nods in approval. "Changing the world with kindness. One of my father's favorite phrases. Your parents were quality folks."

"My dad still is," I say. "When you talk to your father, ask him to pray for me, David, and Heather."

I momentarily reflect on how odd my request is. What do they say about foxholes? Kevin pulls the door shut behind him. I walk to the living room window and watch him back out of my driveway. A car parked across the street does a U-turn and takes his spot. It had better not be pretrial services again. I have no piss to give right now. They are worse than cops.

She exits the car and is at once recognizable. The television. The *Trib*. The shiny, smooth news anchor's haircut curling at her shoulders. My infamous, "I'm Innocent," headline. It's Erin Campanara.

I press my eye against the peephole. She's at the porch, and I still haven't decided whether to answer the door. I slap my palm over the hole. This is silly. She can't see in. I looked through it from the outside to make sure when I had it installed. My hand, however, is frozen in place. She knocks twice. I shake my head and chuckle at myself. What are you doing, Jason? Grow up. I remove my hand and peer through the hole. Three more knocks follow.

"Mr. Feldman, Erin Campanara from the *Trib*. I know you're home. I'd like to ask you some questions about Heather Brody."

Maybe I should call Shel. She'll tell me to keep my mouth shut, and I'll get billed for it. No thanks.

"Jason, if you're not going to answer the door, please look through the peep hole. I want to show you a photo."

All I see is the white border of what appears to be an old Polaroid, but the image is distorted.

"Back up. You're too close," I yell.

She's probably been sitting out there watching and saw Kevin leave. What's the point of pretending I'm not here? The Polaroid pulls away, and the picture comes into focus. Halloween 1988. I dressed as Freddy Kruger with the mask, rubber claws, the whole bit. Heather was Cyndi Lauper. She stood behind me with one hand over my chest and the other on my crotch. Trent, dressed as Beetlejuice, snapped the photo with a new camera his dad had bought him. It was a gag. We were all hammered. The photo was in the box that was on the floor after my house was broken into. I had long forgotten it was there. How the hell did she get it?

She yells through the door. "Can you see the photo now?"

"I have nothing to say. Please talk to my lawyer, Shelly Kowalczyk."

"That's fine, Jason, but you should know we are running this photo tomorrow afternoon. You're front-page news. This is your chance to tell your side of the story. The truth. Doesn't Heather's family deserve that?"

"I said I have no comment. You're trespassing. Please leave."

Campanara puts the photo in her purse and walks back to her car. The moment she's gone, I'll call Shel. Erin however, stands there for ten minutes talking on her phone. My eye socket begins throbbing from the pressure on the peephole. She finally gets in the car, pulls into the street and drives away. I bolt into the living room for the bat phone.

"Shel, we have a new problem."

"What will it be today, Shel?" a voice asks.

"Sorry, I'm grabbing a bite to eat, and it's as loud as a sold-out Steelers game in here. I'll step into a quieter area."

I'm under house arrest, facing life in prison, and a photo connecting me to Heather is about to go viral. She's grubbing and sipping a brew. I'm not angry. I'm jealous and want my life back, at least parts of it.

"I'm sorry," she says. "I've stepped into the bathroom and checked the stalls for privacy."

"Shel, Erin Campanara was here at the house."

"I hope you told her to pound salt."

"Kind of but—"

"No buts. Please tell me you booted her off your stoop."

"I didn't say squat to her, but she sure did to me. She's in possession of a photo of me with Heather when we were kids. The *Tribune* is publishing it. Knowing Campanara, the national media will be next."

"Thank you for coming in Ms. Kowalczyk. We hope to see you again soon."

"Shel? Are you paying attention? There is a photo of Heather and me together. It's crap, though. We ran into each other at a high school Halloween party. Trent took the photo. This is part of the setup."

"I'm on the move. The bathroom got crowded. Yeah, I heard. You ran into her at a party. Big deal. I can neutralize the impact."

"But I didn't tell them about it. I said I didn't know her."

"You didn't tell me either and as I recall, you said that you didn't know her well. You forgot, and so what. I can't remember parties from last month, let alone thirty years ago. The hit parade continues, however. There are more prints, not yours, on the hammer, and they have a witness who puts you at the scene."

My already Indy 500 pulse rockets to a SpaceX launch. "That's impossible," I say. "Who's the witness and whose prints?"

"You're not going to believe this, but a second set comes back to Heather Brody from a public intoxication bust when she was sixteen."

As if for effect, she leaves me hanging for an annoying ten seconds of dead air. Willie walks in and sits at my feet, staring up at me with his feed-me eyes. I stroke his head, wallowing in a brief mixture of calm and sadness. Willie knows I didn't do it. Who will love and care for him when I'm in prison or dead? "This isn't a legal pundit show, Shel. Spare me the vocal theatrics and tell me what it means for my case. Didn't they have an obligation to tell us about her prints?"

"You're referring to the Brady Rule which requires the prosecution to turn over exculpatory evidence. I'm surprised a personal injury lawyer knows about that."

"I saw it on a *Law & Order* episode but yeah, that's what I'm talking about."

"Well, we know she didn't beat herself to death with the hammer, so I suspect the prosecution will claim it's evidence she fought back, and you were stupid enough to bury it with her body. I'm going to make a stink, but their position will be since it's not exculpatory, they had no obligation to tell us. They also probably knew we'd turn them up when my forensics person examined it, which is what happened."

"What about the witness?" I ask.

"An old man who lived in an apartment overlooking the alley behind Stodgehill Toys & Novelties. I haven't seen the statement yet, but I'm told he's certain he saw you running from the alley the night in question."

There is no one to blame for this new development but myself. I put myself at the previously unknown scene of the crime when I bared my soul to Sonya. The upside, however, is it also corroborates parts of my story—the real story.

CHAPTER 28

When Trent called me that night to come over to the toy store, I was watching television with David. Trent's voice was slurred, a sign he'd been drinking.

"Yooo dude, you wanna come by the store? My dad had a poker game upstairs at the Odessa Club, but everyone's gone now, and they left a lot of beer. I'll leave the back door unlocked."

I covered the mouthpiece and yelled to David, "Trent's on the phone. He wants us to come over."

As expected, David balked. "I'm tired, and you know I don't like him. He's such a bully."

"Wait a minute, pleeease," I implore.

David sighed and stood with his arms crossed, staring and tapping his foot.

"You there? Trent? He hung up. Come on. Let's go over. My dad won't be home until the morning and when those games end, there's always extra beer, doughnuts, and those sandwiches we love from the deli. I'm starving."

The mention of food piqued David's interest. He shuffled toward the front door and said, "I'll go, but I can't stay long. We can grab sandwiches and a couple brews but after that, I'm going home."

I grabbed my jacket out of the closet, and we walked the five blocks to the toy store. The door to the Stodgehill Toys stockroom was in the alley behind the building and had a white, handwritten sign that said, "Deliveries Only."

David was about to press the buzzer when I said, "Trent told me the door would be unlocked." David pulled, and it opened. The hallway was lined on either side with wooden pallets, stacked to the ceiling with boxes of board games and novelty knickknacks: Nerf balls, G.I. Joe, Bingo, and Memory. The closer we got to the storeroom, the louder a strange noise became, a metallic sound. I had butterflies in my stomach as I rested my ear flush against the door.

"Are we going in or what," David said. "I'm starving."

"Shhh, I hissed, keeping my voice in whisper mode. A creaking noise, like old bed springs, stopped, and started again.

I stepped back from the door and placed three fingers on it.

The door swung forward, seemingly on its own. Trent was on a cot in the corner of the stockroom. His pants and underwear were around his ankles. I couldn't make out who was beneath him, but he was the only one making noise.

David's foot bumped a wooden pallet. I stopped breathing, and Trent's hips stopped moving. He braced himself with his arms and craned his head around.

All I could think of to say was, "Hey Trent, what's up?"

He rolled onto his feet and yanked his jeans up. The girl's eyes were closed and her body limp. Around each wrist were rows of black rubber bracelets that were all the rage at the school after Madonna began wearing them. Dangling from one ear was a gold Egyptian-type earring that she had worn in school. I overhead her telling someone that it was Queen Nefertari, who I recognized from the movie The Ten Commandments. It was Heather, naked from the waist up, her shorts around her ankles.

Trent stumbled toward the circular card table littered with beer bottles, drinking glasses, and crumbs of food. Conspicuously visible in the mess were lines of white powder and a crack pipe. He seemed to be on the verge of toppling over and managed to slur out, "Man, I'm shit-faced." He then bent over four lines of blow. Two of them disappeared up his nose through a red straw. "It's a paaarty, help yourself," he said, wobbling back toward the cot where Heather lay, still motionless.

"Is she okay?" I asked.

Trent nodded, and swigged from a beer bottle on the table. "Too much to drink, and we did some blow. She'll be fine."

David moved closer to her. "She's barely breathing," he said. "We should call 911."

Trent pushed himself away from the table and staggered over to her. "Nah, she's cool. Jason, you're up."

I hadn't snorted cocaine since the prior New Year's Eve. Still, the incredible self-confidence emanating from a tiny white line of powder had stayed embedded in my memory. When the high had ended, the shame swept into my gut. I would have to lie to my dad for the rest of my life. I'd woken up and practiced my confession, but the words hadn't materialized. I had no intention of dealing with that guilt again and stood frozen in place.

Heather's chest heaved, and a foamy substance seeped from the corners of her mouth.

"She's OD-ing," David shouted. "We need to get her to a hospital."

"Mind your fucking business," Trent said. "Who invited you, anyways." He glared at me and said, "I didn't say you could bring him."

Out of the corner of my eye, I spied David inching to the side of the cot. "I'm getting her out of here," he said.

Trent lunged at him, grabbed his arm, and jerked him backward. "You're not doing shit. Leave her alone. She's fine."

Heather was gagging and her skin had taken on a bluish tint.

"Dude, she's choking on her own vomit," David said, wrenching away from Trent and turning Heather's head to her side. A combination of greenish slime and foam seeped out of the side of her mouth and onto the cot. Trent walked over to a steel toolbox sitting on an empty pallet. He opened it and pulled out a revolver, aiming the barrel at the back of David's head.

"I'm going to count to three—"

I picked up a hammer from the toolbox and screamed, "What the fuck? It's David. Put the gun away."

Trent wheeled around, and I was face to face with the barrel. His eyes were glazed and vacant, like he didn't know who I was. I swung the hammer at him, a wild swing without a precise target. It flew by his head but made direct contact with the gun barrel. The gun went off, and a bullet whizzed inches past my right ear, the blast turning my brain to pulp and causing me to lose my balance and fall backward. My head bounced off the concrete floor.

"Shit," Trent said. "Why'd you hit me? I wasn't gonna do anything."

I struggled to my feet as the room spun and my ears rang. Waves of nausea and pain rolled through me. A small pool of blood, where my head had struck the floor, seeped around the hammer, turning the ball-peen red. Trent grabbed me under the armpit.

"Let me help you up. I didn't mean to hurt you, honest."

"Get off me," I said, grabbing his wrist.

He broke my grip and wrapped his hands around my neck.

I wrenched my body away, pushed myself up, and looked at David for help. He had Heather in his arms and was struggling toward the stockroom door. His eyes were scared and desperate.

"She's too heavy. Help me get her to the alley," he wheezed.

The only sound I heard was my labored breathing as I bolted out the door. I sprinted the length of the hallway to the exit, right into the arms of Hit the Hole Yanzer.

"Whoa," he said. "Where's the fire?"

I pointed back to the door. "In there," I said.

"Wait right here," he said. "Don't move. I'll be right back." He opened the door and disappeared inside. I waited. The alley was darker than when I had come in. My heart pounded, and my chest ached. I wondered if it was what a heart attack felt like. I wasn't waiting for Yanzer to come back and sprinted to my house.

CHAPTER 29

"This whole thing's a setup," I say to Shel. "It's utter bullshit. I don't deny I was there. I'm a witness, not a perp."

"Well, he's given a statement to the AG, and I should have it shortly," Shel says. "I'll ring you after I've reviewed it. Sit tight and stay chill."

I see no point in debating the merits of the witness's claim when I don't plan on being here for trial. I grab a bottled water from the fridge, turn on the television, and sink back in the recliner, exhausted.

"Bombshell out of Pittsburgh. The ex-husband of Allegheny County DA charged with the murder of his high school sweetheart. Stay tuned for *Crime and Justice* with Melinda Barron."

The Halloween photo pops onto the screen. Now we were sweethearts. The power of visuals. It works wonders with juries. The show is five minutes in when the doorbell rings, followed by a knock and a shout: "Pretrial services. Open the door."

I chug the rest of my water to make it easier to give them a piss sample. The moment they are out the door, I head upstairs and collapse on my bed.

The bat phone text alert wakes me up. I struggle to reorient. What time is it? I must have crashed hard. Pretrial services were here hours ago. I open the secure messaging app.

Open your door.

I text back: *Who is this?*

Open your door.

I pull back the bedroom curtains less than an inch. It's still light out, and the front porch is empty. Do they have the balls to try again in broad daylight? An abundance of trees and shrubs in the park offer enough concealment to take a shot at me if I expose myself.

I creep down the wooden stairs. Every groan and creak is amplified ten times over. I swallow twice, turn the dead bolt, and open the door enough to peek through the crack. A large, bulging manila envelope leans against it. The trick here is to grab it without exposing myself to a shooter. Get a grip, Jason. No one is going to shoot you in broad daylight unless they have a high-powered rifle and scope. Better safe than sorry. I drop to my hands and knees, reach around the door, and snatch the envelope. I shift into reverse and back myself out of the kill zone.

The envelope is glued shut and has substantial heft, weighing at least three or four pounds. I grab the scissors from the kitchen and slide them across the top, stopping with each slice to expand the envelope and ensure I'm not cutting wires that will trigger an explosion. Two inches into the process, I'm able to make out the envelope's sole occupant—a Glock 45 automatic. I didn't ask Kevin for a weapon but who else can it be from? Zev is also a possibility. Where the hell is he?

I inch the Glock out of the envelope like it's an unwanted insect. The last gun I fired was a Daisy air rifle my dad bought me at Stodgehill Toys. A search of YouTube brings up hundreds of videos on how to fire a Glock. I sort through multiple clips of people shooting cans, trees, and paper targets while explaining the intricate workings of the weapon. I've heard time and time again—don't point a loaded gun at a person unless you're ready to pull the trigger. None of the videos explain how to work up the courage to blow a person's head off, which is the skill I need. Can anyone predict how he will respond at the moment of truth? My hunch is, with the right motivation and stakes, anyone can kill, regardless of temperament or morals.

A new bat phone text: *2200, ACA N420G 2100 alley.*

After internet research and a bit of deduction, I believe I've figured out the text hieroglyphics. A plane with the tail number N420G is wheels up from Allegheny County Airport at ten p.m. tonight. The rendezvous will be in my alley. I'm not surprised Kevin has his own plane. Don't all drug kingpins?

I stuff the Glock back in the envelope. Where can I hide it until I'm ready to go? The attic in the master bathroom is the perfect spot. I mean, who looks at the ceiling when he takes a piss or shit? I pull the rope to release the attic hatch and place the envelope on the inside ledge for quick access.

My insides ache like my appendix is about to burst. I must see Sam before I run. He needs to hear my explanation for why I kept what happened to Heather from him and his mom. More than anything, before I board the plane, I need to hear that he believes me. He should be in town by now.

I dial Sam wondering about the phone protocol when your son might suspect you of murder. Who speaks first? Should I start it off proclaiming my innocence?

"Hello?"

Shit, I forgot that he won't recognize the bat phone number. "Sam, it's Dad."

"Hey Dad, I didn't recognize the number."

"It's a new phone."

"Did you do it, Dad? Did you?"

"You have to believe me son, I didn't kill her. I'm being framed. Please let me see you. I need to explain it face to face. It's a long and complicated story."

As I wait for his response, I once again flash to Trent's bathroom with regret. I could use artificial confidence right now. The next random urinalysis isn't a concern since I won't be here. Maybe this is the moment I unconsciously anticipated when I flushed my stash.

"Have you spoken to your mother?"

It's an idiotic question. Of course he has spoken to her.

"I'm staying at her place," he says. "I'm flying back to London in two days and want to see you, but I know you can't leave the house. If it works for you, I'll swing by tomorrow evening."

Goddammit. That won't work. After tonight, I'm a ghost and don't think Dad as a fugitive from justice will solidify our new bond and engender trust.

"Please don't ask me to explain, but I need to see you sooner. Can you come by now? Will you do that for me?"

"How about this evening, after I have dinner with Mom?"

I'm about to ask what she's told him but pull it back.

"After dinner is fine. Thank you, Sam."

"See you soon," he says.

The phone disconnects before I can tell him I love him in the hope of hearing it returned.

CHAPTER 30

The prosecution's eyewitness statement arrived by text attachment from Shel. Moses Sterenberg, the one-time suit king of Squirrel Hill, claims he saw me running in the alleyway outside of Stodgehill Toys the night Heather disappeared. Moses, a Polish Holocaust survivor, was an entrepreneur in his own right, earning a living by peddling dress shirts, socks, and ties out of a black steamer trunk with "Suit King" painted on the lid in yellow block lettering.

Growing up, it wasn't unusual to see the king wheeling his chest along the sidewalk of Murray Ave. or slurping on a giant bowl of matzo ball soup in the local deli. The king also made house calls and, on more than one occasion, wheeled his wares into our living room. My dad loved the heavy-duty work socks that supplied an extra layer of cushioning during long nights on his feet sorting mail. While my dad rummaged through socks, shirts, and pants, the king showed me the number tattooed on his forearm. He said, "You must not forget what happened to our people, Jason. This number should be a reminder never to forget."

Apparently, Moses and his wife were watching the news when they heard what sounded like a car backfiring in the alley. He walked to the window to investigate and recognized me running toward the street. I had passed directly under a spotlight he'd bracketed to the wall of his building so he'd be safe from muggers while taking out the trash.

The moment I'm finished reading, I dial Shel.

I have trouble hearing her when she answers. There's a familiar, heavy dubstep beat pounding in the background.

"Shel, where are you?"

"I'm out having drinks with my new beau. The music is a bit loud, I'm sorry."

I cover my left ear and shout, "They're going with the fleeting observations of a ninety-something-year-old to convict me of murder? Is this a joke?"

"Not quite," she says. "They are going with a ninety-something-year-old Holocaust survivor who's still sharp as a whip. It shouldn't be difficult to trip him up, but let's not pretend he is a drooling, senile geezer."

"Like my dad, right?"

Ten seconds of nothing but dubstep announces her regret. "I'm sorry, Jason, I didn't mean to suggest..."

Dementia is so unfair. On a good day, my dad asks about Sam and understands Sonya and I are divorced. He talks about the Pirates and complains about the nosy widow, Mrs. Schulman, bothering him while he's watching *Jeopardy!* When he's sundowning, he screams racial epitaphs, swear words and bangs his head against a padded wall.

"Forget about it," I say. "What about Mr. Sterenberg's wife?"

"She passed eight years ago," she says.

"How'd they find him?"

"What's the difference, they have him," she says.

"Would you and your handsome hunk like a lap dance, Shelly? Why don't you come upstairs to the Everest Base Camp private club?"

Holy hell, Shel is at Mt. Everest. Even Yak can't get into the ultra-exclusive Base Camp swinger's club on the third floor. To walk into the private elevator requires a five-thousand-dollar initiation fee and monthly dues of one thousand dollars. Swinging isn't my thing, but I did try to bribe my way up to get a look around by slipping a Benjamin Franklin to the bouncer guarding the elevator. He laughed, handed it back to me, and said, "This is what I tip the bathroom attendant."

"Why is his statement crucial to their case? I admit I was in the Stodgehill Toys stockroom that night."

"I'm getting in an elevator, so I may lose you. Pay attention. Trent has given the AG a sworn statement that you had a key to the storeroom. He says when his parents were out of town, you kids threw beer parties upstairs in the Odessa Club. He wanted you to be able to haul beer up there, so he made a copy of the key and gave it to you. Their circumstantial case is shaping up nicely. If the jury believes Trent Stodge, you had access. He has the rehab alibi. The photo connects you to Heather. The Holocaust survivor puts you at the scene. DNA evidence wraps the bow."

"Shaping up nicely? Whose lawyer are you? It's total bullshit. Trent called and asked me to come over. The door was unlocked, there was no key, and I explained the photo."

"What can I tell you? You're not paying me big money to bullshit you about their case. That's his story. Keep your chin up. This is what you pay me for."

It's time to break out the Legos. "Shel, I'm positive Trent murdered Heather and there's a person who can help me prove it. His name is David Chaney."

"David who? I'm sorry, it's loud in here. Let's talk later."

"Chaney, we need to find him. He was there that night."

"Grab her around the ass, Andre. Yeah, I like that."

Shel says, "Before I forget, The Commonwealth is filing a motion to revoke your bail and there will be a candlelight vigil protest in front of your home the day after tomorrow. Close your shades, don't answer the door, and stay away from the windows. Gotta go. Talk soon."

"Slap her butt, Andre. That's hot."

Andre? Is that her new guy?

"Shel? Hello?"

A fucking protest in front of my home, my neighbors, and every runner, walker, and car that drives by. Great, just great. I think back to the candlelight vigil for Heather my father and I attended. Her parents walked out of the house and addressed the crowd, letting us know they loved each and every one of us and asking us to pray for her daughter's safe return. Unlike that vigil, I won't be present at this one. I'll be a fugitive from justice.

CHAPTER 31

The banging on my front door. Did I fall asleep? What time is it?

I orient myself and peek through the living room window curtains. It's Sam. I take hold of the doorknob, rotate it, and pause, contemplating the greeting. Should we hug? Should I kiss him on the cheek? It's very European. An old-fashioned handshake? Maybe I should go with the talk show guest greeting. The celeb strides out from behind the curtain, the host stands up and puts out a hand. They shake and mutually pull their bodies together for a chest bump.

I open the door, and my heart palpitates with joy. My son.

"I rang the bell a bunch and was starting to worry. My dinner with Mom finished early, so here I am. It's good to see you, Dad."

"You too, Sam. I'm sorry, I fell asleep. It's been a long few days."

He steps forward and embraces me, putting his hands on my back. Nothing fancy. An old-fashioned, years-melting hug fathers and sons replicate around the world. Nothing I remember beats this feeling, including booze and blow. He steps back and says, "You look healthy, Dad—maybe a few pounds heavier, but you wear it well."

"You've grown a few inches," I say. "Can I offer you something to drink? I have soda and bottled water."

"Nah, Dad, I'm fine." He inspects his surroundings. "It's been a while since I've been in here. Not much has changed, minus Mom's furniture and decorative touches."

"I've never been much of an interior designer. Sit and take a load off."

Sam sits on the edge of the couch cushion, silent and rigid. He probably doesn't trust me, and I don't blame him.

"Thanks for coming," I say. "My ability to travel outside my house is restricted."

He's trying not to be obvious checking out my right ankle. We might as well get past this part. I pull my pants leg up.

"You can inspect it," I say. "It doesn't bite, but don't yank on it, or it may go off."

Sam doesn't accept the invite but continues to study the device like a law student preparing for a final exam. "How does it work?" he asks.

"Without becoming too technical, if I leave the house and walk beyond a designated perimeter, it sends a signal to a monitoring station. They then contact pretrial services, who will call first, then come check to see if I'm here. If I'm gone and haven't been given permission to leave the area, a warrant for my arrest will be issued. It's annoying, but infinitely better than jail."

"Do they let you go to work?"

"Yeah, I have to make a living, pay the rent, and keep your grandfather in the lifestyle he's accustomed to. Speaking of which, have you been to see him?"

Sam stares at the carpet in silence. That's a no. I don't press.

The hours counting down to wheels up move in slow motion. Keep your eye on the ball, Jason. The problem is there are two balls. One is sitting on the couch.

For a prolonged moment, I study his eyes, searching for any sign he is open to my version of events. "I swear on your mother and grandfather, I did not kill Heather Brody."

"What happened, Dad?"

I thought I'd have a pat answer, but this is my son, not my lawyer, not my ex-wife, my only son. Sam jerks and reaches for his ankle. Willie is circling, rubbing, preening his head for a scratch.

"Willie," Sam says, scratching him behind the neck. Willie's head stretches upward for more. Sam picks him up and drapes him over his shoulder like a baby, stroking his back. "I've missed you, Willie."

"He's clearly missed you as well," I say.

Sam sets Willie on the carpet and says, "Mom thinks you're guilty. She says the evidence is strong enough for a jury to convict you."

"I know she does," I say. "I want to explain my side of what happened that night. Whatever you believe after I'm finished, I'll have to live with it, and I'll still love you."

Sam is stoic as I spend the next thirty-plus minutes outlining the hidden beats of my life, ending with my theory that Trent is trying to silence the witnesses to his crime by any means possible.

I can't tell from Sam's eyes or body language whether he's buying any of it.

"I take full responsibility for staying silent about what happened for all these years and for not being the man your grandfather taught me to be."

I put my head in my hands and sob. Sam rests his hand on my shoulder.

"You have to help that poor girl's family find peace and justice."

"I have a plan," I say, as I wipe my face dry with my forearm. "I want you to catch the first flight back to London tomorrow."

"What the hell are you talking about, Dad?"

My pitch spikes. "Please, go back home. For your own protection, I can't tell you anything more. I'll contact you when I can."

Sam leans into me, grabs my kneecap, and squeezes. "No way I'm leaving you like this. I'm calling Mom. She'll know what to do."

"Please don't," I plead. "She thinks I'm both a liar and a paranoid basket case."

Sam's eyes shift away from me to the front door. He also thinks I've gone insane. We both stand.

"Do you promise you won't say anything to her?" I ask, fighting not to become hysterical.

"I promise, Dad," he says, sounding like a little boy swearing to do his homework. He's patronizing me and will tell his mom everything. It will be out of love and concern but will fall on deaf ears.

"I love you, Sam." I pull his chest to mine and bear-hug the air out of him. "We'll talk when this is all resolved. Look after your mother."

He steps onto the front porch.

"Dad!" he shouts in surprise as he's propelled backward, past me and onto the staircase. The barrel of a gun crosses the threshold into the house. The arm attached to it follows. The face is a picture on my office wall. I saw him in the alley the night Heather disappeared. My dad worshipped him. The face of Hit the Hole Yanzer.

CHAPTER 32

While recognizable, Yanzer no longer bears any resemblance to the photo in my office. His once compact, fireplug body that blasted through open holes and dragged opposing players into the end zone is now soft and bloated with a yellowish tint. His enlarged and crooked nose reminds me of a boxer whose taken one too many direct hits to the schnoz. Entering behind him is an acne-scarred guy with a grotesque, cauliflower left ear resembling something a beaver gnawed on for a snack. Yanzer marches in and sticks the muzzle of his Glock against my forehead.

"I should congratulate you for slipping away from us. Jumping out a second story window while tied to a chair during a rainstorm. Hell, if it were an Olympic sport, you'd win a gold medal." He wiggles the barrel of his gun and says, "Abe, help the kid to his feet, and let's all go to the living room."

Yanzer uses the gun barrel to push me backward. I take the hint, turn, and fall in behind Sam, whose hands are in the air like a stickup victim.

"Lower your hands, kid," Yanzer says. "This isn't a cop show, but as the saying goes, no sudden movements, please."

Sam drops his arms to his side and sits on the couch. Abe shoves me down next to him.

"I should have thrown you out the window with your friend," he says. "You and your kid sit there and keep your mouths shut. If you even pick your nose, I'll paint the walls red with your brains."

Yanzer pulls out his phone and dials. "We're inside, and we have him. His son is here as well. No, we weren't expecting him, but it increases our leverage." The conversation goes on for about five minutes, with Yanzer nodding his head and an occasional "yeah" and "I got it."

The gun. I have to talk my way to the attic.

Abe returns from upstairs and says, "All clear up top."

I bolt to my feet and announce, "I need to use the bathroom."

Abe pistons the barrel of his gun into my stomach. I moan, tumble backward on the couch, and put my hand up under my shirt to check for blood.

"Shut your pie hole," he says. "No one said you could talk or stand."

Yanzer's eyes are vacant, and his face is blank. "What happened to you, Mark?" I ask. "You were good to my dad and I."

Out of the corner of my eye, I see Abe's gun arcing toward me. Oh, fuck. The butt slams against my right temple, knocking me sideways into Sam, who wraps his arms around my head to shield me from another blow.

"Leave my dad alone!"

"We talk, you listen," Abe commands.

The room is spinning, and I slump against the cushion. The next twenty minutes pass in silence as Yanzer occasionally checks his phone and texts.

Abe breaks the quiet. "I'm going upstairs to use the pisser."

Risking another pummeling from Abe, I say, "Can I please go as well? My bladder's about to explode."

Yanzer's eyes roll up to the ceiling, and after a few seconds, he says, "Abe, check the john before he goes in. I'll keep an eye on this one."

Yanzer looks at his phone again, walks over to Abe, and covers the side of his mouth with his hand. I can't decipher the whispering, but I'm sure they're not talking about the weather or last night's Pirate's game. Abe glares at Sam; his eyes are narrow and evil. My heart jumps to my throat. Something's wrong.

"You have to go, so go," Yanzer says.

I walk upstairs with the barrel of Abe's gun in my back. I try to pull the bathroom door behind me, but Abe sticks his foot in and rummages through vanity drawers and the towel closet.

"Didn't you do a search of the house already?" I ask.

He growls. "Shut the fuck up." Seemingly satisfied there are no hidden weapons, he turns and says, "Well?"

I raise my eyebrows. "You're going to watch?"

He waves his gun at the toilet. "Let's get this over with."

I drop my pants and underwear. As I squat, Abe turns his head away and draws a full breath. After holding it for ten seconds, he exhales. "I thought you were only going to piss. Fuck this shit. I'll be right outside the door. If I hear anything weird in here, I'll put a bullet where your dick is."

Abe backs out of the bathroom, pulling the door shut behind him. My heart races as I stand, raise my pants, and gently place my palm flush against the attic hatch, raising the door a few inches. My other hand takes hold of the envelope, inching it off the inside ledge. I remove the gun and ease the door back into place. This is taking too long. Two raps on the door.

"Let's go. Now."

I tuck the gun inside my front waistband against my belly button. I then untuck my shirt and let it fall loose over my jeans. After a yank on the shirttail, I flush the toilet. I hope they don't notice the slight bulge or style change. Downstairs, Sam is sitting with his hands folded in his lap, his eyes closed. Yanzer is on the phone.

After multiple head nods, he says, "Yeah, I got it. I understand. We'll take care of everything."

I pull the lever on the mental slot machine of who he could be speaking with. It comes up three Trents every time.

Yanzer pockets the phone and stares down at me, head tilted. "There's good news and bad news."

"Am I supposed to ask for the bad news first?" I say.

Argh. A brutal open-handed slap to the right side of my face snaps it almost parallel to my left shoulder. My cheek is on fire like a thousand needles penetrating simultaneously. Is this how my clients feel? If I live through this, I'll never doubt their injuries again.

"Shut up and listen," Abe barks.

"That was a love tap," Yanzer says. "Spare us the wisecracks."

I massage my face, trying to restore feeling.

"What are you going to do to us?" Sam asks.

Yanzer checks his wristwatch and says, "We're moving you both to a private location for a more intimate chat. The good news is, if you cooperate and give us what we need, you'll both be drugged, blindfolded, and dropped off somewhere safe and sound. The bad news is, if we don't like what you have to say, you'll turn up as bloated and crab-eaten floaters in one of the three rivers, that's if a motorboat propeller doesn't chop you up first. They'll need dental records to identify you."

I glance over at Sam. Now he knows I didn't lie to him. Not about this.

Risking another smack from Abe, I say, "I've been arrested. I'm about to take the fall for Heather's murder. Why all this?"

"Because we need your pal, David. Tell us where he is," Yanzer says.

"Leave now, and I'll keep my mouth shut, and so will Sam."

Abe interjects, "That train left the station. You're both coming with us, and one way or another, you'll give up David's whereabouts and what you've told the cops. You and the kid had better believe me when I tell you that you don't want to find out what the other is."

I lay my hand on Sam's lap. They wouldn't dare kidnap the son of the district attorney of Allegheny County. The law enforcement shitstorm rained down on them would be of cataclysmic proportion.

"You can't be that stupid. You know who his mother is."

Abe laughs but thankfully doesn't swing his gun again. "You should be more worried about who I am and the people I work for. This isn't good cop, bad cop. What's the name of that song, 'Bad to the Bone'? That's me, and it's my job to protect my employer's interests. You and your friend are screwing with our business."

Sam's eyes are pleading with me for help. "What's going on here, Dad? I don't understand."

Yanzer ignores Sam's question, glances at his watch, and says, "It's time. Stand up and move to the kitchen door."

Sam takes my hand and says, "We're not going anywhere with you."

Abe shifts his gun to his left hand, and his right balls into a fist, arcing up into Sam's gut. Sam cries out, doubling over in pain. I reach toward him and grab my stomach with the other hand like I'm the one Abe slugged. Dammit, Sam, I need them relaxed. *Don't fight this*, I want to scream.

Abe shifts the weapon back to his right hand, raises it over his head, and slams the butt between Sam's shoulder blades, causing him to cry out and fall to all fours. I scream, "There's no need for this. I'll cooperate."

Abe's face contorts into an evil grin as he draws his leg back like a soccer player. "I know you will, but I'm enjoying myself." His foot arcs toward Sam's stomach, but Yanzer steps between them and grabs the ankle, stopping the forward momentum.

"That's enough," Yanzer commands.

Abe backs away from Sam and glares at Yanzer. "I don't answer to you or your boss—you do what I tell you."

"Don't be an idiot," Yanzer says. " Beat on these two enough and they'll tell you where Jimmy Hoffa is buried, but that doesn't make it so."

His boss? If Trent's not calling the shots, who is?

I kneel beside Sam, take his hand, and help him to his feet, whispering, "I'm sorry."

"Mark, do you ever think about my dad?" I say. "He has dementia but still remembers you."

Yanzer's lips purse, and his eyes roll up like he's accessing long-blocked memories.

He muses, "Yeah, the past. I liked your dad. It was a long time ago. Let's go."

We walk out of the house and into relative darkness. With the clouds and the oak trees in full glory, the moonlight has no illuminating effect which could be an advantage. I can traverse my backyard to the alley with my eyes closed. Abe trips over a decorative rock and stumbles forward. "Turn on the yard lights," he says.

"Let's not draw attention to this house," Yanzer says. "Use your phone to light the way."

Abe's phone flashlight flicks on, and Yanzer shoves me forward. I put a death grip around Sam's wrist, dragging him with me. He's not leaving my sight.

"Where are they taking us, Dad?"

Rats and syringes flash in my mind, but he's better off not knowing Yanzer is Dr. Kevorkian. I have to devise a way out of this before we get in their car.

Abe's voice rings out from the darkness. "Go back through the house and bring the vehicle around to the alley."

They storm my place at gunpoint but forget to bring the car around. Go figure. We can't get in that car.

Yanzer calls out in exasperation. "Let's go out the front door."

Abe's voice rises in anger. "Do what I fucking told you to do and hurry."

Yanzer grunts and sticks his gun in my lower back. "Move your asses back in the house." He pulls on the sliding door, but it won't budge. He tugs it again. It doesn't move. I locked it from the inside when we exited the house.

"Who locked this thing?"

I raise my shirt, taking hold of the Glock.

Yanzer continues yanking on the door and says , "Open it now." He turns and does a double take. He's face to face with my muzzle, but the barrel sways back and forth with every breath and the gun is heavier than when I first held it. I inhale every oxygen molecule my lungs will hold. If I squeeze, his forehead splatters across the porch. It looked easy on YouTube with paper targets and trees. Hold your breath, look at the target, and apply five pounds of pressure to the trigger.

Yanzer's eyes twitch and narrow. Before I can react, his hand is around the barrel, forcing it downward. His other arm comes up under mine, landing a direct hit to my gut. I gasp and the Glock clacks on the wooden deck with me collapsing beside it. Yanzer grabs Sam by the arm, points his gun at the door latch, and fires. He slides the door back, dragging Sam into the kitchen.

I pick up the gun and raise it to eye level from a kneeling position. It's so heavy, and I'm exhausted. I could miss and hit Sam. Yanzer steps backward into the living room, his eyes on me, his muzzle flush against Sam's temple.

I struggle to my feet and start forward into the house after them.

A bang from behind echoes through the yard, causing the windows to vibrate. Something whizzes past me, disturbing the air and creating a puff of wind. The sliding glass door shatters. Another crack, and a wooden patio swing sways back and forth as if pushed by a ghost. Yanzer screams from inside the house, "Don't kill him, you idiot."

I turn and aim in the direction of the second shot, close my eyes, and squeeze the trigger. The muzzle jerks upward.

Abe howls.

"He shot me in the ass. I'm shot in the goddamn ass."

I turn to go after Sam. Two massive tree trunk arms wrap me in a bear hug. "No more shooting. Let's go. We must leave." It's Yak.

"My son. We have to go back for him."

"No time. We must go."

"No, they have Sam. I have to go back inside."

He's squeezing my body so hard, I worry my ribs will crack. My arms are pinned to my side, gun in hand. Yak lifts me off the ground and carries me across the yard past Abe, who is sprawled face down, still yelling about being shot in the buttocks. Yak releases his embrace and aims his Sig at Abe's head.

I grab his arm but can't force it down. He's too strong. "You said no more shooting."

Seconds that seem like a lifetime pass before Yak lowers his weapon. "It is a mistake not killing him, but this is your home. I let him live," he says. He forces me through the fence door into the alley that divides two rows of homes. I turn toward the house as if Sam will magically appear, and we can escape together. He's not there. They have him, and at this moment, I'm helpless to do a thing about it. A guttural, primal scream only a parent can understand emerges from a deep, compartmentalized area of my heart. It explodes from my contorted mouth like a mortar shell.

Yak drags me to a black SUV, opens the door, and shoves me inside. I look up, relieved to see Zev in the front passenger seat.

"They took my son. We have to go back."

Zev turns and looks toward the house. "That's not happening. The police will be here soon."

I can't argue with him on that score. Houses are lighting up like dominoes tumbling against one another. Another bang, and Doc Allen's trashcan tips over, suspended in the air for a moment before falling on its side. The next shot finds its mark. Yak doubles over, clutches his rear quadriceps, and yells, "Blyad."

Abe was down but not out. Yak was right. He should have killed him.

I jump out of the SUV, and Yak wraps his arm around my neck for support, almost toppling us both over. "You're too fucking heavy—a little more effort on your part, please."

I do my best to dump him in the backseat and run around to the front of the car, jumping in on the driver's side. Another pop and the rear window glass shatters. The tires spin gravel and dirt into a dust cloud as we drive away.

"My God," I shout to no one in particular, trying to focus on the dimly lit street. "Where the hell did you two come from?" In the rearview mirror, I see Yak tending to his leg. "How bad is it?"

"I'll live. Hurts like a motherfucker, though."

"We have to find my son before we leave."

Zev's response conveys no tension or distress. It is disturbingly matter of fact given what's transpired. "Where would you suggest we search? A guided tour of the city is not advisable."

My plea is both desperate and resigned. "We can't leave without Sam. I think I know where they will take him, at least a general location."

"We stick to the plan," Zev says. "Half of your neighborhood proba-bly called the police, and they will be here soon. We can't find your son from jail."

"How did you know they'd make a play on us?" I ask, still fighting through the confusion of the backyard firefight while struggling to road map the safest escape route to the airport.

Zev shrugs, "We didn't." We showed up early to bypass your ankle mon-itor. A strange car was parked in your driveway. We assumed it wasn't a cable repair technician and decided some reconnaissance was in order."

"Did the Glock come from you?"

"Yes, Kevin was worried and suggested that you have something to defend yourself if needed."

I turn around to check on Yak while keeping my ears tuned for sirens. At least disabling my ankle monitor is now a moot issue.

"Promise me you'll find my son."

Yak grimaces, nods, and says, "We will find him."

CHAPTER 33

We pull into the parking lot of Clear Skies Aviation. Zev presses the button on a remote intercom and recites the tail number of the plane. The gate opens, and a young woman in a golf cart drives up to greet us.

Zev lowers the window and says, "Hello, Melissa, my apologies, but we're running a bit late."

Melissa peruses her clipboard, gives Zev a thumbs up, and pulls away with us following. She either doesn't notice it or doesn't care about our shot up vehicle and missing rear window. There are only shards of jagged glass lining the rim that once held it in place. She leads us to what appears to be a small jet.

"Does this belong to you?" I ask.

"Kevin owns it," Zev says. "We are flying a Cessna Citation with decent range. Absent having to circumvent severe weather, we'll stop once to refuel."

We follow Melissa to about ten feet from the aircraft. She waves, turns around, and heads back to the main terminal building.

"Don't get out until I tell you to," Zev says.

He exits the vehicle, gun drawn but inconspicuously relaxed at his side.

Yak limps a perimeter and loads a duffel bag on board. He has a slug in his leg but continues business as usual. He would have kicked the Mt. Everest bouncer's ass.

The tense seconds creep forward like a turtle crossing a busy street. I wonder who will burst through the gate first—the cops or Yanzer. Finally, the two engines start.

Yak opens the copilot cabin door and says, "You get in."

"You need medical attention," I say.

He winks and says, "Yak's been shot worse."

I nod and manage a weak smile. I want to embrace him but refrain, thinking he's probably not a hugger. "Please, find my son."

He nods and says, "I'll make him safe."

I climb into the copilot's seat next to Zev.

"I guess we're adding pilot to your resume. You Mossad guys are versatile."

Zev laughs and says, "You Americans think all Israelis are former Mossad. Too many television shows. You, however, are now a copilot." He hands me a headset. "Put this on."

I slide it over my head and fumble with the microphone. "You're sitting next to me. Why do I need this? I can't help you fly this thing. It looks like the cockpit of the space shuttle."

"Trust me," Zev says. "When we're airborne, you won't be able to hear yourself think, let alone anything I say. Don't worry. Sit back and enjoy the flight unless I tell you to do something."

I scratch at my ankle. "When can we cut this monitor off?"

Zev toggles switches and reviews his takeoff checklist.

"There's no time now, and the police are probably swarming your house. They know you're gone."

"I get that, but it itches like a son of a bitch."

He puts his right hand up in a signal for me to be quiet. "N420G requesting a VFR departure westbound."

The response crackles over the radio: "N420G, you are cleared to taxi to runway twenty-eight."

The plane lurches forward. Minutes later, we're climbing into the night. Of course, I've flown on many commercial flights, guzzling overpriced mini bottles of Jack Daniel and complimentary Diet Cokes. Stressing over first-class upgrades and silently cursing passengers who remove their socks. This, however, is my first time in a private plane. I find myself gripping the edge of my seat.

Zev smiles in amusement at my anxiety. "Are you a private jet virgin?"

"Yeah," I say. "I've heard these smaller planes are like roller coasters."

He laughs and says, "Relax, my friend. We will arrive in one piece."

Relax? Who is he kidding? So many things can go wrong with this stunt and probably will.

"Are they able to track us by flight plan or tail number?"

"No," Zev says. "We're ascending to 3,500 feet, which is under Class B airspace. We are not required to file a flight plan. Oops, almost forgot to turn off the transponder."

He reaches forward and toggles a silver switch.

"Don't take this the wrong way, but the sky is black as the moldy bread in my fridge. Can you fly at night?"

He adjusts his headset and says, "If I say no, does it matter now?"

"No, I guess not."

"Not to worry," he says. "I'm fully rated for night flying."

I wonder what chaos is raging at my house. Shel is probably pulling her hair out. A national manhunt for both of us is imminent or already in progress. Keane and Romo are probably frothing like rabies-infected dogs, volunteering to hound me to the ends of the earth and drag me back. Fuck them both.

"How long until we land?" I ask.

"We will refuel in Homer Wyoming, weather permitting. At a lower altitude and this airspeed, we are in for a long flight. Sit back and relax."

I rotate the monitor around my ankle, the torque easing the itching. "Why are we landing there? I've never heard of it."

"The airstrip is isolated, within our fuel range and has a suitable run-way. The fewer prying eyes and questions, the better."

My stomach growls and twitches. "Do you have any food in this plane?"

Zev jerks his thumb toward the back and says, "There are peanut butter bars in the duffel bag."

I shrug. Not exactly first-class fare, but beggars can't be choosers.

After unzipping the bag, it's clear that Zev leaves nothing to chance. Besides the bars, it holds a bolt cutter, a Sig Sauer, money, and two leather billfolds. The gun. I glance at my right hand and frantically dig through the contents. It's not there. Yak has my Glock.

Zev says, "Until I say otherwise, you have one and only one responsibility. You are the guardian of the bag. The bag will not leave your side. If you need to defecate or urinate, you take the bag. What is your function?" he asks as if I am ten years old.

"Guard the bag with my life," I say, like a dutiful son trying to please his dad.

I take a billfold from the bag and open it to find only a California driver's license with a passport-like snapshot of me. David and I once bought fake IDs out of the back of a comic book using photos we had taken at a four-for-a-dollar booth in the mall. I combined the first and last names of my favorite movie stars and became River Cruise. The liquor store owner chuckled and confiscated them when we attempted to purchase beer.

I hold the ID up to Zev and say, "My name is Brian O'Reilly? Do I look Irish to you?"

Zev eyes me, squints, tilts his head one way, then the other. "You have reddish curly hair and a few freckles. Yes, you kind of do. The identification won't survive a thorough analysis by law enforcement, but for our limited purposes, it will pass muster."

I open the other wallet. The identification has Zev's photo with the name Lev Simon.

"Why does yours have a Jewish name and mine doesn't?" I ask.

He shrugs and responds in deadpan: "Do I look Irish to you?"

Point taken.

The backyard gunfight replays in my head. I analyze and dissect the chain of decisions that ended in Sam's abduction. If I had only done this or the other thing, he'd be safe. Selfishly asking him to come to the house was the apex of my stupidity, and, even worse, I had the chance to save him and didn't pull the trigger. My weakness may have cost my son his life. It won't happen again.

Despite the noise of the engines and the howl of the wind against the fuselage, my eyelids droop, and my head slumps forward. I'm not sure when my last sound sleep was.

A fist bump to my shoulder and a crackle in my headset rouses me.

"Wake up. We're almost there." Zev says. "We are ten miles out of Homer and should be wheels down in thirty minutes, give or take."

I fight through the sleep confusion and stare out the passenger window. I've slept through the night. The morning sky is already crystal blue, giving me an unobstructed, panoramic view of farmland, silos, cows, and not much else.

"What do you know about Homer?" I ask.

"Enough to land, my friend," Zev says. "We won't be doing any sight-seeing."

He's being glib, but we need to refuel quickly and go wheels up—milliseconds matter.

"After we touch down, I will check in with Yakov on your son. Fill me in with background on David. The more information I have, the more prepared we will be for what will go wrong."

Thirty minutes into my Lifetime Network monologue, Zev holds up his right hand.

"I need to do my landing checklist."

The plane touches down and bumps along an asphalt runway. We taxi up to the refueling area and stop behind a smaller, single-engine plane.

Zev says, "You can stretch, but stay with the aircraft while I pay for the gas. Let's also not announce you're a fugitive from justice. Hide the ankle monitor under your pants leg.

I'm dozing off in the plane when Zev bangs on the door. "Let's go. A cab is on the way. Troy at the desk told me there is a small, privately owned motel called Grandma's Inn. They won't blink at cash."

I stare at him in disbelief, wondering if I heard him correctly.

"We're not wasting time in this shithole overnight," I say. "Let's fuel up and take off."

Zev returns the stare. "There is a massive storm system moving toward us, and another one right behind it. I'm the pilot, and I don't have a death wish. We stay in Homer. End of discussion."

The fuck it is. He knows my son's life is on the line, the bastard. "Fly through the storm, around it, or above it. You're former Israeli Intelligence. This is the shit you do!"

We're interrupted by a dusty, brown, Ford F-150 pickup pulling alongside us.

On the driver's side door, hand-painted in white letters is WYATT'S CITY CAB. He lowers the window and says, "You the fellas going to Grandma's?"

I note he pays particular attention to Zev. His beady-eyed, suspicious gaze moves from head to toe. I don't have to be telepathic to know what's on his mind.

"That's us," Zev says. "We will finish this discussion at the motel."

He opens the passenger door and slides across the seat. Wyatt's truck has no meter, no medallion, no heavy plastic separating the driver from the passengers. A piece of white cardboard is taped to the window. Handwritten on it in black magic marker is, "$15 FLAT RATE WITHIN TOWN LIMITS. ALL OTHERS NEGOTIATED BEFORE TRIP BEGINS."

We pull away, and Zev says, "I take it you're Wyatt. How far to the motel?"

The rearview mirror gives an unobstructed view of Wyatt, once again sizing Zev up.

"That'd be me, owner and operator so to speak. The motel is a few minutes away. Where are you boys comin' in from?"

"Philadelphia headed on to Los Angeles," I say.

"Philly, huh? That's a long flight. This your first stop?"

Wyatt doesn't seem to be watching the road as he speaks. He's all about the dark-skinned guy sitting next to me.

"Where are you from, fella?"

"Like I said, I'm from Philadelphia, and yeah, this is our only stop before we reach our destination."

"Not you, your friend. The dark guy."

Here we go—racial profiling in Small Town, USA.

Zev doesn't flinch. His response is calm and probably borne of countless similar episodes. "I'm from Philly as well. Any place to eat around here?"

"You're close to town," he says. "There are lots of places. What about before Philly?"

His tone changes to accusatory.

"My mother's womb."

"You're a funny fella. Here's Grandma's," Wyatt says.

From the outside, Grandma's appears less hotel and more no-tell motel with a malfunctioning, blinking neon sign in the parking lot. The last three letters of Grandma's are burnt out, spelling, "Grand Motel—Kitchenettes, Low Rates, Clean Rooms, Free HBO and Internet." I doubt the drab, yellow-brick, single-story structure with a row of weather-faded red doors shows up on any best-of travel lists. Walking through the office front door, we are greeted by a thirty-something clerk sporting a Grateful Dead T-shirt.

Zev approaches the counter and says, "One room, please. Two beds."

"Do you have a reservation?"

Yeah, right. People are dying to stay here instead of the Holiday Inn down the road with the indoor pool.

"No," Zev says. "We're passing through."

The clerk squints at his terminal. "The cattle auction is going on this week, so we've been full up, but you're in luck. We had a no-show. Two double beds, a fridge, and a microwave for fifty."

"We will take it," Zev says, handing him three twenty-dollar bills.

The room is about what I expect. The stench of cow manure mixed with stale cigarette smoke does it's best to trigger my gag reflex. Cigarette burns dot ancient carpet, and the mattresses are covered with multicolored floral polyester bedspreads circa 1980, more appropriate in a San Fernando Valley porn shoot. An assemble-yourself nightstand, a wood-veneer dresser, and a coffee table constitute the balance of the furnishings. The TV is bolted to the wall with a steel bracket.

"You sure pick the high-end places," I say, pulling back the bedspread to inspect for lice and bedbugs. "If they're not mixing bathtub meth here, they're shooting adult movies or renting by the hour. At least we have Wi-Fi."

Zev sits on the edge of his bed, checking his phone. "I won't be connecting to it, and you won't either. Hotel internet is as secure as the idiots who use their birthdays for passwords."

He reaches into his computer bag and pulls out his iPad and a portable hot spot. "Let's see what's going on at home," he says, powering it up.

"I want to speak with Yak," I say, raising my voice to impress the sense of urgency.

Zev ignores my plea and hands me the iPad. "Check this out."

The browser is directed to the *Trib* website. The headline reads, "Manhunt Continues for Fugitive Lawyer."

I lock onto every letter, every syllable, in the body of the article: "Gunshots heard. District Attorney Sonya Kim-Feldman frantic over missing son. Nationwide search underway for son and ex-husband."

I must call Sonya, but what can I tell her, and what will she believe?

"I need to call Sam's mother and let her know what's going on. Why are we here? Let's go back to the airport and get in the air."

"You're not calling your ex," Zev says. "If the police are doing their jobs, there are wiretaps on her phones. We can't circumvent back-to-back storm weather systems, and flying them is a suicide mission."

"Don't tell me who I can and can't call. You work for me," I say, tossing the iPad on the bed. "I paid you ten grand."

Zev sighs and says, "Understand this, my friend. Kevin paid me the ten grand and I don't work for you. If you thought your money bought you all this, you need to rethink things. We will locate David, but Kevin and I have urgent business in California, which is not your concern. If you want your son to survive this, please do as I say without question or hesitation from here on out." He holds up his hand to shush me. It's becoming an annoying habit. "This is Yakov on the phone. Stop talking."

"Yakov, we're on the ground, one leg to go. What's the situation there? Got it. We'll check in from Fort Bragg."

He tosses the phone on the bed and says, "Everything is proceeding as planned."

My temperature soars to boiling point. Is he kidding me? Nothing has gone as intended.

"You're an asshole. I wanted to speak to Yak. They will murder my son."

I swing at Zev. A weak and awkward roundhouse from a guy who hasn't thrown a punch since a fight at a pony-league baseball game with Lonnie Rankin when he told me I was so fat I'd run faster to first base if I pretended I was chasing a refrigerator. Zev doesn't raise his arms to protect himself. His head and neck shift two inches back, allowing my fist to fly past him.

"Let's not do this," he says, his voice clinical. "I understand you're upset and tired, but if they kill your son, they lose their leverage."

Easy for him to evaluate leverage when it's not his kid. I was in that basement, not Zev. Fuck leverage.

"I'm calling Kevin. Let's cut the shit here. I know Kevin is in the cross-hairs of the DEA. Before this is all over, you're going to need my help as much as I need yours."

Zev tosses me his phone and says, "Keep the conversation short." He then takes his Sig and a cloth from the duffel bag, humming to himself as he massages the gun with the same gentle touch as Roger wiping my fingerprint from his Roadster. I wonder what Freud would say about these guys and their toys. I wish I had my Glock. I pulled the trigger once, and I can do it again.

"Kevin, it's Jason. We're almost to Fort Bragg. Tell me something good."

"Jason, the shit has hit the fan big time. The FBI, DEA, U.S. Marshals, and local cops are looking for you and Sam."

"Yeah, I'm a popular guy. You're familiar with Trent's operation. Where would they take my son?"

"Trent has four mill houses scattered around the city. I have general locations but not exact addresses. If I were him, I'd stash Sam at one of them."

Dr. Kevorkian. The Odessa Society. The crime scene. Of course.

"I may know the place. They may have taken Sam to the house where Trent's goons held me in the Hill District. I don't have an address but can give you landmarks and streets."

"Give me what you have," he says.

I recite as many location markers as I remember from my gimpy mad dash home through a veritable monsoon.

"This bit of information may help you find him," I say. "The house is walking distance from where Heather's remains were found. How's it going on your end?"

"Well, I'm not quite Moses leading the Jews out of Egypt, but within forty-eight hours, all my drug couriers, except for you will be out of the country. I'll put out a press release that I'm bleeding money and can't raise more capital, so I have no alternative but to file for Chapter 7. The safes will be removed from the WarpMobiles by the end of the week." WARP will be just another failed startup.

"That's long enough," Zev says, his tone tense and impatient.

"Kevin, I have to go. You're my only shot at finding my son. You have to save him."

A blast of a train whistle muffles his answer. "Kevin, I didn't hear what you said."

But he's hung up. Zev holds his hand out, and I toss the phone back to him. He removes the bolt cutter from the bag.

"Let's cut this thing off," he says, wedging the blades between my ankle and the black, unbreakable, thick plastic strap securing the monitor.

He huffs and grunts, struggling to make the first cut into the thick plastic.

"Be careful. That fucking hurts," I yell as the metal digs into my skin. "You're going to cut my damn ankle off."

"I have no doubt it does, and lower your voice," he says, opening and closing the jaws.

In sixty seconds, he's cut through and I'm free of it. I pick the pieces off the floor.

"What should we do with this?"

"Put it all in the bag. It goes with us," he says.

I take another peanut bar from the bag and collapse on the bed. The springs sag like a hammock. So much for a good night's sleep.

CHAPTER 34

Thunderstorms throughout the night, a rattling air-conditioner, and intermittent dreams of a five-year-old Sam calling out for Daddy leave me drained as I roll out of bed. Fortunately, we are able to get a cab to the airport not driven by racist Wyatt. Troy is engrossed in his laptop as Zev and I walk into the terminal. He glances up and slams the cover shut. I chuckle and think, I understand dude. What else is there to do in this cow town but watch online porn?

"You fellas out of here?" he asks.

Zev plucks two mints out of the candy bowl on the counter and says, "Yes, we're wheels up as soon as my preflight is complete. How is the weather westbound?"

Troy peruses a computer printout and says, "A five-mile-per-hour breeze coming out of the west with ten-mile visibility. It's a beautiful day to fly."

"What's the plan when we land in Fort Bragg?" I ask. "How will we find him?"

Zev takes the printout from Troy and studies it. "I'm confident he's using an alias, so we'll engage in some old-fashioned gumshoe leg work."

I hadn't thought of that. When he texted me, I assumed he was always David. It makes sense he might have used a false name all these years.

"Why do you think he's living under a fake name?"

"Because I haven't found him yet."

"How did you figure out he's there in the first place?"

Zev shrugs and says, "It was not difficult. People miss simple stuff. I didn't track David. I tracked his father, utilizing genealogy websites. There's an obituary in the *Fort Bragg Advocate*. Simon Chaney, originally from Pittsburgh, is buried in Rose Park Memorial Cemetery. He was survived by his only son, David Solomon Chaney of Fort Bragg."

If it was that simple, not a chance in hell Trent hasn't figure it out as well.

As we walk to the plane, two words from Zev quadruple my pulse like I've been injected with pure adrenaline. "The police."

I jerk my head toward the terminal where a car is driving toward us. The classic black and white paint job spelling out, "Homer Police Department."

"Keep quiet," Zev says. "I'll handle this."

I respect Zev's expertise, precision, and stealth, but I'm the lawyer here, even if only an ambulance chaser, and if push comes to shove, I will be lawyerly.

A cop gets out of the passenger side and opens the rear door. He claps his hands once and says, "Out, Hercules." A black and tan German shepherd bounds out of the car and sits facing the officer, snout tilted upward like he's waiting for a treat. A tug of the leash, and they both walk toward the Citation.

Zev cups his hands around his lips like a megaphone and startles me with a yell, causing me to jump. "Do not let your dog near our plane. We do *not* consent to a search."

I breathe a sigh of relief when the cop stops and circles back to the squad car

The other police officer walks toward us. He doesn't appear agitated, but something triggered them to come out here to check us out. I think back to Wyatt. Zev shouldn't have made that womb crack.

"Where is the bag?" Zev says.

The cop is on us before I can answer.

"Morning, fellas. Where are you flying off to this morning?"

"We're headed to Los Angeles—is there a problem?" I ask, keeping his partner and the dog in my peripheral vision.

"LA, huh? This is an out-of-the-way place to refuel. What's your business there, and where are you coming from?"

His partner walks Hercules back to the patrol car on the driver's side. He reaches in and takes out the mic. He's probably calling in our tail number.

"Who's the pilot here?"

Zev raises his hand and says, "I am." He's calm and composed like he's having a casual conversation at Starbucks. He leans forward and squints at the officer's name tag. "This is a business trip, Officer Tulley. We were coming from Philadelphia."

"What business are you fellas in?" he asks. "And why'd you pick Homer to fuel up? This is a bit off the normal flight path."

"I'm in corporate security. We intended to refuel in Cheyenne but encountered harsh weather and veered off course."

Tulley glances toward the plane and says, "That's quite a veer. If this is legitimate business, why the objection to the dog?" He presses hard. "Seems to me, you'd let us do what we need to and go on your way. I'm not going to pump any sunshine up your skirt. We got a tip you boys are hauling drugs."

That's my cue. "I'm an attorney, and your accusation is ludicrous." I place my hand on Zev's shoulder. "This gentleman is my client. We're not narcotics traffickers. We're on our way to LA for an important business meeting."

Zev nods in agreement, clearly pleased at my new tactic, and for now, appears content to let me take over.

"You're a lawyer, huh?" He eyes me from head to toe. "We don't get too many big-time Philly lawyers flying through here. As a matter of fact, you're the first. Wouldn't it have been quicker to fly commercial? Let's see identification from both of you."

We're screwed. Not only is my fake ID in the back of the Cessna, but it's a California license, not Pennsylvania. This is one contingency Zev didn't plan for.

My Civil Rights Law class in law school is about to pay off.

"Profiling us with the excuse of a bullshit tip because my client is the wrong color and accent is a violation of the Fourth Amendment prohibition against unreasonable search and seizure, and the Equal Protection Clause of the Fourteenth Amendment to the Constitution, as well as Title VI of the Civil Rights Act of 1964. We're law-abiding businessmen, and this is 9/11-style harassment."

"We're not profiling you," Tulley says, on the defensive. "We received a credible tip—"

"Your tip is from Wyatt the cabbie who can't tell the difference between an Israeli and an Egyptian. Anyone brown is a terrorist in your book." I'm at risk of aggravating and escalating, but this isn't the time for détente. "Unless you produce a warrant to search our aircraft or you're placing us under arrest, we're walking to our plane, getting in, and going wheels up."

Officer Tulley massages his chin, never taking his eyes off us. He takes three steps backward and motions for his partner to join him. They huddle together, speaking in hushed voices, each occasionally glancing in our direction. Tulley shrugs and ambles back to us.

"Flying coast to coast in a small plane. Stopping here. You paid cash for your fuel. I can't prove it, but you're both bullshit. Maybe not drugs, but something is on that plane you don't want us to find. My partner took down your tail number, and you can bet dollars to donuts I'm alerting Homeland Security about your"—he raises both hands and gestures with air quotes—"business flight."

"Are we free to go?" I ask.

Tulley rubs his chin again and tugs his pants up at the belt loop. "Yeah, you can go. Don't come back here ever again. We don't want your kind of trouble."

Zev and I stroll toward the plane like we don't have a care in the world. Neither of us looks back or says a word.

Zev doesn't bother with the checklist. I glance over at Tulley, who has his hands on his hips, observing intently. Within three minutes, we're rumbling down the runway, picking up speed while Tulley and his partner trudge back to their patrol car. Next stop, Fort Bragg, and David.

I slide on my headset, adjust the microphone, and glance over at Zev with a shit-eating, smug grin. "Like I told you in the room, you need me. How long until Fort Bragg?"

"About six hours, give or take," Zev says.

More than enough time for the sheriff of Mayberry to alert authorities, I think, taking a bite of a cardboard tasting peanut bar

"Who's waiting for us when we land?" I ask anxiously.

"The people from Emerald Leaf Blends," Zev says. "The airstrip is within their secure facility."

That's good news and lessens my anxiety about being detained on landing. A marijuana research and processing installation won't allow the DEA or FBI to waltz in without a damn good reason.

"We're coming in below radar," he says. "If anyone is surveilling us visually, they'll be looking at Ells Field in Willits or another Emerald triangle airport, not a private facility like Emerald Leaf."

"Who'd be tracking us? The feds?"

"Homeland Security, DEA—who knows, maybe no one. We assume the worst and make the best happen."

Zev must sense the spike in my body temperature and breath rate. My raging pulse swells the left side of my neck with each pass through my carotid artery.

"Try to relax." he says. "No one is going to find us. We're in town to check out a legal marijuana-processing operation. The plane will be safe behind a barbed wire fence with armed guards."

How am I supposed to relax? I rest my neck against the seatback and shut my eyes. I don't think I can sleep, but I can propel myself back to a happier time, if only for a few hours. Before my dad lost his past. Before Sonya left me. Before I looked at Heather's limp body and did nothing.

Finally, we begin our descent.

"See the greenhouses?" Zev says. "Those are all marijuana farms. This is the Emerald Triangle. We've been studying this opportunity for a while."

I wonder how involved Zev is in Kevin's operation. I don't recall Kevin ever mentioning him. How and why does a Pittsburgh-born piano prodigy disappear and end up here?

Zev nudges my shoulder as the sprawling facility that resembles a prison comes into view. High concrete walls are topped with rolled barbed wire. On two opposite sides are guard towers occupied by uniformed guys with Uzi-looking weapons slung over their shoulders. As we descend, one speaks into a walkie-talkie and waves at us with long, sweeping motions.

Zev waves back and says, "We're cleared to land."

The runway appears as we descend over the outer wall, close enough to the Uzi guy to high five him. My pulse is stroke worthy. Can you land there?" I ask. "My driveway is longer."

"Plenty of room for this baby," he says, his voice steady.

I white-knuckle my armrests, and time slows to a crawl as the plane creeps toward touchdown. At the end of the landing strip, a guy in a light blue suit, leans against a black SUV, talking on his phone.

A female computer voice counts out the feet in descending order. Zev is singularly focused on the task at hand, his breathing is relaxed and soft. I, on the other hand, replay movie airplane disaster scenes in my mind, and envision tomorrow's headline, "Fugitive's Plane Crashes. Pilot Error Blamed."

The rear landing gear impacts the concrete with barely a jolt. Three seconds later, the front gear bounces on the asphalt. I sit up, open my eyes, and exhale. I've had rougher landings on American Airlines.

CHAPTER 35

Zev glances at me, shakes his head, and says, "Do you need help prying your hands from the seat rests?"

I reach for the duffel bag, but Zev grabs my arm and says, "Leave it here. No one will bother it."

I open my mouth to remind him of the Sig but catch myself. He knows what he's doing, and there's probably enough firepower between these four walls to repel an alien invasion, and the two guards on the wall could drop either of us in our tracks. They're not concerned about a handgun.

The guy with the van strolls our way, his hand extended. "Welcome to the Emerald Leaf Institute. I'm Geraldo Picazo, but everyone here calls me Pic."

Pic is thin and fit, with jet-black hair, reminding me more of a suave Latin movie star than a marijuana mogul.

"Let's head to my office to chat," Pic says. "After that, we can give you a tour of the facility. By the way, *Emerald Triangle Gazette* recently named us the best marijuana-related company to work for in the state."

"Congrats. That's quite an honor," I say.

I tap Zev on the shoulder. He swats my hand away and whispers, "What did I tell you earlier? Back off and let me finish what I'm here for."

"How was the flight?" Pic asks. "That's a long haul in a Citation."

"Uneventful," Zev says.

He thankfully doesn't mention the cops or my hysterics. I hope whatever we are here to do doesn't take long. I understand Kevin's predicament with Trent, but whatever happens, he will be alive. There won't be a do-over with my son's life if we fail.

We arrive at a ten-story glass building that more resembles a modern college student union than a corporate hub.

"This facility is only two years old and state of the art," Pic says. "We have a full-service cafeteria where our employees can select anything from vegan to sushi. We also have a kick-ass gym, as well as a meditation and yoga room."

Pic punches a code into a digital keypad, and after three beeps, places his thumb on a tiny scanner, disengaging the lock to the front door. He pulls it open and says, "State-of-the-art security as well."

"Do you store the product in this facility?" I ask.

"No." He motions us forward. "But we have several labs and lots of proprietary work going on. This is a competitive industry with a ton of espionage."

We walk up to the reception desk, where we are greeted with a cheerful smile by a thin, pale twenty-something with long, shiny red hair and a severe case of freckles.

"This is Tiff," Pic says. "She will handle your biometric security clearance."

"I'll need your driver's license or passport," she chirps.

I present my faux identification.

"Please stand in front of the camera and give me a big smile," she says in a bubbly tone. I position myself over the X painted on the floor.

"Let's see those pearly whites," she says.

As if hoping that monkey see, monkey do, she contorts the corners of her mouth into an ear-to-ear demonstration. I do the best I can. Zev nudges me and says, "She asked you to smile, not imitate a kidnap hostage."

"One last step," she says. "Please put your thumb in the biometric scanner."

My hands are lead weights at my sides as I stare at the device. Tiff repeats her request, but I continue my statue posture. I glance nervously at Zev, who nods and says, "Go ahead."

I appreciate Zev's comfort with the process, but even so, we're talking about fingerprints that can expose my actual identity.

"Please forgive me for asking, but I'm a bit paranoid about Big Brother. Why do you need my prints?"

Pic intercedes and says, "This entire facility is secured biometrically. Tiff will match your security clearance to the print and upload the data to our system. We delete all personally identifying information from the system when you leave the facility."

I eyeball Zev again. He simply says, "Trust me."

I place my thumb on the pad, and Zev follows with his.

"It'll be a few minutes," Tiff says, her fingers working the computer keyboard.

"You're booked at our corporate chateau in Fort Bragg. You'll love the view," Pic says. "It sits on a cliff overlooking the bay."

Concerned about time wasted not looking for David, I ask, "How far is it from here?"

"It's about sixty miles," Pic says. "There's nothing around here but ganja."

Tiff lays two name tags with photos on the counter along with two empty cloth bags.

"You're all set, and these are for your phones. We'll return them and your identification when you leave."

I don't relish being cut off from communication with the world, but I have no choice. Zev and I place our phones in the bag. Tiff secures each with a plastic zip tie, places a coded label on each, scans them, and inserts both bags into numbered cubbyholes.

"You take your security seriously here," I say.

Pic hands me my name tag and says, "Welcome to Emerald Leaf Institute, please follow me."

A turnstile scanner accepts our thumbprints. Inside the elevator is another biometric device. Pic places his thumb on it and presses the button for the second floor.

"Different floors have different levels of access restrictions," he says. "The higher you go, the greater the security built into the biometrics."

We exit into an expansive warehouse-type environment with nothing but cubicles. Pic waves his arm across the room and says, "This is the heart and soul of our organization. Our sales and marketing force. It all happens here."

We follow Pic to his office where he sits at the head of a glass conference table. I nudge Zev, lean over, and say, "What are we doing here? Haven't you heard of Zoom? We're wasting valuable time."

"This isn't the time for discussion," Zev says under his breath. "If I'm not here doing this, I'm not at your place the other night, and you and your son are in the morgue."

I shoot back, "He's dead regardless if we keep screwing around here."

"Gentlemen," Pic says, "After speaking with Kevin Goldman three weeks ago, I've been very excited about the possibility of a fruitful partnership when Pennsylvania legalizes marijuana for recreational use."

The forty-five-minute meeting ends with an agreement for Pic and Kevin to speak again in the next few days. Pic escorts us back to the reception desk, where Tiff hands us back our counterfeit identification and phones.

"Your driver, Alex, will transport you to the corporate chateau," he says. "Text him when you're ready to fly back to Pittsburgh. He'll pick you up and return you to your plane." Pic sticks out his hand. "It was a pleasure to meet you both, and I anticipate continued fruitful discussions about potential synergy between our two organizations."

I exhale as if I've been holding my breath for the last forty-eight hours. I don't know what awaits, but at least we're finally moving forward. After a detour to a Walmart for clothes and toiletries, we arrive in Fort Bragg.

The chateau turns out to be a two-level home overlooking the Pacific. It could be the South of France or on a mountainside in Italy. As if for effect,

Alex drives past the house to the edge of rocks where the driveway ends. We are now looking straight out into the ocean. I exit the car and walk to an Adirondack chair by itself on the grass. A sense of calm and quiet comes over me. I wish I had time to sit in it and clear my head.

"We should check on my son and put together our plan to find David," I say. "Or do you have one?"

Zev holds up his hand like a crossing guard and says, "As soon as Alex leaves, we'll talk."

I glance at Alex, who's busy removing our belongings from the vehicle.

The butterflies in my stomach are proximity detectors—David's close.

Alex slams the trunk shut and calls to us, "Let's go inside, and I'll give you a tour."

Zev hands Alex two one-hundred-dollar bills and says, "No need, we'll self-guide."

Alex gives Zev the house keys and says, "When you are ready to leave, I need a two hours' heads-up to come get you." He points to a boathouse about twenty yards away and says, "There's an old wooden staircase down to the cove but be careful if it's dark out. There's no lighting."

He hands me his business card. "If you need anything at all, text me," he says.

"I will," I say. "Thank you for the ride here."

"Happy to do it," he says as he gets back in his car. "It's what I do."

The backyard bloodshed was barely two days ago but minutes still seem like hours, and I know why. The pull of a trigger or the plunge of a needle happens in under a second.

Zev holds his phone up, motioning me over. "It's Yakov with news on your son."

My heart skips as I snatch the phone and take a deep breath. "Yak, make me happy."

"We've learned valuable information, and I hope, soon we will locate him."

"What did you find out? Where are you looking?"

"Don't worry. We'll find him."

Did a bowling ball drop on his head? Worrying was yesterday. I'm beside myself with fear and frustration at the lack of progress. Zev grabs my hand and pries the phone away.

"You wanted to speak with Yakov, and now you have."

I grab at his wrist to snatch it back, but he stiff-arms me and switches to Ukrainian with Yak. I've picked up a few words in my business dealings, but the back-and-forth dialogue moves so fast, I can't decipher the conversation. Zev disconnects and jingles the keys at me.

"Let's head inside," he says.

"You speak Ukrainian?"

Zev shrugs and says, "In my trade, being conversant in many languages is mandatory."

My bat phone text message alert beeps. I can't get it out of my pocket fast enough. Maybe Yak has located Sam. My heart sinks. It's only an internet link from Kevin. I tap on it.

"DA Under Pressure to Resign." The next sentence tells the whole story: "...allegedly shared confidential narcotics task force investigation with fugitive ex-husband."

Goddammit, she was only trying to keep me out of hotter water than I was already in. I, however, can't do anything about that right now. One step at a time.

"Where do we start our search?"

Zev says, "As I told you, he probably no longer goes by David Chaney."

"He was using his real name in the obituary you showed me," I say.

He hands me a computer printout. "Would you dishonor your father by using a fake name in his remembrance?"

Imprinted on the paper is the unmistakable image of David at seventeen years old in his high school graduation photo.

"Many high school yearbooks are digitized and searchable online," Zev says. "You keep it. I have a copy."

I sigh, fold the printout, and put it in my pocket. "Let's find David so we can go home, and I can get my son back."

"What if David doesn't want to come back?" Zev asks.

I cross my arms and say, "Listen carefully. He's coming back with us, even if we have to carry him onto the plane. That's non-negotiable."

CHAPTER 36

"The cab will be here in fifteen minutes," Zev says.

I head upstairs, find the master bedroom, quickly change clothes, and open the balcony door. The salty Pacific air floods into the stuffy room. I inhale as much as my unexercised lungs allow. I don't know why David chose this place, but gazing out toward the serene horizon, I see nothing but water and understand why he would stay. Lying out on the beach and barefoot walks through the surf have never been my thing, but there's something about the way the ocean blots out the past.

Zev's voice booms from downstairs. "The taxi is here."

I take in the serenity one last time.

"Where to?" the driver asks.

"Downtown Fort Bragg," I say.

"Any particular destination?"

"Where do the locals drink?" Zev asks.

"Silver's at the Wharf is one of my favorite hangouts," he says.

"Silver's it is," Zev says.

I spend the entire ride studying the features of David's face, wondering what he envisioned for his future when the shutter clicked. Julliard music school. A recital at Carnegie Hall? A national concert tour to sold out arenas and stadiums of screaming fans? I had dreams as well at seventeen years old and knew I wanted to be a lawyer, but unlike Sonya, for me it was about the prestige and money. I was determined to rise above my father's station in life and make him proud of me.

Twenty minutes later, we pull up in front of Silver's. I tap the driver on the shoulder.

"What's your name?"

"Dylan," he says. "The fare is fifteen dollars." I hand him two twenties and the copy paper with David's image on it. "You can keep the change. By any chance, do you recognize this guy? This photo is old. He'd be in his forties now."

"Wow, thanks for the tip," he says. "I may take the rest of the evening off." He studies the printout and hands it back to me, shaking his head. "He doesn't look familiar, sorry."

"Take another ten seconds. Are you sure?"

Dylan raises the paper to eye level and says, "Sorry, man. I don't know the guy."

"No worries," I say. "It's an old high school friend, and I heard he lives in the area."

He stuffs the bills in his pocket. "I wish I could help."

"One more question. What are other popular bars in town?"

Dylan rubs his chin. "It depends on what type of crowd you like," he says.

Where would a forty-something David hang out? "Where do they have live jazz or piano music?" I ask.

There's another long pause as he processes. "You might check out North Coast Brewing's Sequoia Room. Another one is the Headlands Coffee House. They feature local talent every evening."

Dylan pulls away but stops abruptly. He sticks his head out the window and says, "You may also want to head over to the Golden West Saloon. Lots of locals drink there."

I slap the roof of the cab twice and say, "I appreciate the help."

"No problem. Good luck locating your friend and thanks again for the generous gratuity."

This wasn't a fair trade. His tips were exponentially more valuable than mine.

Zev taps me on the shoulder. "We should split up to save time. I'll start here, then head over to the Golden West."

"Works for me," I say.

Zev turns and walks into Silver's. I cross the street and walk toward the coffeehouse. The sidewalk is crowded with people going in and out of stores and talking about the best restaurants for a late evening bite. I'm approaching Headlands when a couple strolls past pushing a baby carriage. Memories of syringes and lying face up in the park bounce around in my head. I freeze in my tracks, turn around, and duck into a hobby store. A pimply-faced teenage kid holding a Batman comic book looks my way and says, "Sir, we're closing up. Can I help you find anything?"

I track the couple through the window. They appear to be having some sort of disagreement. She's jabbing her finger at him, and he's shaking his head with his palms raised in a *what did I do wrong* posture I know well. When they pause in front of Headlands, my fight-or-flight nerve endings fire into my extremities. If they go inside, I'll hover outside for a bit and wait for their next move. I pull out my phone and text Zev.

May have something. Stay tuned.

The pimple-faced kid shelves the comic and raises his voice. "Sir, can I help you? I'm about to lock up."

The couple hasn't moved. Their discussion is loud and hostile.

"Did you remember to buy the Skunk Train tickets?" she asks.

"You asked me the same thing three hours ago and an hour before that. Same answer. Yes."

"I wouldn't have to ask if you paid attention the first time. You never listen to me."

I shake my head and laugh at the familiar spat. They look nothing like the couple in the park. Is this what PTSD feels like?

I text Zev: *False Alarm. You have anything?*

He responds: *Not yet, showing picture around.*

Headlands is alive with music and packed with customers drinking and eating. In the back, there is an instrumental trio dressed in kilts and playing a tune I recognize as the title score from the movie *Braveheart*. I pull open the glass door and squeeze my way through the dining tables to the back of the room. How am I going to find David in this sea of humanity or have a conversation with anyone who might know him? I decide the best place to start is the barista. They're the coffee shop equivalent of hairstylists and bartenders. They hear everything and know everyone.

As I make my way to the bar, the confluence of sandwiches, soups, and the distinct odor of red onions on the lox-and-bagel platter pulls at my empty stomach. A server informs an irritated diner handing her a credit card that they only accept cash. This is my kind of place. I'd love to sit and lose myself in music.

I take the photo out of my pocket and raise my hand high to signal the barista. In the hodgepodge mix of music, chatter, and ambient dinner conversations, a gravel voice at the other end of the counter stops my heart.

"Have you seen these two guys before?"

I slide off my seat and circle to the back of the room. It's Mark Yanzer.

The employee studies the pictures, squints her eyes, then tilts her head, clearly giving it serious consideration. I suspect Yanzer obtained the photos breaking into my house. How did he find us? The obituary? Did I crack in the basement? Sam didn't tell them because I didn't say anything to him. She hands the photo back. Her mouth is moving, but the music and the crowd drown her voice out. As if he senses my presence, Yanzer's head snaps in my direction, then swivels from left to right.

I stagger back, colliding with a server. Hot, pungent coffee soaks the back of my shirt. The skin on my back might as well be crawling with fire ants. I grunt and clamp my hand over my mouth to keep from yelling out. "Careful, sir," she exclaims, as surprised as I am.

I pick a napkin off her tray and drop to all fours while not letting Yanzer out of my sight. He's still scouring the bar, but I don't think he's seen me.

"I'll clean this up," I say apologetically. Yanzer is walking a semicircle around the room. It won't be long before he's on top of me. Keeping my head down, I slide my hands across the hardwood floor like I'm searching for a dropped contact lens. All I see are feet as I crawl away from him. There's nowhere left to go. Yanzer moves toward me, eyeing every table. He takes two more steps when a man sitting with a young boy stands, blocking his path.

"I'm sorry to bother you, but were you the Stygian Knight in the WWF?"

"That would be me," Yanzer says, his posture relaxing. "I played a little football as well."

"I loved you," the guy says. "Your world title grudge match against Hulk Hogan is my all-time favorite. I thought he had you until you pinned him with your signature Triple Flop Suplex."

Yanzer grins. "Your boy looks a little too young to remember me. Are you sure this isn't for you?"

The guy rubs his son's head. "We're both huge fans."

I'm watching from my knees, praying Yanzer doesn't look in my direction while I grimace from what has to be first-degree burns. Yanzer picks a napkin off the table and takes a pen from his jacket breast pocket, allowing me to glimpse a shoulder holster.

"What's your kid's name?"

The redheaded boy looks up, wide-eyed, and says, "My name is Josh."

Yanzer hands him the autograph and says, "I don't scribble many of these Josh, so promise you won't hawk it on eBay."

"I promise, Mr. Knight."

The dad prods his son on the shoulder. "What do you say?"

"Thank you, Mr. Knight."

Yanzer takes another step toward me when his phone goes off. He answers and says, "They're not here. I'll meet you at location number two."

"Sir, can I help you find something?" It's the server I collided with, and she's staring down at me.

"I dropped a contact but found it, thanks."

As soon as Yanzer leaves, I head for the exit and inch the door open, taking in as much of the street and sidewalk as possible. Even offset by streetlights and storefront illumination, the lateness of the night makes it difficult to discern one pedestrian from the other. I enter the Sequoia Room address into Google Maps and double-time my way there, eyeballing every person, store entrance, alleyway, and parked car. A large picture window gives me an excellent view of the Sequoia interior, but I don't see Yanzer. I retreat to the rear of the building and text Zev again.

I'm at Sequoia. Where r u

Enough of this texting shit. I dial his number.

"This mailbox has not been set up by the user. Please try back another time."

The Sequoia bartender, a slender, punkish type with short black hair, reminds me a bit of Joan Jett. She slides a bottle of beer to a customer and flashes me the *I see you and will be there in a sec* facial expression all bartenders excel at.

Joan makes her way to me and says, "What can I get you, sir?"

I point to the beer of the month postcard. "Give me a Red Sea Ale."

"That'll be four-fifty."

Along with a twenty-dollar bill, I place the picture of David in front of her. "Do you, by chance, recognize this guy? We're old childhood friends, and I heard he might be a musician around here. I leave in the morning and would love to surprise him."

She holds the paper at eye level and tilts her head. "Even with the age difference, this looks a lot like William," she says. "They have the same eyes." She squints. "Yes, I'm sure this is him." She loosens a five-by-seven cardboard flier taped to the window and hands it to me.

"Billy Martin Jazz Quartet, Saturdays at nine p.m." Below the band's name is David seated at a black Steinway baby grand piano, not much different from the one he played at Trent's house when we were kids.

"You're one lucky guy," she says, scooping the twenty off the bar. "His band is playing tonight."

I'm stunned. "Right now?"

"Yep. They're probably finishing their last set for the night, but you can go surprise your friend. Don't excite him too much," she says. "He recently had an awful car accident and is using crutches. He still shows up and plays, though. He's a trooper."

I stick my finger into the beer foam and watch the bubbles pop and hiss until there's only liquid. Neat trick. I push it back to her without taking a sip.

"Keep the change."

CHAPTER 37

The crowd is filing out as I approach the entrance. David is sitting at the piano and appears engrossed in a conversation with the drummer seated at her kit. There are no crutches, but I spot a cane on the floor at his feet. I check my phone, but there's nothing more from Zev. He wouldn't leave me hanging unless something was wrong.

David converses with the band as I work my way around the perimeter of the stage. If he's seen me coming, he's not letting on.

"You look a lot better than the last time I saw you," I say.

He turns his head in my direction, takes a hold of his cane, and pulls himself upright. "I'll come to you," he says. "I've gotten surprisingly adept at this."

His first step shows a marked limp and triggers a pronounced grimace. He slowly and with noticeable difficulty descends the three steps to the floor, swinging his stiff right leg out and around to his front, propelling himself forward. David motions to an empty table and hobbles toward it. I move to assist him, but he waves me off.

"It's not as bad as it looks. You should have seen me yesterday."

That he finds humor in this mess both amazes me and tugs at the past. David was always a laid-back kid. I sit across from him and wait for the right words to come, but they elude me.

"I wasn't sure this moment would happen after you left the hospital," I say.

The quartet waves as they exit. David smiles and shouts, "Kick ass set. See you at the next jam."

He rests his cane on his lap and says, "Do you want a drink? The bar's closed but I'm sure they will make an exception for us."

"For fuck's sake, David, forget the drinks." The people looking for us may walk in here any second. Let's get out of here."

"Tell me something I don't know," he says, motioning to a woman cleaning off the tables. "Cheri, can you please bring me some paper and something to write with?"

I glance nervously around the room. Why the hell are we sitting here like we're waiting for the next band set? Cheri returns with a blank order slip and a pen.

"Here you go, Will. It's all I could find."

"This works fine. See you tomorrow."

Not if I have anything to say about it. He can phone her from the plane. "What's with Will? When did you take on a nom de plume?"

"I've been Will Martin longer than I was David Chaney," he says quietly. "I'm off the grid, but not off the planet. You skipped bail, and Trent's after me. I get it. Let's go someplace that offers more privacy. Even quiet conversation carries in here."

The best idea of the evening, I think, wondering if we'll make it out of the building before Yanzer catches up with us.

He jots on the slip and hands it to me.

"Meet me here in an hour."

"The lighthouse?"

"It's a tourist spot close to here," he says. "At this time of the evening, it's deserted. I occasionally go there after sunset to meditate."

I'm no fan of isolated spots in unfamiliar towns, but I'm not letting him out of my sight.

"We don't have a lot of time. They've kidnapped my son and will kill him."

"Unless you do what?" he asks.

"Unless I bring you back with me. I have a plan, but time's running out. We have a plane fueled and ready to go."

He closes his eyes, takes a deep breath, and holds it like he's jumping into the deep end of a swimming pool. "Then we have a lot to talk about. Let's get out of here."

"You lead, and I'll follow," I say, standing up with him. His movements are agonizingly slow, limp by limp. I'm amazed he's recovered enough to manage this pace after the mangled mess I saw in the emergency room.

My heart stops. I shake David's shoulder and manage a raspy whisper. "It's them."

Yanzer and Abe are standing at the door and blocking our way. Where the hell is Zev? As if he's telepathic, and with an awful smile, Abe holds up an iPad case with the state flag of Israel on it. Even with David's disability, we match them backward step for step as they advance on us. Abe pulls his jacket open to expose his gun. Message received.

Our backs are against the stage when David takes my arm and says, "Back door exit. My car's there."

We retreat up the same steps David descended fifteen minutes earlier. I glance at Cheri, who finishes wiping off a table. She walks toward the two advancing thugs and says, "The show's over for the night, gentlemen. Can I help you with something?"

David puts a vice grip on my wrist. I know what he's thinking. Please, don't kill her.

Neither says a word to her, and they continue toward the stage.

Cheri follows up with a more assertive, "Can I help you?"

Yanzer quickens his step.

"Let's go," David says. "Cheri, get out of here and call the cops!"

His pace is now faster than I could have imagined with his injuries. He pushes open the back-exit door with the tip of his cane and motions to a red Jeep Wrangler convertible parked in a handicapped spot. I sprint to the passenger door while David deftly maneuvers his bum leg into the driver's seat. Yanzer rounds the corner of the building, his arm outstretched. The streetlight reflects off the gun barrel. A muzzle pop and a flash. A piece of concrete shrapnel flies from the building wall and ricochets off the Jeep's hood with a metallic bang. I dive into the passenger seat—another pop and a ping off the roll bar.

"Duck," David screams as he slams the stick shift of the Jeep in reverse and floors it so hard, we slam into a light pole. The windshield becomes a spider web of cracks around a hole the size of a quarter. I grab at my shoulder and scream in pain. A burning sensation travels the length of my arms and into my fingertips.

David shifts gears again, and the Jeep lurches forward over a grass medium and into the street. I turn around in my seat and check our rear. Screaming employees pour out the front door of the Sequoia and scatter to their cars.

The roar of the wind through the Jeep has me practically screaming at David. "Where are we going?"

I inspect the damage to my shoulder where a shard of glass entered, grimacing as I probe the entry wound with my finger, but I can't extract it.

"Do you have any suggestions?" David asks.

This isn't my freaking backyard, I think, looking behind us again as the sound of a police siren pierces the otherwise quiet night.

I open Google Maps and show David the address. "Take us here."

"I know the place," he says. "A big cannabis company uses it as a corporate VIP lodge."

"How do you know that?" I ask, surprised.

"This is a small town, and weed is the primary industry," he says.

"That's where we're staying."

David nods. Blood is flowing profusely from my shoulder. I press my shirt into the wound to soak up the excess.

"The Will Martin Band?" I ask.

"When Billy Joel was starting out, he played Los Angeles bars under the pseudonym Bill Martin." David runs a red light and turns onto the tree-lined street leading up to the chateau. "Martin is his middle name."

Of course. The not-so-obvious. Zev asked me for inside information about David, but I gave him only the obvious and easy. I didn't turn inward, probing memories that I fought hard to forget, and it cost us the most valuable asset there is—time. I choke back tears thinking of Zev. I was sure it would be me. James Bond has to survive for the next movie installment. I'm not sure he'd approve of a Jewish Hail Mary, but I have nothing to lose.

I text Trent: *David is with me. Call it off.*

The headlights pierce the pitch dark, bringing the chateau into view. I'm halfway out of the car before it comes to a complete stop. I bolt around to the driver's side and yank the door open.

"Let's go, let's go," I plead, as David manipulates his broken body out of the car, one leg at a time.

I reach into the car and shut the headlights off. The area goes dark except for the porch lights of the chateau. I yank David's arm, dragging him toward the house and almost toppling him over. He stops and pulls back, breaking my grip.

"I got this. Go inside. I'm right behind you."

The darkness is unsettling. The wind whistles in from the Pacific and over the cliffs composing an eerie sonata as the waves crash against the rocks in the cove below. The porch light supplies only enough illumination to ensure I'm moving in the right direction. I reach into my front pocket, and my body convulses with panic. Zev has the keys to the house.

Argh.

A bullet tears through me like a red-hot poker, shattering my collarbone. I slam back against the front door and fall face first onto the wood deck. My left arm is dead at my side.

"Get up, get up."

David's panicked voice stirs me from convulsion to reality. I've been shot, and I have to move—now. David bends over and struggles to help me to my feet. I wrap my fingers around the shaft of his cane and pull myself upright. A pool of my blood on the porch expands outward like an oil slick. I teeter on the edge of passing out. There's no point in looking for a way into the house. We'd be trapping ourselves. The cove. If we make it down there, we can call the cops and hide in the rocks. Two cripples scaling a cliff in the dark isn't the best Plan A, but with no Plan B, it will have to do.

What had Alex said about a staircase down to the cove? Our only chance is to cover the twenty yards to the boathouse and get down those stairs, but it will be like crossing a minefield.

My phone vibrates. God, please let it be good news. It's Kevin.

Sam is safe-he's w/ your x.

I hold my healthy arm out to David. "Does your phone have a flashlight? Turn it on and give it to me."

My sense of direction is out of whack, but the surf crashing against the rocks orients me on which way not to go as we creep toward the boathouse. Each agonizing, crippled step seems to echo like a beacon inviting another bullet. The outline of the boathouse takes shape.

"We're almost there," I say.

"No...you're not." Yanzer's voice is behind us coming up fast, the grass crunching under his lumbering feet. I turn and make out his outline taking shape. David's grasp turns into a death grip.

"Speed the fuck up," I say. "We have to make it to the stairs."

My right hamstring explodes in pain. The muscles tear as the bullet slices through them. I grab at the entry point and topple onto my face. My finger finds the bullet hole and the blood pouring out of it. I stick it further in to plug the wound. Bad idea. I scream and push myself to my knees, but my right leg won't budge any further.

"On your knees next to him, kid."

David kneels next to me, sobbing. I'm still patching the hamstring wound with my palm as I close my eyes. The muzzle touches the back of my head. Aqua Velva.

A strong thud from behind startles me. It's like a sack of wet cement dropping into a mud pit. David falls forward face first. Oh God, no.

Yanzer screams in pain. The muzzle pressure against my skull is gone. I roll onto my side and over the Sig lying in the grass. Yanzer drops to his knees, and we both grope for the gun. My fingers touch the cold steel barrel. I wrap my right hand around the grip and roll toward the sound of the ocean, praying I don't go over the ledge.

"David, get out of here and call the cops."

Yanzer struggles to his feet, his body tilting to one side. He reaches around behind his back. The moonlight glistens off his blood covered hand.

"Give me the fucking gun," he says.

Behind him, Abe limps toward us like a maimed horse. He's feet away when I raise the gun and fire in the direction of Yanzer's head. There's a splattering pop like a water balloon hitting the pavement from fifteen stories up. Abe, without making a sound, collapses forward into Yanzer, who flops on top of me, pile-driving me into the grass, belly to belly. I press the gun barrel into his head and pull the trigger. Click. I pull again. Click. The gun is empty. His hands are around my throat. I can't pry them off. I release the gun and thrust my hips upward to buck him off me, but he doesn't let up.

Yanzer uses his grip and the full weight of his body to inch me toward the cliff. Even with the bullet hole in his back, he's too strong. Blood continues to ooze from my numb shoulder. His hands tighten more around my neck, and he thrusts his right knee into my groin, inching me toward a free fall to the rocks and water below. Consciousness and the will to fight ebb from my body. That massive nose. I reach up and squeeze it like I'm trying to turn a lump of coal into a diamond. Yanzer yelps; his grip releases from my neck and is now around my hand, trying to pry it loose. I let go and plunge two fingers so far into his nasal cavity I think I hit skull. The blood rushes out like a faucet's been turned on, gushing over my face and eyes, blinding me.

He squeals, "Take it out! Take it the fuck out! I'll kill you, you motherfucker."

I gasp for air, muster all the strength I have left, and piston my right knee into his groin. He groans and growls, "If I die, your son dies."

I take my fingers out of his nose, grab his belt, and pull hard as I roll in a backward somersault. There's panicked confusion in his eyes as my knees continue their arc past my head, pulling him up over the top of me. A move he's probably done a hundred times in the wrestling ring. He latches on to my right ankle as the force drags us both toward the cliff. I manage to wrap my hand around a rock to stop my momentum.

I draw back my knee and slam my foot against his head.

"Fuck." I strike again. "You."

His grip breaks free, and he disappears over the cliff. All I hear is, "Shit."

The release of his body weight allows gravity to take over. I lose my grip on the rock and slide to the cliff's edge. A hand locks around my right wrist and halts my forward progress. David. We both lie wheezing on the cliff's edge. There are no more voices. No muzzle pops or flashes. The only sound is the water in the cove below, washing over the rocks and the body of Hit the Hole Yanzer. If there's anyone else out there, I'm toast. I have nothing left.

I crawl on my hands and knees to the Adirondack and open the bat phone again. The message from Kevin has disappeared but Sam is safe. A new text comes through.

> Got held up. Wanted a head shot with Yanzer but too dark. Glad you're safe.

I text back: *Zev? Are u ok? Where are u?*

> I won't be sticking around for the cops. You got this. Take care.

I push myself to my feet and with my good arm wind up in my best major league pitcher imitation, heaving the bat phone into the bay.

I look into David's eyes and think about something Keane said in my kitchen. He was my best friend, and he left without saying goodbye. Who does that?

"Why didn't you tell me you were moving? You were my best friend, and one day you were gone," I say.

David looks toward the cliffs and picks at a splinter in his cane. "I didn't want to leave like that. We didn't have a choice."

"What do you mean, you didn't have a choice?" I ask.

He props himself up, the tip of his cane digging into the grass, his fingers unable to fully grip the handle. Those mangled fingers. It starts to make sense.

"I mean, the decision was forced on my dad the night it happened. I didn't want to leave."

There were four of us in the stockroom. What happened to him after I left? The nausea of the truth surges from my stomach, up my throat.

"You killed Heather didn't you."

He sighs and gazes into the star-filled sky as if the answer is in a faraway solar system.

"I've justified it to myself in so many ways over the years. There was always a new reason to let it be."

I think back to something Trent said about reasons and excuses. He was right. There's no difference.

"You murdered Heather and framed me? Why? We were friends."

"The framing wasn't me," David says. "It was Trent's dad taking out an insurance policy in case the body was ever discovered. Your locket was on the floor of the storeroom."

I rub my neck where the locket once hung. It must have fallen off when Trent grabbed me around the throat.

"She hurt me," he says.

"What do you mean, she hurt you? You barely knew her."

David holds up the hand with the mangled fingers. "She did this. I was accepted to Julliard. I was going to be a concert pianist. Instead, I'm a musical afterthought with a tip jar. She ruined it all. I only wanted her to stop."

I'm more confused than ever. Stop what?

"When does the flight leave tomorrow?" he says. "I'll be on it with you. I'm so tired, Jason. I'm so tired."

"How did she hurt you?" I ask. "I need an answer, and I need to understand."

He points toward where Yanzer went over the rocks. "After you left, guys came and took Trent away. Yanzer told me to wait there until he came back."

I glance toward the chateau and wonder if this is truly the end of it. Odessa and Trent probably have lots of other guys.

David continues, "I was dabbing her forehead with the cloth. I was sure they would call an ambulance or take her to a hospital when they came back. I didn't understand who they were. Anyways, she regained consciousness and sat up. It scared the shit out of me. She was screaming so loud. I was certain the entire city could hear it."

The wail of multiple sirens comes into earshot.

"I tried to tell her she was safe and calm her down," David says. "She kept screaming, 'Don't touch me, don't touch me,' and jumped to her feet. She grabbed the hammer you dropped and swung it on my right hand. I felt the bones shatter. It hurt so bad. I couldn't see straight." His voice breaks. "Then she swung the hammer at my head, breaking my jaw."

How the hell is my print the only one left on the hammer? The story of my life. The luck of the fake Irish.

Sirens are louder and coming up the long driveway, the aura of blue and red lights reflecting off the trees. The first car to the chateau is a black SUV. Right on its tail are two Fort Bragg cop cars.

"I wrestled the hammer from her," he says. "I was in agony and enraged. I wanted her to stop hurting me. I don't remember swinging the hammer at her, but she fell to the ground and hit her head on the corner of a wooden pallet. Her blood was everywhere. I wanted to vomit. I dropped the hammer and ran, Jason. I ran home as fast as I could. My father made me take a shower and took my clothes."

I can't see anyone through the emergency lights rotating in pitch dark. Doors slam, and voices bark orders as feet pound toward us. "Federal marshals. Drop your weapons, put your hands up, and don't move a muscle."

The tears stream down David's face. "Yanzer and another guy showed up at my house and made my dad and me go with them to a house in the

Hill District. They said that I could go to the hospital after. They took us into the basement, and I helped them dig a hole while my dad watched with a gun to his head. They wrapped Heather's body in a tarp and put her in it. I thought they would kill us both. A well-dressed guy with shiny silver hair showed up and said we both had a choice to make and had to make it there. He said we could keep what happened to ourselves forever, or they'd dig two more holes. It was an easy choice."

"I said put your fucking hands in the air."

"Yanzer wiped the hammer's handle with a rag and put it in the tarp with the locket." David says.

Figures, I think to myself. Yanzer couldn't even get that right, leaving my prints on it.

I glance at David, shrug, raise my arms, and say, "I guess we won't be catching our flight tomorrow, though I'm not sure how much you can help me anyways. Why would anyone believe you killed her when all the evidence points to me?"

"Not all of the evidence," David says, reaching behind his neck and unfastening a necklace.

"Open your hand," he says.

He lays a chain with a piece of jewelry attached into my hand. A gold Nefertari earring.

"They searched high and low for this before we left the storeroom. I had hidden it in my sock. I've carried it with me as a reminder of what I did, so I would never allow myself to forget."

A minute later, my arms are violently yanked behind me and cuffed. Two of the Fort Bragg cops pull me to my feet.

The federal marshal says, "Jason Feldman, we have a fugitive warrant to take you into custody."

"I understand," I say, looking over at David, who's on his feet and cuffed.

Two women exit the SUV and walk around the front of the vehicle—Jeanette Keane and DEA agent Denise Webber.

"Well, Detective Keane, you got me."

"It was a foregone conclusion from day one," she says. "Old-fashioned, methodical police work isn't quick, but it generally leads me where I need to be."

She turns her attention to David. "You're a hard man to track. Uncuff this one and give him back his cane."

"I've been a wiz at running and hiding," David says.

"Here's the tricky part, David," Keane says. "I'm confident you have a lot to say about Heather Brody, but I can't force you to come back, at least not yet."

Agent Webber takes the cane from the cop and hands it to David. "My name is Agent Denise Webber. I'm with the Drug Enforcement Agency. I wish this could be a kumbaya moment, David, but whatever you have to say about Detective Keane's case, this isn't over. You're in grave danger from powerful and dangerous people who are into a whole lot of criminal shit. You won't last a month here. I strongly urge you to come back and let us put you in witness protection while we sort this out."

"I'll come back with you," David says, leaning heavily on his cane.

I can tell he's struggling to stay upright.

"Where's Mark Yanzer?" Keane asks.

I shrug. "We both need medical attention."

One of the Fort Bragg cops says, "An ambulance is on the way. Do either of you want to tell me what went on here?"

I glance over at the lifeless body of Abe.

"You might want to check the cove below. There's a wooden staircase. Watch your step in the dark."

EPILOGUE

The Duquesne incline jerks to a start and again begins its journey to the top of Mt. Washington as it has every day since I last sat on this wooden bench, climbing towards my confrontation with Trent. The Christmas lights strung along the roof are a reminder of how much time has passed. The excitement of a nighttime game in Heinz Park, Steelers against the Dallas Cowboys, replaces the summer glow of the brightly lit PNC Park.

Returning to the Allegheny County Jail sucked, but I knew it would be my home for a while. You don't make bail after you skip bail. After my release, I made the most humbling phone call of my life and took Mary up on her offer. I spent a month at a lawyer's-only rehab in Minnesota. Mary is dating a commercial litigator whom I've run into at the courthouse a few times. He's a good guy and a straight arrow. I'm happy for her.

Shel took David's case pro bono, and with the blessing of Heather's family, managed to negotiate a no jail time plea bargain for voluntary manslaughter. Shel did all she could to convince him to take it to trial. She had a real shot at an acquittal, but David was adamant about taking responsibility.

Shel told me she took the case gratis because she felt sorry for him, but I suspect it was more about being a fixture on the true-crime cable circuit and what I hear is a six-figure offer to host her own show. The rumor is that the first episode's devoted to the new shocker coming out of Heather's former resting place in the Hill District. The discovery of a skull, at least eighty years old. A bullet hole in the back of the head. The Odessa Society continues to spill its secrets.

I wish I could talk to David. I'm told he's in the WITSEC program. Shel says it has something to do with a federal sealed indictment but even she can't squeeze anything out of the Feds.

Yesterday was particularly brutal but also cathartic. After many stops and starts, I finally called Heather's mom and to my surprise, she agreed to see me. I'd intended to reach out sooner but had always managed to talk myself out of it.

It was a fearful and anxious walk from my car to her mother's door. It wasn't about reasons or excuses—that would be an insult to her, and to Heather's memory. All I could do was apologize. She made it clear she couldn't forgive me for my silence and blamed me for her husband's suicide. As I got into my car, however, she ran up to the passenger door and said, "Whether I forgive you is not as important as whether you forgive yourself, and how you make amends for what you've done moving forward. I hope you eventually find a path to redemption."

I exit the gondola into a frigid, star-gazing-worthy evening. The walk along Grandview takes me right past where Trent once lived. The Justice Department unsealed another indictment charging him with drug trafficking and money laundering, as well as conspiracy under the Racketeer Influenced and Corruption Act, but Trent was already in the wind. The word is he's somewhere in Eastern Europe with a new identity. Part of me believes he won't be found. Odessa taking care of their business.

Lana filed for divorce from Trent and moved to Florida. The kids are in the federal lockup, unable to make bail after the feds hit them with RICO charges as well and seized all Stodgehill assets. The scuttlebutt from Shel is the kids may cut a deal to testify against their dad. They are represented by Cal Langdon, of course. I guess blood isn't thicker than the prospect of spending the next twenty years in prison. Interestingly, the feds made no mention of Kevin. Is his name in that sealed indictment? Is mine? One point of significant relief is a California grand jury electing not to indict me for killing Yanzer and Abe, finding that I acted in self-defense.

I forgot my gloves and keep my hands jammed in my pockets for the walk to the Lamont restaurant, where Sonya and I agreed to meet.

One unenjoyable aspect of Mt. Washington is the winter wind, and this evening is no exception. I hunch my shoulders up as far as possible, but my ears have no protection and are numbing. I should have taken an Uber. WARP's no longer a possibility. Kevin and Yak have gone, as David would phrase it, off the grid, as has Zev. WARP shuttered virtually overnight after I told Kevin he was a federal target. We haven't communicated since I returned to Pittsburgh.

Station Square is glowing with lights strung through the trees, as is the docked Gateway Clipper. I can't help but notice the bowling alley Yak loved to meet at for our drug transactions. I'll miss that crazy Ukrainian, and I hope he's healed up and safe, working on his bowling championship trophy.

Sonya is standing on the sidewalk in front of the entrance to the restaurant. Despite the frigid air, she's smiling and more appropriately dressed than I am in a long, black winter overcoat, earmuffs, and mittens.

"Why are you waiting outside?" I ask. "My ears are Popsicles."

She places each mitten on the sides of my head and rubs up and down over my ears, warming them up. "Any better?" she asks.

I take her right hand in mine. "Much better." I want to kiss her but don't want to ruin the moment by assuming too much.

"Let's go inside and warm up," I say.

Before I can pull the door open, a familiar face exits.

"Well, well, my favorite client and his always beautiful dinner companion." Of course Shel would eat here. This froufrou atmosphere is more her style than mine or Sonya's. Exiting behind her is a buff guy at least thirty years younger. I didn't know she had a son. She takes him around the arm. "You two, this is my new beau, Andre. He has an incredible tech startup going public next month. It will be worth millions."

Andre from the swinger's club. Shel's next ex-husband. For his sake, he had better have more sexual stamina than the last multi-millionaire she put six feet under.

Sonya's arm tenses, and she bites her lower lip.

"I'm happy to meet you, Andre," she says.

Shel takes a five out of her wallet. "Well, we'd love to stay and chitchat, but I'm freezing my beautiful big butt off, and there's my car." The valet screeches up in her Porsche, banging the curb. She cringes and reprimands the driver, putting the five back in her purse. "Delicately, please—this isn't a Honda."

I extend my hand to Andre and say, "I hope you and Shel enjoy the rest of your evening. Good luck with her; she's a wild one."

He gives me an eyebrow raise and gets in the car. The wheels spin on the ice-splotched road, and the car zooms away.

Sonya and I eye each other and bust out laughing. You could water-board Shel, and she wouldn't violate client confidence, but this? Sonya and I both know her reputation for loose lips where city gossip is concerned. The ex-DA with her former fugitive husband. Oh, yeah. Page six, Pittsburgh-style.

"Heeere we go," she says. "I'm glad the office rumor mill is no longer a problem."

We both shrug our shoulders and sigh in unison.

"We have time before our reservation," she says. "Let's walk for a bit like the old days."

I'd endure the brunt of a blizzard for this walk.

"I'd love to. Which way?"

She buttons the top of her overcoat and says, "Let's head to the city overlook bench we used to sit on and snuggle."

I shove my hands in my coat pockets. "Lead the way."

"You don't have gloves?" she says. "You're a mess. Give me your hand."

I take my left hand out of my pocket. She wraps her mitten around it. For about twenty yards, we don't say anything. I'm searching for a starting point. I wish I could read her mind. Current events are as good as anything to break the ice.

"I visited Heather's mom yesterday."

"I was wondering if you would," she says. "How did it go?"

"It was rough on both of us, but I'm glad I went."

We stop and take in the view. Downtown Pittsburgh is lit up like a massive Christmas tree on steroids.

"Have you been to see your dad?"

Sonya loved my dad. I'm glad that hasn't changed.

"I've been twice a week since I got out of rehab and given him the broad strokes. I'm not sure how much he absorbs. I think he's simply happy I'm back visiting. Schedule and routine are important with dementia."

A sad smile comes over her face. "I'd love to visit him with you."

"He may not recognize you. There are good days, and really bad days."

"I understand," she says. "Few people know, but my dad is struggling with the mid-stages of Alzheimer's. I'm constantly surprised at what he remembers."

"I wasn't aware. I'm sorry."

We all have secrets.

As we approach the overlook, she says, "Let's sit for a bit. We can be tardy for our reservation."

I wink at her. "I will if you rub my ears again."

"I'm happy to help defrost you," she says, giggling. She leans against me and rubs her mittens up and down my ears. This could be one of those weak moments like the night we made love or a step forward in the rebirth of our relationship. I wrap my arm around her and pull her closer.

"What's next for you?" I ask.

She's quiet for a second or two, staring out over the city. "I'm not sure," she says. "I'm taking it one day at a time. Alan didn't think a disgraced, former district attorney currently fighting to keep her law license was compatible with his DC lobbyist image. I don't blame him. I'd have dumped me too."

"His loss," I say, secretly ecstatic it didn't work out but sad there was so much collateral damage for her. "I'm sorry about what happened. I didn't intend to cause you problems at work."

Sonya shrugs. "I'm an adult and knew what I was doing when I let you see the file. It was impulsive and stupid, but part of me believes it was intentional self-sabotage."

I nod my head. "I have an advanced degree in that. I am curious about something, though. Didn't Alan say anything about the photo of us in your house? I know I'd be jealous if someone I was dating had a photo of her ex on display, unless he was dead or something."

"Alan's never been to my place. When he came into town, we stayed at hotels. Maybe not inviting him to my house was a sign I wasn't ready. Maybe I didn't want to take it down and his coming over meant that I would have to. I wasn't ready to let go."

My muscles tense, but as if Sonya knows where my mind is wandering, she says, "We never stayed at the William Penn. I told him I wouldn't spend the night there."

My pulse slows, and my shoulders relax. It will always be our place regardless of what happens down the road.

"So, what will you do?" I ask.

She continues, "I won the election on the platform of fundamentally reforming this county's criminal justice system. It hasn't worked out the way I hoped. I wanted addiction and mental illness to be public health issues and not jail issues. It hasn't happened. I wanted more diversion programs to reduce the jail population. It hasn't happened."

Snow flurries begin to swirl around us. She stares at a flake that lands in her lap. Is she mentally tabulating her failures? She's accomplished so much for so many with no voice. "I've been politically thwarted, back-stabbed, and otherwise opposed at every turn," she goes on. She smiles, but it makes me sad. I see more resignation than happiness. "I'm tired, Jason. Oh well. I guess that was a long way of saying I really don't know what I'm going to do. What about you?"

"Taking it one day at a time, focusing on my sobriety, and ready to do something else, or at least be better at what I did do."

I take a giant breath. I'm sitting on the edge of the plane again, ready to push myself off. This is the moment to trust that the parachute opens.

"What's up with us? Is there anything?"

She places her hand over mine hand and says, "I care for you, Jason. That never went away, but..."

I hate buts, and I want her to stop there. I know, however, that my quest for self-honesty isn't enough. I must allow others to be as well.

"You broke my heart, and your son's, with so many lies. So many broken promises. I don't know if I can take going through it all over again."

I could beg and plead. I could regurgitate the bullshit addicts loves to spout, and tell her none of it will happen again.

"I've given you no reason to feel any differently. I understand."

Sonya gets up and says, "We should head back before they give our reservation away."

I tug at her coat, pulling her back. "Let's sit for a bit more. If we miss our reservation, I know an incredible hot dog place across from the law school. Remember when you bit into your Dirty Dog with chili, and the pressure squirted con carne all over my clothes?"

She smiles and says, "That was funny. You went home to change, and I had to explain what happened to our torts law professor. The entire class got a giggle out of it."

I take in the city lights and the darkened outline of the Cathedral of Learning towering above Oakland. "If you think about it, our history is pretty much contained within this landscape, law school, the courthouse, ball games."

She nods. "I hadn't thought about it, but yes, you're right. The bad stuff as well."

"Yeah, the bad stuff as well, I agree."

There will be more difficult situations to come, but I'd rather focus on the nostalgic romance of this moment. I may not have my law license or my freedom once the nature of Kevin's actual business comes out, and it will. Zev knew what he was talking about. There's a trail if you know where to look. The DEA will look. Keane will look.

"I'm guessing you'll be going into private practice?" I ask.

"I suppose I might," she says, "or I may transition out of the law altogether." She stands again. "Let's walk. I'm freezing and need to move my feet."

I stand with her and say, "I have an idea. Let's warm up on the incline and get those hot dogs.

We take our seats in the gondola across from a young couple leaning against each other with their heads touching. The girl takes the glove off her left hand and adjusts her diamond solitaire ring. The guy places his hand on top of it and kisses her.

"Feldman and Feldman has a nice ring to it," I say.

Sonya's eyes drift upward toward the roof. "Honestly, Jason, I'm thinking more social justice, class actions, and save-the-whales type of litigation. Aren't you tired of the same auto accident grind day after day? What happened to the kid who almost bowled me over running out that elevator with dead roses? He had such big dreams."

I think back to what a retiring, jaded, curmudgeon plaintiff's lawyer told me when I was a baby lawyer. He said, "You don't believe it now, but you'll come to despise your clients."

He was wrong. In the end, I despised myself, in large part because I allowed myself to become a legal caricature, and it started in the Stodgehill Toys storeroom.

"I'm sorry, I didn't mean to imply—"

"Don't be," I say, cutting her off. "You're right. I wasn't a lawyer. I was a bad used-car salesman."

The girl again rearranges her ring. They both seem oblivious to our presence. Sonya removes her gloves. Her left hand leaves my lap and lies on top of her right. Her lips part slightly, and her index finger moves along the length of her ring finger.

"Well, we'll see," she says.

The gondola lurches to a stop. The newlyweds are still smooching. I take Sonya's hand and help her out. Yes, we'll most definitely see.

ACKNOWLEDGMENTS

I wish to thank the following people who guided, educated, and inspired me every step of the way.

As always, my wife, Amanda, who patiently endures and loves me through the voids of writer's block to the heights of creativity, allowing me to continually redefine who I can be as I continue my addiction recovery journey.

To my brothers Mark and Jeff. I love you and probably wouldn't be here today without your love and support.

To my mother, Shirley. You've shown me how to live life on my own terms as you've always done. I love you.

To my mentor Bonnie Hearn Hill. You've worn many hats, structural editor, copy editor and critic to my many awful ideas as I struggled to transition from memoir to fiction writer. You always tell me what I need to hear not what I want to hear. Thank you for always wearing the important hat of all, my friend.

To Luke Gerwe. You've been with me as a structural editor since my first non-fiction book which seems like a lifetime ago. Thank you for keeping me from making many rookie fiction mistakes like using "vocal fry."

To my wonderful Pittsburgh legal crew, who continually answered my many questions about the nuances of the Allegheny County legal system and took the time to critique those portions of my manuscript through multiple revisions.

Lisa Middleman Esquire

Phil DiLucente Esquire

Lea T. Bickerton Esquire

To Ray Balestri-We've known each other over thirty years but only really got to know each as you guided me with wonderful critique. I'm glad to call you a friend.

To Drew Rossow Esquire, who has some of the best Uber driving stories. Thanks for your friendship.

To Pittsburgh police detective(retired), and fellow Mt Lebanon High School grad, Valerie Milie. Your input on police and jail procedure was invaluable. Enjoy your well deserved retirement.

To my Fort Bragg guru, Jon McColley. I now understand what you mean by, "No one comes to Fort Bragg by accident." Thank you for being a wonderful guide through your incredible town.

To my friend Bryant Zadegan, if I ever want to create a disappearing message app, you are the man.

There are many others who I bounced ideas off and guided me at various points through the writing journey. I particularly want to thank:

Emily Madden

Geoffrey William Melada Esquire

George Heym Esquire

Alex Vinokur

Sergei Nezhurbida

James Rosenberg Esquire

Pilot Jeffrey Taylor

David Delugas Esquire

David Samuel Levinson(editing)

Sabine Morrow (editing)

Lisa Wagner Freeman

Karmen Harris, BSN, RN, SANE-A

Joe Otte Esquire

To all the hard-working employees at my publisher, Post Hill Press. Thank you for believing in me twice.

ABOUT THE AUTHOR

Author photo by Noah Purdy

Brian Cuban, the younger brother of Dallas Mavericks owner and entrepreneur Mark Cuban, is a Dallas-based attorney, author, and person in long-term recovery from alcohol and drug addiction. He is a graduate of Penn State University and the University of Pittsburgh School of Law.

His book, *The Addicted Lawyer: Tales of the Bar, Booze, Blow, and Redemption* is an unflinching look at how addiction and other mental health issues destroyed his career as a once successful lawyer, and how he and others in the profession redefined their lives in recovery and found redemption.

Brian has spoken at colleges, universities, conferences, non-profits, and legal events across the United States and in Canada. His columns have appeared—and he has been quoted on these topics—online and in print newspapers around the world. He currently resides in Dallas, Texas with his wife and two cats.